# LEFT TO YOU

DANIEL J. VOLPE

*This one is for my mother. Mom, here's a book you can finally read. And yes, I would do the same thing.*

## ACKNOWLEDGMENTS

I just want to thank a few people who made this book possible. My editor, Patrick C. Harrison III. His input brought this book to a new level of professionalism. Mort Stone, who offered key recommendations and helped me clean this up further. To my fellow podcast brethren, Aron Beauregard, Carver Pike, and Rowland Bercy Jr. These guys help me with every project, and I can't thank them enough. And finally, the two people that brought this book to life, Dawn and Tim Shea. I cannot express how happy I am to be a member of the D&T family. Dawn and Tim are truly dedicated to their authors and publishing some of the best horror out there.

# I

# AN UNLIKELY FRIENDSHIP

# 1

Robert Sinclair pushed the wobbling shopping cart down the aisle. The good ones, which the employees hid for themselves, were all gone. He was stuck with one of the worst carts that always pulled to the left. It was full of merchandise that needed to be restocked on the shelves. It was one of the more mundane tasks he performed as a valued employee of L-Mart, but it was a job.

He walked around, making notes as to what was low so he or someone else could restock later. Robert stopped in front of the plastic wrap, grabbed a few rolls from his cart and restocked the shelf. The store brand always sold better, even though it was an inferior product. People had to choose when to skimp and it appeared most did with their choice of plastic wrap. Next was tinfoil; again, the store brand was low.

He was tall, which was a plus when putting product on upper shelves. Robert had a full head of dark hair which had a perfect natural wave. Even though he was 21, he had very boyish looks. He only shaved three times a week and could probably stretch it further. He looked slim and athletic, but hadn't seen the inside of a gym in nearly a year.

He finished with his cart full and headed back to the stockroom to see if there was anything else that needed re-stocking.

"Did you finish in aisle 7?" asked Mike. When Mike was promoted to assistant manager six months prior, he redid his name tag with bold letters. Anyone short of being completely blind could read he was the assistant manager.

"Yeah," Robert said, looking at an inventory form on a clipboard hanging from a nearby shelf.

Robert had been working at L-Mart for nearly a year. He hated it, but times were tough all around, so he took what he could.

Mike put his chewed pen up to his chapped lips. He pursed them around the end, looking at the list in front of him. He didn't hate Robert, but he wasn't his biggest fan. Before Mike was promoted, no one really talked to him. He normally had a shitty attitude and took it out on everyone, especially the females. Mike wasn't much of a ladies' man. He was 27, stood a whopping five-seven and tipped the scales at 230 lbs. His face was always greasy looking, along with his brown hair. The lack of power over the opposite sex was evident. He was sure to let everyone know he was the boss, at least behind the automatic doors of L-Mart.

A year prior, Robert had graduated from community college and was prepping to head to a state school. His grades were good and he'd gotten a partial scholarship, which was a plus because money was tight.

His mother, Helen, who was a single parent for all of Robert's twenty-one years, worked her ass off to give him the best life she could. For twenty-five years she worked for Ashmore central schools as a secretary. It didn't pay great, but it was steady money. Until the cancer.

It started as nothing, or so they thought. His mother never smoked a day in her life. What she thought was Bronchitis, turned out to be stage 3 lung cancer. After three surgeries and one lung removal, the cancer was gone, at least from her lungs. Her lymph nodes were riddled with malignant tumors. The Oncologist gave her six months to live. That was about a year ago. Helen Sinclair was on borrowed time.

"Ok, well, grab a few packs of hotdogs and go check the stock. Memorial Day is coming up and you know how people love their wieners."

Robert saw the hotdogs on the clipboard and crossed them off. He wheeled his cart over to the cooler and began filling it.

Jordan rolled his cart into the stockroom, the batwing doors closing behind him. Like most of the employees who did stock work at L-Mart, Jordan was young. He and Robert graduated high school together a few years back and became work-friends. He grabbed the stock sheet, found the next item to be restocked and crossed it off the list.

Jordan stopped his cart by Robert, who was still loading it with hotdogs. He started filling up with various cheeses.

"Your buddy is out there," Jordan said, stacking blocks of yellow American. He looked at Robert from the corner of his eye.

Robert gazed over at him. "Mr. Lazer?" he asked.

Jordan stopped and looked at him. "Yeah, of course. Who the hell else would it be?" He started back up again and chuckled. "Hell, I think I'm your best friend and I'm right here."

Robert knew that was pretty much the truth. Since his mother had gotten sick, he didn't have much of a social life. His closest friends left their little town for college. Besides, with his mother's treatment, he didn't have the time or money to go out. Every now and then Jordan would take him out for a beer or two, but that was it.

If his social life was weak, his love life was abysmal. From Senior year until his last year in community college, Robert had a steady girl-friend. It was three years of crazy sex with a crazy woman. After years of fighting and fucking, the couple called it quits when she left for college. Since then, he'd been on a dry spell.

Robert pulled out his phone and checked the time. It was just about 1 pm.

"He's a little late today," he said, putting his phone back. He finished stocking. "Where was he?"

Jordan said, "Near the cereal aisle."

"Thanks," said Robert, rolling his cart away from the cooler.

Six months prior Robert had been stocking toilet paper a few days before Christmas. The store was a madhouse. People were scrambling for last minute gifts, food for their dinner parties, and toiletries. During the most magical time of the year, people could be downright shitty to each other. Robert saw that first hand. He watched an old man navigate through the crowds, his red basket jostling as he moved. A few 'sorry's' and 'pardon me's' accompanied the bumps, but not many. Robert watched the man try to squeeze in to grab the last pack of toilet paper. A large woman, her phone glued to her head, used her girth to move him aside, snatching it for herself. The only packs left were the massive ones, which clearly wouldn't fit in a basket. Robert weaved his way through the crowd and tapped the man on the shoulder.

The man turned and stared at Robert with watery blue eyes. He had large ears with a fair amount of wispy white hairs. He had a full head of hair, but it was snow white. Originally, Robert thought the man was hunched over, but up close he realized the man was just short. Actually, his back was straight and shoulders wide.

"Follow me," Robert said. "I have more in the back."

The old man smiled. "Thank you. That'd be great." He followed Robert towards the back of the store.

Robert came out of the batwing doors with a three-pack of toilet paper. "Here ya'go," he said, handing it to the man.

"Thank you," the old man said, tucking it into his basket. "Josef Lazerowitz," he said, sticking out his wrinkled hand.

Robert took it and was shocked by the strength in it. *Old man strength*, he thought.

"Robert Sinclair," he said, shaking hands.

"Pleasure to meet you," Josef replied.

Robert couldn't place it, but the old man had a slight accent.

"You too," he stated, looking over him at the crowd of customers. "Well, let me get back to the vultures." He pointed over Josef's shoulder at the crowd.

Josef smiled. "Right, right. Well, enjoy your day and thanks again."

"No problem," Robert said, heading back into the maelstrom.

Six months later, Mr. Lazer, as Robert had taken to calling him, was at L-Mart at least three to four days a week. He always looked for Robert and if the store wasn't busy, they'd talk for a little while.

Robert didn't mind; it broke up the monotony of the day. Plus, if customers saw him talking to another person, they wouldn't bother him.

Robert took the long way to the meat cooler, passing through the cereal aisle. Just like Jordan had said, Josef was examining a box of oatmeal.

"Is that any good?" Robert asked, sneaking up on the old man.

Josef wasn't startled; he knew he was there. "Eh, it's ok, but it's on sale," he said, putting it in the red L-Mart basket. He looked at Robert's cart full of hotdogs. He let out a whistle. "That's a lot of tube steaks."

After the meeting, Robert found out Josef was originally from Poland. Even being in the States for years, some Americanized food still didn't resonate with him. Sure, they ate sausage in Poland, but the processed, pink slime, last-forever hotdogs, didn't appeal to him much. At least, not anymore.

"Memorial Day is coming up," Robert said, reciting Mike's quote. "You know, 'honor your dead with a hotdog' kind of thing." He smiled, but noticed Josef wasn't.

"Yes, you should always honor the dead. Your country lost many brave men in their wars," he said, his eyes wandering. He snapped back. "Oh, well. I won't keep you," he said, looking at his basket absently.

Robert started to move as the old man did.

"Otis is cooking tonight, if you don't have any dinner plans," Robert told him. Besides the grocery store, he also worked in the Blue Star Diner. He didn't mind it, especially when Otis was working. The burly cook would make him whatever he wanted and not charge. When Simon, the brother-in-law of the owner, was there, he made sure to charge the staff for their meals. He'd give them a discount of a whopping ten percent. If you went in hungry, you could eat up a day's pay and not even notice.

"Oh, well now you've gotten my attention," Josef replied, smiling. Otis was one of the few people who made authentic Polish stuffed cabbage. This reminded Josef of the old country he'd left so long ago. "Do you think he's making the cabbage?"

Robert shrugged, getting to the meat cooler. He began shifting product around. "I'm sure he is. That's his favorite thing to make and eat, so I'd say you'd be in luck."

Josef smiled. "Well, you've convinced me. I'll be seeing you tonight." He patted Robert on the shoulder and walked away.

## 2

ROBERT LOCKED the bathroom door and sighed. His shift at L-Mart was finally over, but now it was time to get ready for his dinner shift at the diner. Robert undressed and grabbed the pair of pants and shirt which he wore at the diner. They were simple, but had the greasy diner-smell embedded in them. There was no point in using too many different pairs; that smell never came out. He finished changing and put his L-Mart clothes in his bookbag. He threw a little cold water on his face and looked in the mirror. He felt tired, but hoped he didn't look it.

He walked out of the bathroom and almost bumped into Sarah Denbrough.

Sarah would never be called sexy or a smoke show, but she was an attractive woman. Her dirty blonde hair hung in a tight ponytail, resting between her shoulder blades. She had an almost cherubic face, with round cheeks, and a slightly upturned nose. Her eyes were green, but not in a stunning way. She had a large pair of breasts her smock couldn't hide, which made up for the lack of an ass.

In Robert's mind, she had the perfect girl-next-door look. Plus, besides her physical attributes, she was the nicest person in L-Mart.

She would often cover for someone if requested, but wouldn't get walked over. She wasn't afraid to help, if it was truly needed.

A few months prior, while Robert and Sarah were on a short break, they shared a kiss. Nothing crazy, but it was enough to start something between the two of them. Robert thought it couldn't have come at a worse time. The last thing he needed in his life was a relationship. He knew he couldn't dedicate himself to anyone with his life the way it was. Sarah understood, and the thought of dating was put on the back burner.

"Hey," she said, sidestepping the distracted Robert.

He stopped and absently ran a hand through his hair, trying to make sure it was somewhat neat. They weren't dating, but no man wanted to look bad in front of an attractive girl.

"What's up?" He asked, wiping at a stain on his shirt. Hopefully the apron would cover it at the diner.

Sarah didn't have much to say. She only stopped him out of habit and just wanted a minute of his time. She had a crush on him. The kiss was one of the best moments in recent memory for her. She felt electric and dreamt of those kisses all over her body. Looking at him now, his hair messed up, a slight sheen of sweat on his forehead, made those thoughts rekindle. She felt flushed.

"Ah, not much," she said, looking away. "Headed to the Blue Star?" she asked, obviously knowing the answer.

"Yeah, I was able to get a dinner shift, so hopefully the tips are decent tonight," he said. He was running late, but didn't want to be rude. One day, Robert wouldn't mind dating Sarah. He couldn't expect her to wait around forever, so hopefully it would be sooner rather than later.

Sensing his tension, she said, "Oh, well good luck." She forced a small, half-smile. "I won't keep you. Shoot me a text later, if you have a break."

Robert smiled. "Yeah, sure. Well, have a good rest of the shift, and watch out for Mike."

"Why, did he say something?" When Mike had just been promoted, Sarah turned him down when he tried to kiss her. He must've thought because she kissed Robert, it meant it was open season for everyone. She wasn't that type of girl, especially for a cretin like Mike.

"No, he's just an asshole," Robert said, smiling.

Sarah smiled back, her green eyes lighting up. "Yeah, tell me about it."

Robert adjusted his backpack with his L-Mart clothes in it. "Alright, take it easy."

"You too," she replied.

Robert walked through the automatic doors and outside.

It was one of those beautiful Spring days. He liked to think of them as Goldilocks days, not too hot, not too cold, just right. The sun was still high in the sky even though it was getting close to 4 pm. Robert was ok with that. Longer days usually meant better days. The only problem with nice weather was the customers. Most people would stay home on nice days and grill or eat outside. Most of the bugs weren't in full force yet and the sun wasn't that bad. It would mean a slow night for him, which meant shitty tips.

He got into his old Nissan Sentra and fired it up. Robert shifted gears as the old import slid into traffic.

---

THE BLUE STAR Diner was one of the thousand greasy spoons in the country. It had Formica tabletops, fully equipped with advertisement place mats and utensils rolled in napkins. The countertop was lined with chrome, as were the stools attached to it. The batwing doors leading to the kitchen were much smaller than those at L-Mart. They were labeled 'in' and 'out' and the bottoms had kick plates, which the staff used more often than not.

Robert walked in through the back door near the dumpster. A bag of garbage sat; squat, wrinkled, and black, waiting to be taken out. He grabbed it and turned back around. With a youthful heave, one that didn't care about back pains yet, he threw it into the dumpster.

"Oh, good, you're early," said a voice.

Robert would've recognized that rough voice anywhere. Kitty, the other server, pulled a pack of Marlboro Reds from her apron and lit up.

"It's pretty dead in there," she said, blowing a cloud of smoke in the air. "Can you just walk by table 15 when you get in? I just checked on them before I came out." Another puff, this one followed up by a mucusy cough. "Bill Jenks is at the counter, but he's fine too. I just warmed his coffee and he's reading the paper."

Catherine "Kitty" Aldritch was a staple in any American diner. Most customers came for the service more than the food. She was in her late sixties and looked like she'd been smoking since she was ten. Kitty had shoulder-length reddish hair that had the look of a do-it-yourself dye job. Her cheeks were wrinkled, sagging just a little. The years of smoking gave her lips an unnatural amount of lines. She was crass and could be a downright bitch, but for the most part, she and Robert got along fine. Kitty hated the big groups when they'd come in. She also hated kids, which, with a few chain restaurants in the area, wasn't much of an issue. She was just fine with her couple of early birds and the few two-tops that wandered in from time to time. In other words, Kitty was an American treasure: the diner waitress.

She grabbed a fresh smoke from her pack and put it in her mouth. With the other one just about out, she used it to light the fresh one. Kitty tossed her first cigarette, which she'd smoked to the filter, onto the ground. It hissed in a puddle of dumpster water.

"Yeah, no problem, Kitty," Robert said, avoiding the cloud of smoke. He walked back into the diner. Robert didn't wish ill will on the woman, but he'd seen her smoke a pack of cigarettes in a five-hour shift. Occasionally she'd have a coughing fit, but other than that, she seemed healthy. Unlike his mother, whose body was riddled with cancer and pumped full of drugs.

"Yo, Bobby," Otis called from the oven area.

Otis Thompson leaned his girth against the oven, his cell phone in one meaty hand. Nothing was currently cooking, so Robert knew Kitty was telling the truth about it being dead.

"Hey, O," Robert replied. He didn't mind Otis calling him Bobby. His grandmother would do the same when he was a kid. Once she died, no one called him that anymore. He figured he'd outgrown it until he met Otis.

Otis had been the cook at the Blue Star for over five years. He was almost as round as he was tall. The stained white apron he wore was tight against his belly and his paper cook's hat was always canted. He was light-skinned black and Robert thought he kind of looked like a pug. Looks aside, he was one of the nicest people he'd met.

"Is Simon around?" Robert asked, grabbing a black apron from the laundry bag in the closet. He threw it over his neck and tied it around his back with practiced hands. He put his pad of paper and pen in one pouch. He'd fill the other side of the apron with straws when he went out on the floor.

Otis smiled, his eyes seeming watery, and put his phone away. "Na, he's in tomorrow." He looked around conspiratorially. "You hungry?" he asked.

"A stinker with cheese and fries?" Robert asked, smiling. He could already taste the popular onion-laced burger.

Otis laughed. "You gonna kill your tips with stank ass breath, but I got you." He opened the cooler under the counter and grabbed a burger patty on a piece of wax paper.

"Thanks, O," Robert said as he walked into the restaurant.

Kitty's table and Mr. Jenks were fine. The table was just finishing up and he cleared a few small plates for them.

Robert heard the unmistakable sound of motorcycles and lots of them. He looked up, a few dirty plates in hand, and saw no less than ten bikes pulling into the lot.

He turned and almost bumped into Kitty. She took the dirty plates from his hands.

"That's a lot of bikes," she said, walking to the bus bin, where she dumped the plates.

Robert followed. He was looking around at where to seat them all. He knew they were his. Even if he'd already had a few tables, Kitty wouldn't take them. She hated large groups with a passion and refused anything over a four-top. Of course, she'd help him run food, but as for taking the order or, God forbid, splitting a check, Robert was on his own.

"Let's set them in the back," she said, already with a stack of menus and silverware in her hand.

They had a few tables pushed together and set before the leather-clad bikers were in the restaurant.

The bells above the door tinkled and the men and a few women walked in. Robert swept over to greet them.

"Hello, welcome to the Blue Star. How many are in your party?" he asked in his host voice.

The lead man, who fit the image of a biker to a tee—bald, red beard, earring, big belly, and tattooed arms—said, "Ah, we have eleven." He turned to make sure his count was right.

"Great, right this way." Robert led them to the set of tables.

After they were seated, he went into the kitchen.

"Hey, O, we just sat an eleven-top," he said. His burger and fries were in the back of the kitchen. Robert descended on it like an animal, eating half of it in a few bites. He crammed his mouth full with a few fries and walked over to the soda machine. He filled a plastic cup with water and washed down his food.

"I'm ready to rock," Otis said as he wiped down the griddle, which hissed from the wet rag.

Robert heard the unmistakable sound of the doorbells chiming again. Another customer. It always happened like this: a huge table would come in and then a few small ones would follow. As much of a pain in the ass as it was, it was nothing new.

He walked back into the dining room and watched Kitty seat Josef. The draw of stuffed cabbage pulled him in.

The old man saw Robert and waved.

Robert held up his index finger, 'one minute' he signaled. He took his notepad and pen from his apron and headed to the bikers' table.

Josef waved him off and put his light jacket on the back of the chair.

Robert could just barely hear Kitty asking him what he'd like to drink.

With the bikers' drink orders in hand, Robert stopped by Josef's table.

"Hey, Mr. Lazer," he said, not wanting to be rude.

Josef, like most older men, sipped on a black coffee. He put his mug back on the saucer, a little drop of coffee pooling on the bottom.

"I'm sorry to bother you," said Josef. He looked pale. His face was sunken and eyes dark.

Robert didn't notice any of this when he'd spoken to him in the store earlier. It could've been the lighting, but he didn't think so.

"I was hoping to grab your ear for a little while, but I see you're busy." He gestured to the table of bikers with his left hand.

Robert followed the man's arm as he pointed and saw something he'd never seen before: a tattoo of numbers on his left forearm.

They'd met in the winter of last year, so this was the first time he'd ever seen Josef without something long sleeve on. His gaze lingered on the tattoo for a moment longer, Mr. Andrew's history class being pulled to his forebrain.

He recalled the lessons about the Holocaust and the number system the Nazis would use to label inmates of the concentration camps. A single needle was used to tattoo an ID number on the left forearm of everyone in the camps.

Robert was almost in shock at seeing the tattoo. He did some quick math in his head, not knowing how old Josef was, and figured the man had to have been a child in those camps. The last ones were liberated almost seventy-five years ago.

"Sorry, Mr. Lazer, but I can't really sit down now." The bell above the door tinkled. Robert looked as a family of six walked in, two of which were little kids. The kids were already loud, one complaining how she wanted to go to the restaurant with the clown and not this stinky place. "I have a dinner shift tomorrow, but you know Fridays can be even worse." He looked over his shoulder as Kitty was leading the family towards their table. "Give me a call and we'll talk." Robert walked away, kicking the batwing doors open.

Josef watched the doors swing shut. He knew he wasn't going to be able to talk to Robert in the restaurant anyway, but figured it was worth a shot. His stomach tensed, white-hot pain clenching his guts. With a shaky hand, he guided his coffee to his mouth.

"Here ya go, hun," said Kitty as she placed a steaming plate of stuffed cabbage in front of him.

It looked and smelled heavenly, but Josef felt like he would've died if he took a bite.

"Ah, thank you, but can I be a pain?" he asked Kitty, who was just starting to turn back to the kitchen.

Kitty looked at him, keeping the family in her periphery. One of the kids was throwing sugar packets at the other. The parents kept their heads buried in their menus.

"I'm going to have this to-go if you don't mind. No rush."

Kitty smiled, her smoker's lines stretching out, but crow's feet deepening. "No problem, hun," she said, grabbing the plate.

Josef's gut clenched again. He was starting to sweat. If she didn't hurry up, he was going to have to use the diner bathroom.

"Here ya are," Kitty said, putting a plastic bag and check on the table. She looked at him and noticed the sweat. "Are you ok?" she asked.

Josef had his wallet out, his shaky fingers leafing through bills.

"Oh, yes." he waved at her with a dismissive hand. "It was just a little warmer in here than I expected." He put a twenty on the table.

Kitty forced a smile. She wasn't stupid and wasn't young. She had seen plenty of sick people in her life and knew one when she saw one. She scooped up the money and ticket.

"I'll go get your change," she said.

Josef stood up, draping his jacket over his arm. "No worries. Keep the change," he said.

Kitty smiled. "Thank you and feel better," she told him, but he was already headed to the door.

The bells chimed as he walked out; the cool night air was a blessing. Josef knew he'd need every blessing he could get.

---

## CHAPTER 2

Josef burst into his house like a man possessed. He flung the bathroom door open, hands fumbling with his belt. In a moment of sheer panic, he didn't think he'd get his pants down in time. The belt finally relented and his sweaty ass hit the toilet seat. His bowels released a torrent of waste. Pain seized his stomach as if he was passing nails and not feces. The pain was bad, but the smell was worse. No one liked the smell of shit, but everyone was used to it. This was different, this smelled like sickness and death.

Josef, knowing what he'd see, looked at the toilet paper. His shit was almost pure black. He threw the toilet paper in the bowl and sat for a moment. His elbows were on his knees, his sweaty face in his hands. He shuddered as a quick stab of agony cut through him.

Twenty years ago, the doctors had given him six months to live. Colon cancer had ravaged his body at unseen speeds. The doctors told him six months, but many of them didn't think he'd make it past one. They didn't know Josef. The following week Josef came back for a follow-up and the man that walked into the office was a different man. A week prior he was a shell, sickly, bent, thin and pale. Now, Josef stood tall and had a healthy look to his full cheeks. His doctor stared in shock. Then came the tests. The cancer was gone. Not in remission or shrinking, but completely gone. His tests showed levels of a man half his age and healthy as a race horse. The doctors wanted to study him, but he knew the reason behind his cure and promptly refused.

His cancer was back again, and this time with a vengeance. Days ago, he was fine, but now he felt like he was on death's doorstep and the door was swinging open. He was ready for death. Hell, he was ready for death the day the Nazi doctors took his twin sons. No, this time he'd let death take him. He was ready to pay the price for what he'd done. The only thing he needed was a few days of life, that was it. He needed to talk to Robert.

Josef stood on wobbly legs and flushed the blackness away. He walked out of the bathroom and grabbed the plastic bag with his food in it. He went into the kitchen, passing the basement door, and threw it in the garbage. He walked by the basement door again, pausing.

*Do I have to die?* The thought popped into his head as he looked at the locked door. Was it even his thought? Something called to him. Something evil beckoned him.

*Come, taste this fruit. It's painfully sweet and oh so delicious,* a voice that was barely his said in his subconscious.

Josef shivered, not from the cancer, but from the fear of what he might do.

"A few days," he said aloud, not caring who heard.

*You know the price,* that voice again.

Josef knew the price all too well. This would be the last time he'd pay it and then it would be his turn to be cashed in. He hoped he was enough.

# 3

Robert pulled his car into the driveway just after 9:30 pm and saw Esther, his mother's aide, was still there. Her car was parked on the street in front of their house.

The rest of Robert's shift had turned out great. The bikers, who always seem to get a bad reputation, left him the largest tip he'd ever earned. After them, he and Kitty both handled the family of six with the snot-nose kids. A few more two-tops came in to round out his night and he left with a handful of cash. Plus, Otis slipped him a piece of raspberry cheesecake, which was his mother's favorite. Hopefully, he could get her to eat some of it.

Over the last few weeks, Helen Sinclair's health had been dropping off sharply. Her body, even though riddled with cancer, continued to fight. That was her nature.

When she was twenty-six, she was in a whirlwind relationship with an older man. The flash in the pan relationship was full of sex, deceit, domestic violence, and alcohol abuse. One morning, Helen woke up and found him gone. No note, no message, and no contact ever again. The only thing she had to remind her was the growing life in her belly. She looked for him, but not very hard. Some of the bruises on her body were still healing. From then on it had been just her and Robert. She had a couple of decent relationships along the way, but none good enough to put a ring on.

Robert grabbed the bag with the cheesecake and walked into the house.

Esther was sitting in the living room reading some trashy tabloid magazine. Those were her vice and Robert always made sure he picked some up when he could.

Esther Jean came from a large family. Being one of nine kids living in Port-au-Prince, Haiti, meant a rough life growing up. They immigrated (legally, she'd always remind everyone) to the United States when she was sixteen and found a new home in suburban New York. She started out cleaning hotels, but found a niche in healthcare. Soon she was a health aide, taking care of the sick and elderly. For Robert, she was a godsend.

"Your mama is sleepin'," she said, her accent faint. She closed the magazine and put it on her lap. "She had a cup of broth I made for her, but that was it."

Robert knew his mother hadn't been eating much for a few weeks. He hoped it was just a reaction to some of the medication, but he knew better. Her body, which was once so vibrant and full of life, was shutting down.

He sat down on the couch across from Esther. "I brought her some raspberry cheesecake, her favorite." Robert held up the bag.

Esther smiled, but it wasn't a happy smile. It was the kind of smile you give to a child who has come with a snake in a jar. You're happy for their happiness, but you know it really means nothing.

"That's nice, Robert," she said, setting the magazine on the end table. She stood up, her knees popping. "Keep an eye on her." She walked the few steps to the kitchen table and grabbed her purse.

"I will," he said, a burning question on the tip of his tongue. "I only work the diner tomorrow, so just a few hours tomorrow night."

She smiled, this time in earnest. "I have it in my schedule. Good night, Robert," she said, walking towards the front door.

"Esther," he called out. She stopped and turned. She looked tired and for a second he felt guilty of robbing her of time. "She doesn't have long, does she?"

Esther took her hand off of the doorknob. She was pushing fifty, just a few years older than his mother. She had been a health aide for fifteen years and had seen it all. Helen Sinclair was days, if not hours from death.

She shook her head. "No," she said matter-of-factly. "I will never lead you on and tell you she's getting better. That is not my way and I wouldn't want it for myself. Your mama is a good, sweet woman, but she needs rest. Her body is weary."

Robert blinked away tears, willing them to not fall. "Yeah," he croaked, "I kind of figured as much. Thank you for what you've done."

Again she nodded. "I'll see you both tomorrow. Get some sleep," she said and walked out of the door.

Robert dabbed his eyes with his sleeve. He walked into the small kitchen, noticing a pile of fresh mail on the table. Robert fingered the envelopes, knowing what each of them contained. Bill after bill. They'd cut back as much as possible, but making ends meet was always a struggle. They had canceled cable and their home phone, only keeping the internet. His cell phone was a cheap pre-paid one, that was usually low on minutes. Helen's retirement wasn't much. L-mart was steady, but the pay was low. If he could get a promotion, he might be ok, but as a stock boy, he wouldn't be able to make it. He was scared. Not just for the fact his mother was dying, but for the fact he couldn't afford to keep the house after she was gone.

Helen's parents divorced when she was eighteen and her mother died in a car accident shortly after. Her father, who had a mean streak in him, left and moved across the country with his new wife. At the end of the day, it was just Robert and Helen and no one else.

He was startled as a violent cough came from his mother's room. It sounded wet, full of blood and broken glass.

"Esther," Helen groaned.

Robert dashed into the bedroom, which was only a few steps down the hallway.

"It's me, Mom. I'm home from work," Robert said, sliding into the chair next to the bed. He was careful not to bump into the small nightstand. It looked like a graveyard made of pill bottles of every size. A sweaty pitcher of water sat on a towel next to the medication. Those orange bottles were the only things keeping his mother comfortable and for the time being, alive.

The room smelled. It wasn't unclean, but quite tidy. It had the cloying smell of approaching death. A sweet, sickly odor of medication, sweat, and a hint of urine. Helen smelled like she was already starting to decompose, even though she was alive.

Helen turned to look at him, her nasal oxygen lines pulling taut. She smiled.

Before the cancer hit Helen Sinclair like a freight train, she'd been a full, vibrant middle-aged woman. Even though Robert was twenty-one, she'd never gotten rid of all the baby fat, which she didn't mind. It added to her already curvy body. Her hair was long and rich brown, with just a hint of blond highlights (which were natural, no matter what anyone said). Right before she'd gotten sick, a few greys popped up, which she yanked out by the root.

Now, she was a shell of her former self. Her body was a withered husk, with her skin hanging loosely. No matter how much lotion she used, her skin was still dry and cracked. Another wonderful side effect of medication. Her hair was nearly all gone and what she did retain was thin and dry.

Robert regretted the thought as soon as it entered his mind, but she reminded him of the Crypt Keeper from the old horror show *Tales from the Crypt*.

"Oh, hi Rob," she said, trying to sound cheerful, as if she wasn't just whining a few seconds ago. "Can you get me some water?"

Robert found a glass behind the pitcher and poured her some.

She took it, pressing the cool glass to her parched lips, and drank. Her throat strained, the water working its way down. Her hands shook as Robert took the glass from her.

"Thanks," she said, the oxygen machine hissing. She looked at her son with watery eyes and flashed him a shallow smile. "I'm dying," she said, still smiling.

Silent tears slid down Robert's cheeks.

"Don't say that, mom," he whispered, taking her hand in his.

"It's ok," she said, the oxygen hissing again. "I'm fine. I'm ready to enter the kingdom of Heaven." Helen had a set of black rosary beads on her chest. She grabbed them and began rubbing, reciting the prayers in her head.

Helen was raised Catholic, but as she entered her teens and early twenties, religion fell by the wayside. With all of the death, famine, and unjust in the world, she'd lost faith in God. After the death of her mother, Helen was left alone. She drifted further from the church, until she found out she was pregnant. By sheer coincidence, or perhaps the grace of God, Helen befriended a priest, Philip Carafa. Father Carafa led Helen back to the light of God and when Robert was born, Helen had been attending mass nearly every day. The thought of becoming a nun had crossed her mind, but she didn't want to have any issues with having a child. There was no way she'd give up her son, even for God himself.

Over the years, Father Carafa had continued with the church. His congregations were always thriving and numbers were up. He quickly rose through the church and was the current Archbishop of New York. He and Helen still spoke regularly. Even though she hated New York City, she would make the almost two-hour drive south, occasionally, to see him at mass.

"Can you please call Philip?" she asked. In private, she'd refer to him by his first name. Never in public, though. "I want my Last Rites."

Robert's tears flowed freely now. He was sobbing, his head in his hands.

In the Catholic religion, Last Rites were the final sacrament. They are only administered to those who are near death. It was the final confession and absolution of all sins.

"Shhh," Helen whispered, running a hand through her son's hair. Her other hand was still on the rosary. "I've had my time. I brought a beautiful, perfect son into this world. My life is complete and I'm ready to enter paradise. I'm not afraid." She was smiling. Suddenly her face contorted. A violent, wet cough tore through her.

Robert stared as she struggled for air. There was another oxygen tank, this one with a mask on it, next to the first one. He put it over her face and turned the tank on. Cold, relieving oxygen rushed out.

Helen breathed as deeply as she could without coughing. Finally, it was under control.

"Hand me that bottle." She pointed.

Robert picked up the giant bottle of medication. He read the label and saw it was Fentanyl Buccal tablets. He was familiar with the drug as it was usually all over the news as a powerful opioid. The drug had legit purposes, especially for people with cancer and other illnesses, but it was often abused. The misuse of Fentanyl could cause fatal overdoses by stopping the heart and breathing. He opened the bottle and handed it to her.

Helen shook out a tablet and tossed it in her mouth. It began to dissolve and she had an instant look of euphoria.

"I brought you a slice of cheesecake," Robert said, watching his mother melt into bliss.

As if she were underwater, Helen turned and looked at him.

"That sounds absolutely wonderful." She looked away, staring at the ceiling. "Oh, don't forget to call Philip."

Robert stood. "Yeah, Mom, I'll call him." He walked out of her room and into the kitchen. He took the cheesecake from the Styrofoam container and put it on a small plate. When he went back in, she was asleep.

Helen was still smiling as if seeing something beautiful.

Robert left the room, closing the door behind him. He sat at the kitchen table and pulled his cell phone out. He was going to call Cardinal Carafa, but first, he was going to eat the cheesecake.

---

CARDINAL PHILIP CARAFA, the Archbishop of New York, sat at his laptop. His fingers hovered over the keyboard as he read over his sermon for the upcoming mass. He typed a few more notes in the list of talking points. With tired eyes, he looked over all of the notes. Satisfied, he saved his work and powered down the machine.

Philip was a large man, standing well over six-foot. He had a full head of short brown and grey hair. He had a decent-sized belly, which he noticed was growing when he put on an old t-shirt.

He walked over to his modest bed, sliding his slippers beneath it. Just as he reached to turn off his small lamp, his cell phone rang. He looked at the screen and didn't recognize the number. It was after 10 pm, so he didn't think it was a telemarketer. *Probably a wrong number,* he thought, just before hitting the decline button. *But then again, what if it isn't?*

Reluctantly, he answered.

"Hello," he said.

"Hello, Eminence," a young man said on the other line. "This is Robert Sinclair."

Philip sat up, his heart racing.

"Your mother, is she OK?" the Cardinal asked. Robert sounded like he'd been crying and Philip expected the worst.

"Well, that depends on your definition," Robert replied. "She's not dead. Yet."

Philip relaxed, but only slightly. If Robert was calling him this late, something must be wrong. For him to even call instead of Helen was odd.

"She's asking for you," Robert sobbed, "to come to give her Last Rites." He was openly crying now.

Philip heard him sniffle.

"Will she make it until the morning?" he asked Robert. He was already thinking about making the drive in the middle of the night.

"Yes," said Robert. "Well, I think she'll make it tonight, but I'm not sure how much longer. She's sure her time has come."

"Ok," Philip said, already thinking of how he was going to rearrange his plans for tomorrow. "I'll be there first thing in the morning." He'd have to wake Father Dinan and tell him to cover his masses tomorrow.

"Thank you, Eminence," Robert said.

"Not a problem, Robert. May God be with you and your mother. I'll see you both in the morning."

"Goodbye," Robert said.

The line went dead.

## 4

At the same time as Helen Sinclair was receiving Holy Communion and being given her Last Rites, Josef Lazerowitz was pulling into the Ashmore Humane Society.

His bowels were cramping again, but he didn't know if he had anything left to get out. He'd awoken in the middle of the night to relieve himself, almost not making it to the toilet. The bloody shit was vile, each movement getting worse. He was happy to have woken up at all.

Josef looked at himself in the rearview mirror. He didn't think he could look any worse than last night, but he'd accomplished that. His face was like an older version of himself when he was in Auschwitz.

*Just a little longer,* he thought. He took a deep breath, trying to bring some color back to his pale skin. Josef plastered a smile on his face, fighting the pain in his gut.

He stepped out of the car. Even though it was early in the day, it was quite warm. That, coupled with the disease ravaging his body, caused Josef to break out in a sweat. He pulled a handkerchief from his pocket and mopped his face.

He opened the door of the Humane Society and was blessed with air conditioning.

A young woman with a shock of red hair sat behind a counter. She wore a pink headband that was made up of pictures of cats and dogs.

She looked up from the computer after one last keystroke.

"Hello, sir. How can I help you?" She said in a high-pitched, cheery voice.

Josef felt phlegm in his throat and cleared it.

"I'd like to look into adopting a dog," he said, the phony smile still hanging on his face.

She jumped up out of the chair and clapped her hands together.

"Excellent," she squealed, walking around the counter. "I'm Jeanine," she extended her hand.

Josef shook it, knowing his hands were clammy.

"Josef," he said, letting go as soon as possible. He broke her gaze and looked around the small room. Pictures of thousands of animals and their adopted families covered the walls. There was a bin for donations, which only held a few cans of dog food and a ripped squeaky toy.

"So, are you looking for any kind of dog in particular?" she asked him. "A puppy perhaps?" She smiled, her green eyes lighting up.

He waved his hand in jest. "Oh, no. Not a puppy," he laughed, painfully. "I'm too old to be chasing a little devil around." He paused for a moment. She was watching him, waiting for him to say something else. "My wife died recently," he said, conjuring up tears. When he thought of the fate of his family, tears came easily. Besides, his insides felt like he'd swallowed a bucket of razors. "I'm just looking for a nice, old gal to keep me company." He felt a tear slide down his face, riding the wrinkles in his skin.

Jeanine was teary-eyed too. She brushed a tear from her eyes and sniffed back snot.

"That's so sweet and makes me so happy," she said, walking towards the door. "Our seniors, the few we have, often die here. It's the worst thing in the world when they're surrendered for any reason." She led him outside and around back. The kennels were kept in a separate building behind the office. "They may not be long for the world, but they have so much love to give." She opened the kennel door.

Josef's senses were overwhelmed. The smell of dogs, shit, piss and bleach was overwhelming. The floors looked clean, but with that many animals, it was nearly impossible to kill the smell. He was glad he was partially deaf because the incessant barking would've driven him nuts. A pair of terriers occupying the first kennel were climbing all over each other, nipping and vying for his attention.

"It gets a little crazy in here," Jeanine said over the dogs, "but I love it." She pushed open a set of double doors towards the back of the room. The walls in the new section were lined with only two kennels each. "This section is where we keep dogs who are recovering from surgery, and the older, calmer dogs." She stopped in front of a kennel. "This is Molly," she said.

Molly was a fat yellow lab, who's muzzle was grey. She had droopy, yet friendly eyes. She stood up slowly, leaving behind her duck-shaped chew toy, and walked over to the chain-link door. She pressed her snout against it.

Jeanine rubbed the dog's nose.

Molly wagged her tail in thanks.

"Molly's owner died last month. No one could take her, so unfortunately she was surrendered to us. She's such a sweetheart." Jeanine kept petting the dog. "You're not going to die on her, are you?" she said jokingly, just before she turned to face Josef. She didn't realize how sickly he looked when he'd first entered the office. Panic set in. "Oh, I'm so sorry. That was a poor joke and I didn't mean it. You look great for your age." She hit herself in the forehead. "I mean, you look great for any age. I-"

Josef's face split in a wide grin, this one mostly sincere. He held up a hand to stop her. The poor girl was talking herself in circles and getting flushed.

"It's quite alright," he told her. "I get it and no offense taken." He looked at Molly, who was splitting her gaze between them. "Can I walk her?"

Jeanine started, as if she forgot why she was there. "Of course," she said, grabbing a leash from a nearby rack. She opened the kennel and Molly stayed still as she hooked her up. She handed the leash to Josef.

He took it and led the old dog out.

Jeanine opened the back door, leading into a penned area.

Josef and Molly walked like they were meant for each other. The dog stayed at his side, tail wagging the entire time. She sniffed, squatted in the grass, and let out a little pee. They walked for a few minutes and even played a game of fetch, albeit a slow-paced version.

"I'm not going to lie, I think we're made for each other," Josef said, sitting on a bench. Molly had her head resting on his lap. Her eyes were closed as he rubbed at her ears.

Jeanine squealed and clapped again. "I knew it from the moment you saw each other. So, when do you think you'd like to take her home?"

"I'll take her right now," he said. Molly, as if she understood, woke up, tail wagging. "I'd hate to think of her spending another night here. She needs to be in a house with a warm bed and no more barking dogs."

Jeanine pulled out her cell phone and checked the time. "There's some paperwork involved, but I think we can get you out of here in an hour or so. Is that OK?"

On cue, Josef's stomach cramped. A grimace shot across his face. He hoped she didn't notice.

"An hour would be fine. I'll just run out and get some housewarming gifts for her." He checked his watch. "I'll see you in an hour," he said, rubbing Molly's head. She licked his hand as he walked her back to the kennel.

Minutes later, Josef pulled into a gas station bathroom. Blackness poured from him. The pain was mounting and he felt as if he'd pass out. *Please God, don't let me die in a gas station bathroom*, he thought. His body was empty of the bloody stool, but only for a little while. He was cold and sweating when he stood up.

He stared at his hollow reflection in the grimy mirror. "One hour," he said. "One more hour."

# CHAPTER 4

ROBERT AND CARDINAL CARAFA were at the kitchen table. Sweaty glasses of iced tea sat in front of them. Most of the ice had melted, leaving a layer of water at the top of each drink.

Robert sipped from his cup, crunching a thin sliver of ice after he swallowed.

"How long do you think?" he asked Philip.

"Honestly, I'm surprised she made it this long." Cardinal Carafa touched his drink but didn't pick it up. He rubbed the condensation between his fingers. "Your mother is a strong woman. I just hope she can find peace in the eternal kingdom of God."

Robert didn't cry. He was cried out. His eyes were red, but remained dry. The visit by the Cardinal not only brought peace to his mother, but to him also. No matter when she passed, he knew his mother would rest, finally.

Cardinal Carafa raised his sleeve, checking the time. "I have to get back to the city, but please call me if anything changes." He rose, putting his hat on.

Robert stood, facing the holy man. "Thank you for coming. It means everything to us." He held out his hand.

Philip took it, pulling him into a bear hug. The embrace was tight and for a moment, Philip had to control himself from bursting into tears. He let Robert go, keeping his hands on his shoulders, and looked into his eyes. "It is in God's hands now." He turned to the front door. "Be well, Robert," he said as he walked out of the house, closing the door behind him.

Robert finished his watered-down tea and looked at the time.

Even though his world was being turned upside down, he still had to put food on the table. His shift at the diner was in four hours and Esther would be at the house in three. Not sleeping well the night before, he decided to lay on the couch and hopefully catch a quick nap.

He jumped up three hours later as Esther walked in.

"Sorry," she said. "I would've let you sleep." Esther put her purse, which had a fresh magazine poking from it, on the table.

Robert rubbed the sleep from his eyes and checked the time. He panicked, not for running late, but because he hadn't checked on his mother. As quietly as he could, opened his mother's door.

Her chest rose and fell. A new set of ivory rosary beads were clutched in her hands. *This is how she'll look when she dies*, he thought. He pushed the image from his head and shut the door.

"She's sleeping," he told Esther.

"That's good," she replied, putting her dinner in the fridge. "Go on and get ready. I'll take it from here."

Robert took a quick shower, which helped to wake him up. On the way out he made a sandwich. Otis wasn't the only cook working tonight and he knew Simon would charge him to eat.

With one hand on the steering wheel and the other holding the sandwich, he headed to work.

---

JOSEF DROVE with the radio on oldies and Molly's head hanging out the window. The old lab held onto her duck chew toy as her ears and lips blew in the breeze. If she turned the right way, the rushing air would hit the noise maker in the toy, making it squeak.

Josef tapped the steering wheel, trying to keep the rhythm of the song. In all honesty, he was trying not to shit his pants and needed something to take his mind off the pain in his bowels.

He saw a green dumpster behind a closed restaurant and hit his blinker. The car coasted behind the building, gravel crunching under the tires. Molly looked at him, confused, but her toy squeaked in her mouth, getting her attention. Josef popped the trunk and took out a large, black garbage bag.

Molly, seeing the bag, perked back up. She knew it was her stuff. The stuff she'd been brought in with: her bed, more toys, some treats, and her favorite brush. Her tail was like a metronome hitting against the windshield as she watched Josef walk over to the dumpster.

He opened the lid and tossed the bag in. A storm of flies buzzed around him. He got back into the car, the air conditioning cooling the sweat on his face. Molly was staring at the dumpster and then looking back at him.

"You're not going to need that, trust me," he said, patting her neck.

The car started forward again, the wind rushing by. Molly put her head out the window, her belongings forgotten.

---

"Here we are, old girl," Josef said, leading Molly into the house. Her duck toy was still wedged firmly in her jaws. A violent spasm hit his stomach like a truck. He dropped the leash and ran to the bathroom.

Molly took it upon herself to lay on the floor and chew her toy. It squeaked with every bite, filling the room with sound.

A very different sound came out of the bathroom. Josef was in agony. Gouts of blood poured from him, with every drop feeling like a minute off his life. When he'd finished, he splashed cold water on his sallow face. The reflection was skeletal.

Molly was waiting for him at the door, the duck in her mouth, and tail wagging. She was still on the leash, which she didn't seem to mind.

Josef smiled, remorsefully, and grabbed the leash.

"Sorry, old girl." He didn't want to say her name. He started walking her through the house. They stopped at the basement door.

The sweet, old dog changed. She dropped her toy, the hair raising on her back, and growled. It was a fearful growl, she hoped sounded aggressive.

Josef picked up the toy, hesitantly, fearing she'd bite him. He didn't think his frail body could take the abuse.

"Oh, stop," he said to her, voice wavering. "There's nothing to be afraid of." He wasn't so sure of that as he opened the door into the blackness of the basement. He didn't need a light.

She stopped growling and began crying. Not a cry of pain, but one of fear. With a splash, she pissed all over the floor. Her tail was tucked deep between her legs, urine dripped from it. Molly's ears were back and feet planted. She could feel the evil coming from the abyss in front of her.

"Come now," Josef said, pulling the leash towards the stairs.

Molly was planted, her nails digging into the wooden floor.

Josef's strength was sapped and the old dog put up more of a fight than he expected.

"Knock it the fuck off!" he yelled as if she could understand him. If anything, it made her fight harder. Realizing he couldn't yank her with one hand, he threw the squeaky toy into the basement. He gripped the leash with both hands, preparing to pull her if needed.

Molly watched her favorite toy, losing sight of it as it bounced down the stairs. She relaxed, just a little, but not enough to follow behind it.

The toy squeaked.

Her ears perked up at the sound and her head tilted in confusion.

Josef looked into the darkness. His skin broke out in goosebumps and his balls pulled up tight against his body.

The toy squeaked again and again as if something was chewing on it.

That was Molly's toy and no other animal would play with it. She stepped forward.

"Atta girl," Josef said, leading her into the blackness. His shaking foot hit the first step, the dog right behind him. "Just a few more," he told her. They descended into the inky blackness.

Slowly, as if by the slightest gust of wind, the basement door closed.

## 5

Josef sat in his favorite chair. He had a glass of bourbon in his hand. It was neat. The drink was untouched for the last 20 minutes. He sat staring blankly at the black TV across from him. He knew it was time to speak with Robert. His secret clawed at him and begged to be released.

He brought the glass up to his lips, sipping the fiery liquid. It burned on its way down, but was only a mild tingle. For the first time in a long time, his stomach felt ok. There was still slight discomfort, but he'd bought the time he needed. In one shot, he finished the drink, grimaced, and coughed. The alcohol hit his empty stomach and delivered slight euphoria. He was pleasantly drunk; not enough to lose his wits, but enough to feel free. This was good. What he had to do in the next couple of hours would involve more alcohol and a terrible story.

He picked up his cell phone and scrolled through his contacts. Robert said he was working tonight and his shift was just about to begin. Josef didn't know how, but he knew Robert wasn't going to work tonight. Something had happened to keep him from the diner. All he had to do was call.

The cursor was over the young man's number. Josef's wrinkled finger hovered above it. *Could I really do this to him?* he thought. He absently put the glass to his lips, forgetting he'd drank it all. He walked into the kitchen, grabbing the bottle from the table. He filled the glass to the brim. *It's the only way, the best way. Not only for me but for him and everyone*, his mind raced. Josef sipped the bourbon; the burn was less now. One of the many gifts of the amber liquid was the more you drank, the better it tasted.

With a little more liquid courage, Josef pressed his thumb down on his phone. He put it to his ear, almost praying it wouldn't connect. Robert answered on the second ring.

"Hello."

Josef paused for a second, contemplating telling the young man he'd called him in error.

"Mr. Lazer, are you there?" Robert asked.

Josef could hear the wind in the background and figured Robert was driving with the windows down.

"H-hello, Robert," Josef said, almost feeling as if he was out of body, watching from afar. The gravity of the situation or just the alcohol was making him feel disconnected. "I was wondering if you had a minute. There's something I'd like to talk to you about."

"Yeah, go ahead," Robert said.

Josef could hear the clicking of a blinker in the background.

He still had time to back out. Josef knew he wouldn't. He couldn't.

"It's kind of long. Would you be able to come by for a little while?" He already knew he would say yes.

Robert paused and Josef could picture him thinking it over. It was almost as if he was in the car with him.

"Ah, sure. Actually, Simon just called and told me the diner was closing for the night. Something about a water leak in the kitchen." He paused and then said, "I can't stay too long. Esther is with my mother, but I'd like to get home early if I could."

Josef was nodding, as if Robert could see him. "Of course. I wouldn't want to keep you." He knew this was a lie. His story was going to be thorough.

"Ok, I can be there in ten minutes."

"Great. Have you eaten yet? I have a frozen pizza I could put in."

"I ate a sandwich, but a few slices would be nice. Thank you."

"Not a problem," said Josef. "See you soon." He hung up without waiting for Robert's reply.

---

Robert pulled into Josef's driveway ten minutes later. He knocked on the front door and heard Josef yell for him to come in.

Robert opened the door and stepped into the house. He knew the address and the house, but he'd never been inside.

"I'm back here," yelled Josef. He popped his head out from the kitchen.

The first thing Robert noticed was how good the old man looked. The last time he'd seen Josef, he looked like death warmed over. Now he looked like a man fifteen years younger, who had just woken up from a great nap.

Robert walked into the kitchen, the smell of pizza leading the way. He stopped short, a confused look on his face.

The small table was covered with hundreds of black and white photos. Given Josef's age and lack of family, it wasn't odd his only memories were captured in grainy black and white. What was odd was the content of the pictures. Twisted bodies in heaps. Men, women, and children being dissected, some still alive. Piles of shoes, jewelry, and clothing. Smiling Nazi guards standing over dead bodies, machine guns in hand. A fierce-looking German Shepherd snarling at a group of terrified children, the dog's handler with an expression of pure glee.

Robert had seen the tattoo on Josef's arm and knew he'd been in the camps, but it seemed so distant. The holocaust wasn't real to Robert. Obviously, he knew it was a real event, but it was so far from the present. He'd never met anyone who'd been a victim of the Nazi party, let alone befriended one of them. This, the pictures in front of him and the teary-eyed man at the table, were real.

"Take a seat," Josef said, wiping his face. He stood and grabbed the pizza from the oven. He put a slice on a plate and handed it to Robert.

Robert took it, his eyes not coming off the pictures on the table. Not everyone was gruesome. Some were happy. A young family, a father, mother, and two twin sons, who looked around nine-years-old. There were plenty of pictures of them mixed in with the atrocities. The man looked like Josef, but it must've been his father. Robert figured Josef was one of the twins in the picture.

Josef set a small glass in front of Robert and filled it with bourbon.

"Ah, no thanks, Mr. Lazer."

Josef looked him in the eye. "Trust me, you'll need it." He poured one for himself and threw it back. He refilled his glass and sat down. "What I'm about to tell you is borderline absurd, but I swear on everything holy, every word is the truth."

Robert gingerly took a bite of the steaming pizza. He wasn't a big drinker and really wanted some water.

"Ok, Mr. Lazer. So, what's so important?" he asked, swallowing the pizza.

Josef looked at the pictures spread out before them. He touched one of the family, rubbing their faces as if they could feel his touch.

"Life in Poland during the war was bad, but the real nightmare started in 1943."

## II

# WORK MAKES YOU FREE

## 6

THE TRAIN CAR stunk of piss, shit, and fear. Polish Jews were crammed in like cattle. The heat was sweltering, only adding to their misery. It had been three days since their ghetto was cleared out and they were taken from their homes. The car, which could've held around fifty people comfortably, was filled with nearly 150 men, women, and children. The doomed passengers hadn't been given any food or water since the start of the trip. They only had what they brought and that was gone within a day. Many of them had resorted to drinking urine and eating bugs that would fly in through the small window. The only area to relieve oneself was a bucket in the corner. Within a day, it was full. Now, the prisoners would either soil themselves or go where they sat. Many were already covered in urine and feces, so it wouldn't have mattered anyway. Some of them were already dead, their remaining family cradling their quickly rotting corpses.

Josef Lazerowitz and his family were the lucky ones. When they were loaded onto the car, they were pushed back near the only window. While at first, this was somewhat discomforting, it became a godsend within hours. The train cars had only one barred window and the cracks in the door for circulation. Not to mention, the heat in the car was stifling with 150 bodies crammed in. It was summer in Poland and the heat was in full effect, only adding to the misery.

Josef, who had his shirt unbuttoned and open, lay with his head against the back of the car. His wife, Ola, rested her head on his shoulder. She was sleeping, her head swaying with the movement of the tracks.

Michal and Piotr, Josef and Ola's nine-year-old twin sons, sat on either side of their parents.

The Lazerowitz's had their meager belongings in front of them. They carried two bags for the family, which contained clothes, a few toiletry items, personal effects, and above all, food and water.

Josef was a theology professor at Jagiellonian University in Krakow. At the onset of the war, many of his peers were questioned and arrested. Their crime was being educated and wanting to start a new school year. Josef, by the grace of God, was on extended leave. Just before the start of the war, he'd suffered from an unknown sickness, which left him bedridden and weak for nearly two weeks. Upon hearing of the persecution of his peers, he and his family fled. Unfortunately, the Nazi war machine had the whole country on lockdown and the Lazerowitz family didn't get far. They found themselves in a ghetto, under constant guard by Nazi officers. Life in the ghetto was rough, but compared to the train car, it was paradise. If only they knew what awaited them.

Before the deportation from the ghettos, many people were talking about where they were going. Some, the naive or just stupid, believed the propaganda of being relocated was for their own good.

From an early age, Josef was taught to think for himself and only believe what his eyes saw. Their occupiers were not in the habit of being gentle. Many Jews were beaten in the streets, had their buildings vandalized, or were raped. No, Josef knew they were not headed towards safety. At that point, he knew the time to fight was over. It would do nothing besides getting him and his family killed. He had seen it firsthand.

A teenage girl who had been raped by an SS officer attempted to stab the officer with a sharpened piece of wood. The girl was disarmed and marched into the center of the ghetto. She was joined by her mother, father, and infant sister. Her voice was raw as all of them were gunned down, one by one, in front of her. She was then executed by hanging from a lamppost. Her corpse was left to rot for nearly a week.

Josef had kept a small ration of food and water in their belongings, just for this instance. His family would discreetly eat and drink, not to make an event of it. Starving and scared eyes would look around at the sound of chewing. Within days, some people had been reduced to animal instincts and would've killed for a drink of water. They only ate at night, and Josef told his family not to chew the hard bread, but let it dissolve for fear of others hearing. He would pretend to urinate in an old can, but in reality, it was filled with semi-clean water.

Josef was on the verge of sleep, when a little voice spoke.

"Papa," Michal said, whispering.

Josef looked down at his son, who was resting on his chest. He didn't speak, just looked.

"I think that lady is dead," he mumbled, moving his eyes across the car.

Josef looked in the direction his son had gestured.

An adult woman was weeping into the hair of a much older woman. The older of the two appeared to be sleeping, but there was no rise in her chest. Josef had seen them around the ghetto, but never knew their names.

"It is not polite to stare," he said to his son.

The boy looked down, ashamed.

Josef, who gave his sons their curiosity, patted the boy on the back.

"It is OK to be curious, Michal, but let her grieve on her own."

The boy smiled, a rare thing in such a place. He put his head back down on his father's chest.

With an abruptness they hadn't felt in days, the train lurched. The rhythm of the tracks changed and the engine was winded down. A loud shriek sounded through the car, rattling fillings, as the brakes were applied.

Grimy and terrified faces looked around as the train came to a halt. They could hear shouting from outside.

Michal jumped, grabbing his father tight as a gunshot rang out.

"What is happening?" Ola asked. Piotr clutched her and began to cry.

Josef looked at his wife. He swallowed hard, his throat dry.

"We are here," he shuddered.

The large doors were thrown open. Dirty hands reached up to block the offensive sunlight.

They'd arrived at Auschwitz.

# 7

CHAOS.

That was the only word to describe the train platforms. Thousands of people poured from the rail cars, taking their first breath of fresh air in days. Unwashed bodies pressed together, trying to see. The cloying stench of filth and diesel fumes permeated the air. Another scent was in the air; something was burning.

"Leave your belongings on the train," said one of the Nazi guards, using a bullhorn to amplify his voice.

Josef and the rest of his family were still stuck on the train, as they were loaded in first. He could see the swelling crowd in front of him. Crisp, uniformed Nazis stood amongst the disheveled passengers.

Ola looked at her husband, tears held back. "We have to leave our possessions?" She half asked, as if Josef would tell her something different. Oh God, how she wanted him to tell her something different. She wanted him to tell her, *'No, not us. There's been a mistake. We shouldn't be here. Just sit down and we'll ride the train back home.'* That would never come. She gripped his hand, her other one squeezing Piotr's.

"Grab food," Josef said. He didn't let go of Michal, but he did let go of his wife. With his hand free, Josef dumped one of their bags out on the floor of the train car. He rifled through it, grabbing a wax square containing hard bread. "Here," he said, pushing it to his wife's stomach. "Hide this," he mumbled through clenched teeth.

Their car was unloading faster and soon they would be the only ones left. This couldn't happen; they couldn't be singled out.

Josef stood, grabbing Ola's hand again. He looked at the woman on the floor, the one who was cradling her dead mother.

The woman sobbed and rocked back and forth. She finger-brushed her mother's hair, her lips moving in silent prayer.

"Out, now," yelled a guard. He, like the others, was tall and in a crisp uniform. In one hand he carried a stick, which he used like an orchestra conductor. He motioned for them to move.

Josef listened to the man, pulling his family into the crowd. He could hear the guard yelling at the woman in the car.

"Leave her and get to your feet," he said.

Josef snuck a glance back at the train car, just in time to see the guard pull his Luger.

The interior of the train car muffled the gunshot, but not completely. People nearby screamed, moving away from the dead women.

Josef grabbed his family a little tighter.

The camp sprawled in front of them, but not much could be seen. Except for one thing. In the distance, a brick chimney belched fire and smoke. Ash, like black snow, fell around it.

"Men to the left, women and children to the right!" A guard yelled over the roar of the crowd.

Josef and Ola looked at each other. The boys were crying now and Piotr had lost control of his bladder.

The column of bodies moved closer to the separation point. Josef squeezed Ola tighter. Finally, he pushed Michal to his mother.

"Boys, take care of Mama," Josef said, looking at his sons. He didn't want to break down in front of them, but each step brought the distinct sting of tears. "You be brave and watch over her." They were all crying now. Another gunshot in the distance made them jump. "I will find you." *In this life or the next*, he thought.

"You," a guard said to Josef.

He broke his gaze off his family and looked at the Nazi guard.

From all of the stories he'd heard, he expected every Nazi to look like evil incarnate. What he saw was far from that. The man standing in front of him couldn't be more than twenty-two. He had a soft face with none of the sharp Germanic features. He could've been a lifeguard or school teacher. Instead, he was a harbinger of death.

"To the left." He pushed Josef aside, not looking as he was swept into the tide of bodies.

Even in the screaming and yelling, Josef still knew the sound of his wife's voice.

"No, no," Ola pleaded.

Josef stopped, the crowd moving around him. He scanned for Ola, who was trying to wrestle their sons from two guards.

"Let them stay with me, please." She was on her knees, and the boys were being sent away. Each boy was led screaming by a guard, who had them by their armpits.

"Mama!" The boys drug their feet, trying to get back to their weeping mother. "Please, Mama!" It was Piotr who yelled. It was the last time she ever heard either of their voices again.

"They are too valuable to be left to you," one of the guards said. He wore the insignia of an *Unterscharfuher*, a sergeant. "If you do not get up, you will be shot." He pulled a pistol from his belt and put the barrel against her forehead.

Josef had a scream on his lips, but a strong hand grabbed his arm.

"No," the man said, "they will kill you too."

Josef couldn't take his eyes off of his wife.

She stared at the ground. Her tears fell freely, not from the risk of death, but the loss of her family.

For dramatics, the Nazi sergeant pulled the hammer back on his gun.

"Sergeant," another Nazi approached the small crowd. "Stow your pistol immediately," the newcomer said. His rank identified him as a lieutenant.

The sergeant glared at his commanding officer, but listened. He lowered the hammer on his pistol and re-holstered it.

"This Jew was causing trouble, Lieutenant Kollmer," the sergeant said. "She was trying to stay with her sons." He grinned something evil. "Her twin sons."

Piotr and Michal were not the only twins taken that day. In fact, the group they walked away with was mostly twins.

Lieutenant Kollmer looked down at her. He showed no sympathy in his expression. To him, she was an animal, an animal that was disrupting his orderly way of things. "Get in line," he said to Ola.

She stood on shaking legs, allowing herself to be swallowed in the sea of bodies.

Josef, who had been holding his breath, finally sighed. He didn't know where she was going, but at least she was alive.

"Thank you," he said, turning to the mystery man who'd whispered to him. The man was gone, swallowed up in the crowd. Josef followed suit.

The men were marched into a squat building, resembling military barracks. They were lined up against a wall and for a moment, Josef thought they were going to be executed.

"Take off your clothes," one of the guards ordered. He was pacing up and down the line of men, cane in hand. Anyone who was too slow or wanted to retain a shred of dignity was hit.

Josef, not wanting the cane, undressed. He and hundreds of others stood nude. They covered their genitals, but were told to put their arms over their heads. Another guard walked up and down the line. He wore two tanks on his back and carried a sprayer in his hand. Each man was coated with a noxious chemical.

When the man reached Josef, he held his breath. The liquid was cold, unless it hit an open orifice, in which case it burned.

After the men were sprayed, they were led into another building.

Josef walked, his hands over his crotch. When he entered the next building, a man in striped clothing handed him his own set. Josef dressed quickly, as the guards were fast to reward laziness with a beating. The fabric was coarse and smelled like chemicals. He itched where the chemicals were still wet in his chest hair. The man in the striped clothes didn't speak, just continued to hand out clothing. His eyes were downcast, like a beaten dog.

"Next," shouted a guard, who was further in the building.

Josef walked up to the Nazi.

"Name," he said, poising a pen over a piece of paper.

Josef looked at the paper. It was filled with names, each one with a corresponding number.

"Josef Lazerowitz," he said, his voice proud.

The man scrawled it on the paper.

"Profession."

Josef knew he was lucky when his friends were taken years ago. Educators were seen as rebels and were usually weeded out. Even so, Josef told the truth. This was his fate and his life was in the hands of God.

"Professor," he said.

The Nazi guard looked up at him. "Ah, a smart Jew," he smirked. "A professor of what?"

"Theology. You know, religion."

His ice-blue eyes bore into Josef. "Yes, I know what theology is." He jotted it down.

Another man in striped clothing walked over to them with a piece of paper in his hand.

"His number," the guard told the man in striped clothes, pointing to his list.

The man wrote the number on the small slip of paper and pinned it to Josef's shirt.

"Follow," he said, walking away.

Josef did, but he could feel the glare of the Nazi following him.

"Next," the Nazi yelled. Another man stood before him.

In the next room, Josef's head was shaved. His scalp bled from a few nicks, but it was over in minutes. Then, his number was tattooed onto his left forearm.

Josef and the rest of the men were led from the building and further into camp. The smell of death was everywhere. They were purposefully marched next to a long trench. Out of curiosity, Josef looked.

At first, he wasn't sure what he was seeing. His senses were overwhelmed with disgust. Human bodies were piled together. Men, women, and children were discarded like trash. Most of them were nude, some wore clothes, but not striped clothing. No, many of them were led off of the trains and shot immediately. These were the undesirables, the human cargo that couldn't work. Elderly, children, or the sick. They were all one in death.

Josef could almost taste the rot in the warm air. A low hum of buzzing flies was constant. Black insects crawled from the mouth of a girl, no older than four. His stomach revolted, but he was able to keep his gorge from spewing.

They marched into a second part of the camp, away from the train tracks. He entered the last building; the barracks. Inside, bunks were stacked to the ceiling. Some were filled with skeletal men, others were empty.

"This is your bunk," the lead Nazi guard told them. "You will live here now, serving the Fatherland." He pulled a pocket watch and checked the time. "You have five minutes to piss and then you start work." He grinned and said, "Work makes you free."

---

BEFORE THE WAR, a normal workday for Josef was quite mundane. He'd get up at 6 am, eat a light breakfast, and go over some of the student's papers (there was always something to grade or evaluate). After that, he'd shower, shave, and pack himself a nice lunch. By that time, Ola and the boys would be up. He'd make his rounds, kissing each of them, Ola he'd kiss three times. That was their thing: three quick pecks on the lips and a smile, always her smile. If the boys weren't looking, maybe he'd slap her on the butt, garnering another one of her smiles. Living in Krakow, his walk to school was brief. Upon arriving (he was always early), he'd review his lesson plans. Once his classes started they'd talk about everything. Sure, the lesson plan would be covered, as per University standards, but his students were free thinkers. They'd often discuss not only theology, but economics, social standings, and the growing Nazi threat.

Josef's workday, now being in Auschwitz, had changed.

He and the other men in his barracks were lined up outside, Nazi guards around them. Most of them had large sticks and all of them had pistols. Once all of the prisoners were out, they marched.

The summers in Poland were normally quite mild, but with no clouds and the sun directly overhead, it was scorching.

Josef shuffled along with the rest of the men. He still had plenty of energy, but the last thing he wanted to do was stand out. They walked through the men's camp and began heading back towards the train platform. The fiery chimney could be seen in the distance. Women and children were being herded around the camp, many of the women in grey dresses. He looked at everyone, scanning for Ola or the boys, but didn't see them.

"My friend, you might want to keep your eyes forward," came a voice from behind Josef.

Instinctively, he wanted to turn and face the man, but took his advice.

"I'm looking for my family," Josef said, trying his best to project his voice back towards the man.

"Don't bother," the man replied. "In Auschwitz, we're all the same."

Josef wondered if this was the same man from the train platform who'd grabbed his arm. The odds were slim.

They continued to walk past more barracks. A volley of gunfire made Josef and some of the others jump. Out of the corner of his eye, he saw two men lying dead in a courtyard between two buildings. Nazi guards stood over them, prodding them with the muzzles of their rifles. One of the men with a smoking gun was familiar. Josef, being a professor for years, had built up a great memory for faces and names. Lieutenant Erich Kollmer, the man who stopped Ola from being killed on the platform, stood over the corpses.

Other prisoners came out and removed the bodies.

"Next," Lt. Kollmer yelled as if auditioning people for a play. A metal door was opened and two nude, stick-like men were pushed out. In their last quest for dignity, they covered their genitals. The men were pushed against the wall, their faces away from their executioners. Lt. Kollmer and the other men aimed and fired. A bloom of brain matter, skull fragments, and blood joined the growing mess on the wall. The men collapsed, their lives snatched away in an instant.

"Next," he yelled. Two more men were marched out, put against the wall, and shot.

"That is the death wall," the man said from behind Josef. Their Nazi guards were too busy watching the executions to notice the brief conversation. "Block 10 and Block 11, two places you'd better pray you don't end up."

Josef didn't want to be here in the first place, but he couldn't imagine what made these places that much worse.

"Why?" Josef asked out of the corner of his mouth, his head turning just slightly.

"Block 11 is a black hole; what goes in, doesn't come out," he said. "From the rumors, the bottom two floors are where they keep the worst of the worst; spies, war criminals, politicians, professors, gays, so on. When they are sent there, within a day or two they're led out to the wall. Unless you get to the third floor." He stopped talking when a Nazi guard was scanning their lines. Not seeing any infractions, the guard moved along.

"The third floor, so I've been told, is the best-kept secret in the camp. Higher classed prisoners are kept there. Germans who angered someone powerful, but had enough backing not to be killed or put in the general population. I've heard some of the higher-ranked guards would keep whores in there too, but who knows. I hope to never go in and find out."

They knew this conversation could get them both shot, but they were too engaged, especially Josef. Since being little, he'd always craved knowledge. If he was trapped here, he wanted to know everything.

"What about Block 10?"

The man was silent for a second. Not for the fear of being seen, but for the horrors that went on in the unassuming brick building.

"Ten is the medical building," he said, looking away from it as if it was repulsive.

"Like an infirmary?" Josef was still in his civilian mindset. He couldn't face the fact he and his family were in a death camp. Nothing was what it seemed. The most innocent indiscretion could get you killed or worse, finding yourself in Block 10 or 11.

Josef was looking forward, this conversation going on with forced whispers. He kept his eyes glued to the shaved head in front of him. Nazi guards were everywhere, but most were occupied with their prisoners or tasks. The man's silence led him to think the conversation was over. Then he choked out a response.

"No, not an infirmary. More like a torture chamber." His speech wavered.

Josef didn't know the man, but could tell from the hurt in his voice, he'd lost someone in those brick walls.

"The fucking doctors experiment on people in there. Men, women, and children, but from what I've heard, it's mostly women. Some sick bastard who is working on female reproduction and the torments the bodies can take."

Josef cringed, thinking of Ola in there being subjected to that.

"That's not the worst fucking part," he said, almost growling. "A few months ago, a new doctor arrived. One even worse, if that's possible. A man who specializes in children, specifically twins. They call him the *Angel of Death*."

For a split second, Josef lost his mind. He stepped with his left foot towards the building, which was far behind them by now. If the thought of Ola in there was bad, Piotr and Michal was torment like no other. His boys were sweet boys, who liked radio programs before bed and playing with toy trucks. Piotr loved to sing and would often serenade the family during some of the radio shows. Michal would paint. He was given a small kit, complete with easel, canvas, and oil paints for his last birthday.

Now, they could be in that building being experimented on by a madman.

A shout from the head of the line brought him back to reality. There was no way he'd even get close to the building without being gunned down. If he was lucky, he'd die from a bullet in the back and not be taken to Block 11.

The column of men continued to walk, passing many more buildings like theirs. They entered a gated area, with a building in the middle. Two trucks were idling outside. The vertical exhaust pipes belched a thin wisp of diesel smoke.

Their German escorts walked over and conferred with a couple more outside of the building. They looked over the prisoners, one man counting them off. This man, a sergeant by his rank insignia, walked down the line of them. He stopped behind Josef.

"From this man," he said, tapping Josef on the back with his stick, "and forward, remain here. The rest of you will follow Sgt. Unger."

Josef stood ramrod straight as the Nazis walked up and down their line. He could hear the gate open and close as the rest of the men left.

"I am Sgt. Kurtz and you are mine. If you do not work, you will be shot. If you are lazy and slow, you will be shot. If you make any attempt to escape…" He trailed off, smiling at them with tobacco-stained teeth. "Well, I think you get the picture."

The wind shifted, blowing the diesel smell away. On the breeze came a new scent, an odd one for the camp. It was a very strong smell of almonds.

When Josef was a boy, his grandmother would always bake *rogaliki,* a crescent-shaped, almond cookie. He would stand on a stool next to her and pinch the little pieces of dough into shape. She always told him his fingers made them sweeter and she'd only eat the ones he formed. He'd loved her, but she'd been dead for years. She was lucky.

"You will load the trucks," Sgt. Kurtz said, pointing to a door at the back of the building. On cue, the door opened. The smell of almonds was now overpowering.

Josef didn't think they were baking cookies in there.

"Oh my God!" a man in the front said. He started backing away from the door, his hands to his mouth.

Josef didn't know the man, but he looked healthy like him, so he figured he was also a new arrival.

Sgt. Kurtz looked at two of the other Nazis and nodded. They grabbed the screaming man and pushed him away from the rest of them.

The realization of what was about to happen struck him.

"No, please. I'm sorry, it was just a reaction. No, I'm ready to work." He was forced down to his knees. He popped back up, turning towards the guards. "Sir, please, I'm strong. I can work. Let me prove it to you." This time one Nazi guard used a heavy stick and smashed it into the man's knee. The second guard drew his Luger from a black holster on his hip.

The prisoner went down in a heap, holding his broken kneecap. He writhed around, making an accurate shot nearly impossible.

The guard aimed at him, but held his fire.

"Oh, for fucks sake," said Sgt. Kurtz. He walked over and placed his black boot on the man's throat, holding his head still. With a practiced hand, he drew his gun and put a bullet in the man's forehead.

All of them knew it was coming, but flinched anyway.

Sgt. Kurtz holstered his pistol and gave his men a sneer. "Here is your first to load in."

Three men closest to the corpse sprang into action and unceremoniously threw it into the bed of the truck.

"Now, get to work," Sgt. Kurtz said, pointing at the open doors.

At the base of the door were bodies. Dozens, if not hundreds of mostly women and children. They were all nude, and almost all of them covered in excrement. Their faces were contorted in pain and fear. Some were embraced, a final act of love in a place where there was none.

Sgt. Kurtz took an exaggerated breath. "Ah, I love the smell of Zyklon." The other guards laughed.

The men shuffled forward, the overpowering stench of almonds permeating from the room. Zyklon B, they'd later find out, was the chemical used to kill the people. The almond smell was one of its signature characteristics.

Josef worked numbly, trying not to look at faces. If he saw his family in the heap of corpses, his thin shred of sanity would surely snap.

They repeated the cycle for the rest of the day. Once the trucks were loaded, they were taken away, only to be replaced with empty ones. The empty ones, which were slick with bodily fluids, were parked and awaited their grim cargo. The doors would shut and Josef and other men would listen to men, women, and children screaming for their lives in the gas chamber. Within minutes the sound would stop and the door opened. A fresh pile of corpses was loaded and sent away.

In the distance, the chimney of the incinerator belched fire all day.

The sun had begun to set. Josef and the rest of the men from his barracks were tired, but still standing. No one else had been shot.

"Form up your line," ordered Sgt. Kurtz. He and the other Nazis had just returned from their dinner break. He smoked a cigarette, which dangled from his lip.

Josef and the men of his camp did just that, they formed up their marching line.

Even though it was nearly dark, the camp was well lit. Guard towers dotted the grounds, usually manned with at least three guards. One man would work the exterior spotlight, which was pointed outside of the wire around the camp. The other would work the interior light, pointing into the camp. The third was at the ready with a rifle in the event someone needed to be shot. Not only were there roaming searchlights, but light towers were spread around the grounds as well.

The men marched back to their barracks.

Josef looked around at the other men, many of whom were lying on their straw-filled bunks. Some were shirtless. They were thin, and not just the kind of thinness of youth or a slim man. No, they were skin and bones. He didn't know how he'd missed seeing it before.

Josef looked for an empty bed. Men were everywhere. When he'd first arrived, it had been such a whirlwind of events and confusion. Now that time had passed, he could take everything in.

The building was long and narrow. Wooden bunks were stacked three high in every inch of space along the walls. Each bunk had a straw-filled mattress and threadbare blanket. There was no pillow.

Josef found an empty bed and laid down. The entire time he worked, he did it with fear for his life. Now, the work had stopped and the weariness of the day set in.

Just recently, he and his family had been in their own place, albeit in a cramped apartment in the ghetto. They'd had breakfast as a family and were preparing for their day, when the shouting had started.

He looked up at the bunk above him, which was inches from his face. There were names scratched into it. Each one a person, each one a life snuffed out. He wanted to cry, but he knew it would do no good.

Josef adjusted himself, but there was nothing comfortable about the bed. His wool uniform was heavy with sweat. The sharp hay used for his bedding, no better than an animal, poked through. Even so, he started to drift to sleep. In sleep, no one could hurt him.

He was nearly out when he heard the commotion. There was a hand on his shoulder.

"Get up," said the man.

Josef knew the voice. It was the man who was in line with him, telling him about Block 10 and 11.

The man was short, but had a hardness about him. Everyone was thin and angular, but this man had something different. His cheeks were hollow, but in almost a dignified way. It was as if he chose to be there on his own accord.

"This is the only time you'll eat, so get up." He offered Josef his hand.

Food was the last thing on his mind, but now that it was being mentioned, he realized exactly how hungry he was. He didn't think the offerings were going to be plentiful here, but something was better than nothing.

"Thank you," said Josef, taking the help out of the narrow bunk. "I'm Josef. Josef Lazerowitz."

"David Ableson, but everyone calls me Abe."

Josef and Abe got in line, following the rest of the men out of the barracks.

Every other barrack was doing the same. Lines of men formed, making their way into another nondescript brick building. The lines were moving with machine-like efficiency, each man coming out with a piece of black bread and small sausage.

"Thank you for earlier," Josef said, shuffling forward in line.

"Don't mention it. I've been here for three months and have seen men shot for less. I could tell it was your first day."

Josef looked around. There weren't many men whose stomachs pressed against their uniform. Those that had a little extra weight were surely new, like him. Many of them had red faces from crying. He hoped he didn't look as destitute as he felt.

"Yeah, I guess it's quite easy to pick out."

"All of the new guys smell like pesticide."

Josef thought back to a few hours before when the Nazi guard sprayed him with the canister of unknown chemicals. He figured it was something for bugs and lice. Through the fear and sweat, he could still smell it on his skin.

The line moved and they entered the building. Guards watched over the service of food, submachine guns at the ready.

Josef took his chunk of bread and dried sausage and left.

Abe ripped his bread in half and put it in his pocket. The rest went into his mouth without hesitation.

"You might want to save some," he told Josef, his mouth full. "You won't get another solid meal until noon."

Josef nodded, thinking of the man's advice. He tried to save some food, he did, but the hunger pangs were too great. In only a few bites, Josef ate both the bread and sausage. It tasted like ash, but he didn't care.

When he returned to his barracks with the other men, Josef crawled back into his bunk. He slept and before he did, he prayed his family was ok, that some miracle of God had lifted them from this awful display of humanity.

His prayers were unanswered.

# 8

It was already uncomfortably warm in the room. Lieutenant Erich Kollmer sat at his desk. A cup of strong, black coffee steamed next to the plate of oatmeal and sausage. His food, while it wasn't the best the Fatherland had to offer, was much better than that of the prisoners. His oats were oats, not a mixture of horse feed and paper. The sausage was mostly meat and not a grain filler. Yes, as high command he did have certain luxuries.

Lt. Kollmer started his career in the Wehrmacht, the traditional infantry division of the military. His keen eye for strategy and intelligence had him moving through the ranks with speed. He was at the front lines of the Blitz through Poland and scored many kills. Not only did he kill with impunity, but he also prevented his men from dying. His tactics, which were discreetly whispered to his commanding officers, kept his men from ambushes, allowing them to set their own. His cunning would've seen him rise through the ranks, possibly commanding his own army one day, but he had another trait: callousness. He followed orders, regardless of what they were, and had the intelligence to make corrections if needed. His superiors trusted his judgment and many would ask his advice on different matters. These traits and qualities led him to the rank of lieutenant and a member of the high command of the Auschwitz-Birkenau death camp.

Kollmer sipped his coffee as he looked over the weekly reports. This was something below his pay grade, but he enjoyed it. He liked to know who was in the camp and how it was running. At the end of the day, it was a giant machine. Instead of petrol, it ran on the backs of the prisoners. Their lives were fed into the war machine, ensuring victory for Nazi Germany.

He wanted to unbutton the collar on his shirt, but maintaining discipline was key. One button could lead his men into insubordination. A long shot, but he maintained his composure anyhow.

A lazy fan spun above him, but his dirty-blond hair barely stirred from the breeze. He sipped again, wondering why he was drinking such a hot beverage on a day like this. His clean-shaven face had a sheen of sweat on it.

Kollmer scrolled through the names of the previous week's deliveries of human cargo. He wasn't looking for anything in particular, but he knew something special when he saw it. Something caught his eye. He set his coffee cup down and grabbed the paper with both hands.

"Theology," he said to himself. He found the man's name and number on the paper. "Private Berg!" he yelled.

A young man, who looked like he was playing dress-up in his Nazi uniform, appeared in the doorway. "Yes, sir," he said, standing at attention.

Kollmer gestured for him to approach his desk. He pointed to the name with a clean finger.

"This man, here," he said, making sure the private could see clearly. "Pull his file and bring it to me, post-haste."

Berg took a pencil and pad from his shirt pocket and wrote the information down. He clicked his heels and saluted again.

"It will be done, Lieutenant Kollmer." He walked out, his boots clicking down the hallway.

Kollmer fingered the name on the list.

"Oh, Professor Lazerowitz, how did you slip our nets?" he asked himself. He smiled, took a sip of his coffee, and said, "Soon, I'll find out. I'll find everything out."

---

It had been a week since Josef arrived at Auschwitz. His once pudgy, forty-year-old body was thinning out. The food, when they'd lived in the ghetto, was horrible. Now it seemed like a feast. Josef learned to save some of his 'dinner,' the black bread and sausage, for breakfast. Breakfast consisted of coffee, which wasn't even coffee beans, rather some kind of grain. Lunch was soup, but as Josef found out if you were first in line your soup was very thin. Every day at noon, the prisoners would try to calculate which place in line would get them to the end of a barrel of soup. The bottom of the barrel, in this instance, was good. All of the potatoes, rutabagas, and grains would sink, making that bowl hearty.

The food was the least of his problems, as of now. Some of the guards, especially Sgt. Kurtz, were sadists. Men were shot and killed for the most minor indiscretion. One man, Josef never learned his name, was suffering from a rather nasty urinary tract infection. While working one day, the man lost control of his bladder and urinated on himself. He completely ignored it, knowing the guards would have no sympathy. Sgt. Kurtz found the smell of the man's urine to be offensive. He was shot and added to the pile of bodies.

Hygiene in the camp was subpar, to say the least. Rats were seen scurrying around, mainly in the area where there were fresh corpses. Almost everyone had lice or some other form of bug crawling on them. Dysentery was another gift of the camp. Horrible cramps and diarrhea made working torture.

Somehow, Josef pressed on. He didn't know if it was in the hope of being reunited with his family or if it was just the human will to live. Whatever it was, he kept moving. Whether it was loading corpses into a truck from a gas chamber or unloading the same truck into the crematorium, he worked hard.

As grim as his job was, Josef knew he didn't want to end up on a construction detail. Those men, most of whom were worked to death, didn't last long.

Josef was forty and in decent physical shape. Even he didn't think he would last on a construction job.

He stood at the door, waiting for it to open to reveal its macabre cargo. The first few days of working either at the gas chamber or the crematorium had been rough on him. Every woman's face belonged to Ola and every boy was Piotr or Michal. He worked without crying, which he saved until he was in his bunk at night. After a few days, the faces started blending together. They weren't humans anymore, just cargo for the truck or fuel for the hungry incinerator. He wanted to live, something he didn't think would be possible without his family. So, day in and day out, he and the other men loaded the corpses of men, women, and children into trucks and incinerators.

The doors opened and the almond stench of Zyklon B washed out. They gave it a little while to dissipate and got to work.

"Josef, here," Abe said, walking to the corpse of a woman who was holding a young girl. The girl was dead on her chest, so they could pick them both up at the same time.

Josef grabbed the still warm ankles of the woman and lifted. With days of practice, he and Abe had gotten in sync with throwing bodies. The corpses hit the metal bed with a resounding thump. Josef and Abe went back to the pile.

The chamber was cleared of corpses, but now it was time to clean. People would often lose control of bladders and bowels when the gas started, making quite the mess. If the next group saw the filth, they might become resistant, realizing they weren't heading into an actual shower. It was the final step before the next group of condemned could be led in for death.

Josef stood straight up, breathing heavily. Sweat poured down his face, but he tried not to show his exhaustion. Weakened men were sent to construction crews, where they worked until death. He did not want to be one of them. His stomach was cramped in hunger pains, something he would need to get used to. He knew it would only get worse.

It was almost noon, which meant a small reprieve from the work and a bowl of thin soup. As hungry as he was, his thirst was even stronger. Every few hours, a water truck would make the rounds, filling a dingy bucket. The men of every work detail would drink from the same bucket, using their hands, which were soiled with human waste. At first, Josef was repulsed by this practice, but thirst is the most powerful human urge.

Josef watched the bulky water truck bouncing towards them. It was beautiful.

Two Nazis rode in the open front of the vehicle. A sergeant was behind the wheel and a private at his side. The truck stopped and the men got out. Pleasantries were made between the Nazis in the truck and the men who ruled over the work party. They lit cigarettes, told knee-slapping jokes, and relaxed like it was just another day at work. For these men, it was.

The truck sergeant must've told Sgt. Kurtz a pretty good joke, because he was doubled over with laughter. It was strange seeing the evil man so happy. Almost an affront to innocent glee. A pleasurable something to be reserved for the goodly people of the world, not the human monsters like them.

"And you, Private Berg, what brings you along?" Asked Kurtz, taking a puff on his cigarette.

All of the men knew Private Berg was the direct assistant to Lt. Kollmer. No one knew how the man landed such an easy job, especially at the rank of private. but he did. Many lewd jokes had been made as to how he received his job and what he was doing to keep it.

"I'm here for a prisoner," he said, pulling a slip of paper from his pocket. He adjusted his glasses on his thin and effeminate nose. He read a number out loud, but not nearly loud enough for the prisoners to hear.

"Here," Kurtz put out his hand for the paper. He read the number and the name with it. "Alright, you rats, listen up." The prisoners, who were watching the guards from the corner of their eyes, turned to face them. Kurtz, who was used to yelling, called out a number.

Many of the men knew their numbers by heart, as that was how they were usually referred to. Josef hadn't quite memorized his.

Abe looked at his friend's chest, where the number was written across his heart.

"Josef," he said, "that's you." He touched the patch.

He stood stunned. *This is it,* he thought. *I'm finally going to die.*

Josef croaked, "It's me," stepping forward. The other men parted as if he were cursed. At that moment, he felt he was. "That is my number, sir." He stood in front of the men.

Sgt. Kurtz and the others looked at the number on the paper and chest. It was a match.

"Jew, what is your name?" asked Kurtz.

"Lazerowitz, Josef, sir." He replied. His tongue was dry and it was a shame to waste saliva on speaking to these men. The spout from the water truck dripped slowly, a crystal drop of water fell to the packed earth.

"Here you go, Private," Sgt. Kurtz handed him the paper, and pointed at Josef. "Your Jew," he smiled. "Or should I say, Lt. Kollmer's Jew?"

Private Berg put the paper into his pocket, habitually adjusted his glasses, and looked away from the bulky sergeant.

"Follow me," Berg said to Josef. He turned and began walking.

As they passed the water truck, Josef had the indescribable urge to drink until he burst. He knew he'd only get a mouthful before he was shot.

They left the area just as the lunch gong sounded. He didn't know what awaited him, but whatever it was, he knew he'd have to face it hungry and thirsty.

Josef walked with Private Berg. They passed the few lunch lines, where men were getting their daily ration of soup. Josef didn't think he'd be eating anything for lunch, if he survived that long. He'd been thinking of his hunger and thirst, not realizing where Berg had taken him. The dreaded Block 11 loomed ahead.

If it hadn't been for his dehydration, Josef may have pissed his pants. This was the block of no return. It even felt evil.

Private Berg led him up the stairs to the third floor. He stopped outside of an office, which was identified as belonging to Lt. Kollmer. He knocked with a thin hand.

"Come in," said a booming voice from the other side of the door.

Lt. Kollmer sat at his desk. His hat and coat were on a rack next to him. The window was open and a fan oscillated lazily. A large fan circled overhead, neither doing much to stifle the heat. His head was down, his pen scratching at a paper on his desk. He didn't look up.

Josef knew this man. He'd seen him the day they arrived, actually helping his wife, preventing her death on the platform. Whether she still lived was another story, but that day she did. He also saw this man executing prisoners with a calm demeanor, as if he were taking out the trash.

Kollmer stopped his writing and gave it a quick once over. Satisfied, he looked up.

Josef stared at him, locking eyes with the SS officer. Kollmer had the glare of a predator and at that moment, Josef thought he was going to die.

"Thank you, Private Berg," said Kollmer.

With a click of his heels and sharp salute, Berg left the room, pulling the door shut behind him.

Lt. Kollmer reached into his desk and pulled out a folder.

Josef's eyes followed it, but stopped when he saw something else: a sweaty, pitcher of water. The metal jug rested on a wet cloth, beads of condensation sliding down the side. He could almost taste the painful coldness of it.

"So, it has come to my attention I have a smart Jew in front of me," Kollmer said.

Josef's gaze was locked on the water as if it were a mirage in the desert. He didn't dare break his eye contact with the pitcher, but he knew the man had just spoken to him. Reluctantly, he looked up.

"Ah, yes, sir." He added, "I am educated." Josef was looking at Kollmer, but keeping the water in the corner of his eye.

Lt. Kollmer saw this, watching the sweaty man's fervent gaze. He was a cruel man, but he was smart.

"Private Berg," he said, just loud enough to not yell.

The door opened. "Yes, sir?"

"Get me a cup, please," requested Kollmer.

Private Berg was back in seconds with a metal cup in his hand. "Here you are, sir." He put it on the Lieutenant's desk.

"That'll be all," Kollmer said.

Another heel-click and salute and Private Berg left, shutting the door.

Lt. Kollmer poured the water into the glass. He held the pitcher high, as if he were a bartender making a fancy drink. The clear, cold water filled the cup to the brim.

Josef never knew torture like this before. His bowels cramped in desire, his mouth yearning for a drop.

Kollmer put the pitcher back on the cloth. With manicured fingers, he slid the cup towards Josef.

"Drink," he ordered.

Josef descended on the cup, careful not to spill a drop. It was so cold, it burned, but he didn't care. His throat screamed in joy and he greedily sucked every drop. He put the cup back down, hoping Kollmer would refill it. He did not.

"Thank you, sir. It's been a hot day today."

Kollmer scowled at him. "I'm not interested in your day, Jew. Honestly, I'm having a hard time deciding if I want to send you to the wall. These next couple of minutes may be the last of your pathetic life."

Josef snapped back to reality. This man was the enemy and not his friend. He'd given him the water because he wanted something, nothing else. He didn't speak, just nodded.

"First, I want to know how a theology professor slipped through our nets for as long as you have."

Josef thought about lying, but he decided not to. If this was the end, then so be it. He told him the truth.

Kollmer listened, not saying anything.

"You were one lucky bastard, I'd say," said Kollmer, after Josef finished talking. "Ok, Professor, let's see what you know."

Kollmer, for the next twenty minutes, quizzed Josef on all aspects of theology, giving him theories and questions. They discussed books on the matter, most of which were pretty common and mundane. Josef was in his element and was impressed with the man's knowledge of the subject. For a moment, it felt like he was speaking with a colleague, not a man who could end his life at any moment.

Kollmer sat nodding. He pulled a pack of cigarettes from a drawer and lit one.

"Impressive, Professor," he said, blowing smoke.

"Thank you, sir," Josef's mouth was dry again, but he didn't think he'd be getting any more water.

"Every day at lunchtime, Private Berg will be sent to fetch you. You will be brought to me and we will talk. One of those days, when I grow tired of our conversations, I will kill you. Until then, we will talk. Understand?" He let a cloud of smoke slither from his nostrils.

"Yes, sir," replied Josef.

"Berg," said Kollmer. The private popped into the room. "I'm done with him. For now."

---

JOSEF WAS LED BACK to his workgroup.

The men looked semi-refreshed if that was even possible in such a place as Auschwitz. He knew, for the time being, they all had some food in their bellies. As if to remind him, his rumbled and cramped.

"Ah, welcome back," Sgt. Kurtz sneered. Even the prestige of the SS couldn't keep the heat away. His collar was damp with sweat. The black uniforms of the guards didn't make things easier on anyone. The heat was enough to sour any person's mood, but it could be deadly if any of the guards were feeling it.

Josef didn't reply, rather nodded and joined the other prisoners loading the truck with corpses.

They worked for hours, with the water truck coming once more. As meager as they were, Josef had yet to miss a meal. After eating the soup since he'd arrived, he never thought he'd miss it.

He and Abe, his only friend, lifted a particularly heavy woman into the truck. Her layers of fat made it difficult to find purchase. With a few grunts, they were able to hoist her.

Abe looked around, making sure the guards were out of earshot. He pushed the woman's leg, which was dangling out, into the bed of the truck.

"So, what did the lieutenant want?" He wiped his face with his sleeve.

Josef's ears were ringing. He didn't know if it was from hunger, dehydration, or both. He heard his friend, but his brain was running slow.

"To talk," he said, wiping his face.

Abe looked at him with a twisted smirk. "To talk?" He laughed. "That man is a butcher. I thought for sure you were dead and you mean to say he only wanted to talk."

They walked back over to the door of the gas chamber, the almond smell of Zyklon-B still in the air. Each grabbed a child no older than three.

"When the Private took me into Block 11, I thought it was the end." He unceremoniously threw the child's corpse onto the pile.

When Josef first arrived, he took care with the corpses, sometimes holding back tears as he lifted them. After a time, he was able to push it aside. Eventually, they became just items to load onto a truck. He hated himself for that.

Abe was hanging on his words, keeping an eye on the guards, who were huddled in the shade, smoking cigarettes.

"He found out I was a professor and wanted to talk about theology."

Abe gave him another odd look. "Theology? I wouldn't have taken him as the religious type." They walked over to the chamber, but it was empty. Other men were already starting to clean it for the next batch of unlucky guests.

Josef shrugged, "I don't know, Abe, he just told me he wanted to talk about it. He said I'd be brought to him to discuss the topic." He grabbed a long-handled wire brush and began loosening the drying shit on the floors.

"Welcome back, Josef," a man, who was scrubbing the walls, said.

Josef spun. "Thanks, Herman. I wasn't so sure I'd be coming back."

Herman was another prisoner he'd become acquainted with. He only knew a few names, which he preferred. Since arriving, ten men on his work detail had been executed. Every day it seemed like one of them was destined for a bullet, yet no one had been shot in days. It wasn't anything personal against the rest of the men, but Josef equated it to naming an animal you were going to slaughter. He knew none of them would make it out alive and what was the point of getting to know a doomed man.

Abe grabbed his arm, returning his attention to him.

"So, he's going to call you back to him?"

Josef scrubbed a stubborn spot. He didn't look at his friend. "I guess so. He also said there was a good chance he was going to kill me." The spot was bare. He moved on to another. "So, I have that to look forward to. I just hope he doesn't pick lunchtime again; my stomach is rumbling."

Abe felt the hard lump of bread in his pocket. He always tried to save something from dinner, just in case he missed a meal.

"I wish I could help you," Abe said, taking his hand away. He looked outside, noticing prisoners on the march. "The good news is the day is done."

The workday, which was normally fourteen hours, ended at 7 pm every night. The prisoners were marched from their work details back to their respective housing assignments. Guards would account for deaths amongst them and submit a final count number. All of them would be accounted for and the evening meal would be served. The evening meal of brown bread, a slice of sausage, a bit of butter, and maybe some cheese, was the most desired.

Josef's stomach cramped at the anticipation of food.

"Line it up," said Kurtz, hand on his gun. He hadn't killed anyone in days and was looking for a reason to.

The men hustled into their lines. Even in their exhaustion, they formed up quickly and neatly. No one would be getting a bullet today.

Like robots, they marched back to their barracks. Their count was done with ease, as no one had been killed that day.

Josef stood in line to use the toilet and wash the blood and filth from his hands. He wished he had a change of clothes, but getting clean clothes was rare.

He washed, glad there was no mirror in the bathroom. He didn't want to know what he looked like. His physical appearance didn't bother him; he knew he was already thin and bordering on gaunt. It was his eyes he feared. What was left in them? He was always told he had soft eyes, something Ola loved about him. Were they still soft? He doubted it. With every corpse he threw, or every order he followed, his eyes hardened. He was turning into an animal. No, these men were making him into an animal. His only thoughts were food and rest, as if he were a plow horse. Work, eat, sleep…and possibly die.

Josef followed the men out and lined up for dinner.

He tried to discipline himself when it came to dinner, knowing breakfast was only weak coffee, but he couldn't help it. Josef nearly choked on his bread, butter smearing on his fingers. The sausage was hard and salty, but to him, it was a filet. When he was finished, he licked his fingers, which were black under their nails, clean. His stomach churned in glee, but wanted more.

The night was a rare reprieve for the camp prisoners. After the evening meal, they had some free time until 9 pm. They could wander between dorms, but not leave their sections of the camp. This was when rumors were spread, trades were conducted, or needed sleep was made up.

Josef lay on his bunk, staring at the one above. He wasn't looking at anything in particular, just allowing his mind to wander.

He tried not to think of his family, but they were always at the forefront. For the first few days of loading corpses, he saw them. Their faces were every woman or boy. His heart leapt when he'd grab a body, flipping them over, sure it was one of them. It never was. He didn't know whether to be grateful or upset at not finding them. He was a man and even though he wasn't a rough and tumble kind of guy, he could endure the camp. His wife and boys couldn't.

Ola was always neat and proper. She'd bathe every morning and night. Her clothes weren't the most expensive, but were always clean. She wouldn't be seen in a pair of hose with a run in them, nor a garment with a stain. Her hair was brushed and styled, an ornate pin usually holding it up. Josef loved when she'd pull the pin at the end of the night. He would watch in awe as she stood nude, her blonde hair cascading down her shoulders. She'd always run her fingers through it, shaking her head at the same time. Her full breasts would jiggle, hypnotizing him with their pink nipples. She would give him a half-smirk and if she was in the mood, she'd gesture him to the bed.

"Josef," Abe said, crouching down to his bunk.

He jumped at the interruption of his daydream. The image of his wife was blown away like dandelion fluff. Josef turned to his friend. He didn't speak, fearing his voice would betray him.

"One of the guys in 7 has a deck of cards. We're going over to see if we can play. Are you in?"

He wanted to go. He needed a distraction from the daydreams he knew would return, leaving him upset.

"No thanks," he said, a spit bubble on his lips. "I'm just going to try and get some rest." Josef's eyes welled with tears he didn't feel coming. They were dry one moment, the next they were leaking.

Abe gave him a pat on the shoulder and a tight-lipped grin. He left without a word.

Josef put an arm over his eyes, soaking up the tears. The almond smell of the deadly chemical was in his clothes. He didn't sleep, but he dreamt. He dreamt of them; his wife and boys and said a prayer. Not a prayer for them to all escape; even God couldn't do that. After a while, he drifted towards sleep and prayed harder. He prayed they were dead, that they died quickly and peacefully.

They did not.

# 9

EVERY DAY STARTED THE SAME. The prisoners were roused from their sleep, the only reprieve from their torment. They were given a few short minutes to try and bathe and use the bathroom. After, everyone had to line up for the morning headcount. Some died in the night or committed suicide, which would cause a delay in the count. Once all people, living and dead, were accounted for, breakfast was served. Breakfast, like every other meal, was sub-par, to say the least. It consisted of a half-liter of "coffee," which was a boiled grain substitute. That was it. Nothing solid to eat until lunch and even then, if you didn't play the line right, you were getting thin soup. The more disciplined prisoners would save a few pieces of bread from dinner to have with their breakfast. Many could not.

The morning was already hot. Josef stood in line with his fellow prisoners, ready to start another hellish day.

He was itchy as they all were. Their uniforms were rough spun wool and had no underwear. Lice were common and even with short hair, the little bugs would feast on the prisoners. The hay in his mattress had been so worn down from his body and those before him, it was like sleeping on tiny needles. Once he could find a position where he wasn't getting stabbed, he would try and hold it for the night.

As soon as the count was finished, they were dismissed. Josef followed the line of men to the waiting area to get his coffee.

When he was a boy, he'd often ask his mother for snacks or sweets before dinner. Like a good mother, she'd tell him dinner would be served shortly. He would then pout, in a final attempt at satisfaction, and cry he was starving. He didn't know what starving was until he was taken to Hell on Earth.

Josef stood in line for his meal. His body was slick with sweat, but not just from the heat. He was starving and in a state of perpetual discomfort. His breath was sour and his stomach cramped. When he'd moved his bowels earlier, there wasn't much and what there was, was mush.

His stomach rolled again when he was handed his cup of coffee. Something was floating in it, but he didn't care. It was something solid for his belly. He wanted to drink it down like a glass of water, but it was steaming hot. Just what he needed on a summer day.

Gently, like he was kissing his kids without waking them, he put his chapped lips to the cup. With a rude noise, he slurped. It was repulsive and delicious at the same time. The coffee cooled faster with every sip and he drank it down, feeling the heat through his body. His stomach growled at getting something in it, but was far from satisfied.

He was doing ok with the meals he was given. Granted, he was always starving, but able to have something to look forward to. After his meeting with Kollmer, that had changed. Even though his lunch soup was thin, he'd usually get a few chunks of something solid in his bowl. Not only that, but this was the halfway point of his day. When his lunch break was over, the day was half over. Kollmer took that from him and there was nothing he could do about it.

---

JOSEF WORKED HARD alongside the other men from his group. He and Abe pairing up like normal.

"Are you OK?" Abe asked.

Josef was more pale than usual. He feared he might be getting sick, which was almost always a death sentence. His stomach cramped again and for a moment he thought he was going to lose his bowels.

"Fine," he said, loading the corpse of an elderly man into the back of the truck. He felt Abe staring at him and forced a tight-lipped grin. He was not fine and he knew it.

After his breakfast and before coming to the gas chamber, Josef spent some time on the toilet. His bowels were watery now and he feared he had dysentery, which was all too common.

Abe knew he was lying, but didn't press the issue. Sgt. Kurtz was looking in their direction, a cigarette dangling from his mouth.

Without taking his eyes off them, he tossed the smoke on the ground and started advancing.

"Come on," Abe said, his voice strained, "Kurtz is b-lining for us."

Josef didn't look back; Abe's face said it all. He wiped an unknown substance on his pants and walked back to the gas chamber door.

Kurtz had a meaner look than usual etched on his face. He walked gingerly and rumors were floating around he'd contracted a venereal disease. The female guards were on the other side of the camp, but it was believed he'd gotten it from a female prisoner he'd raped. This was not against the rules, but was looked down on. He had his stick in his hand already, looking for someone else to feel his pain.

The sound of a truck caught his attention. It was the water truck and in the front seat sat Private Berg.

Kurtz looked at Josef and Abe, a toothy grin on his face. He'd get them eventually.

"All right, you dogs, come get a drink, but make it fast. The next train will be here in five minutes." He smiled at the thought of the arriving trains. The screams from the platforms always made him happy.

Private Berg approached him. "I need the prisoner again," he said to Sgt. Kurtz. As if there were any other reasons he'd be there.

Josef was just out of earshot, waiting his turn for water. He hoped he'd get a drink this time, since he was probably missing lunch again.

He watched Kurtz scanning the line, but looking right over him. It was his turn and he pressed the ladle to his lips. One drop of lukewarm water made it into his parched mouth before Kurtz slapped it from his hand.

"You rat fuck!" he spat at Josef. "You knew the private was looking for you."

Josef, his shirt wet from sweat and now water, put his hands up defensively.

"No, sir, honest. I don't want to interfere." Josef could only watch as Kurtz pulled his heavy stick from his belt.

Private Berg cleared his throat, stopping Kurtz's swing.

"Lt. Kollmer is waiting for this man and a trip to the infirmary might upset him, Sergeant."

Kurtz turned an unholy shade of red, but resheathed his baton. He forced a maniacal sneer, his substitute for a smile.

"Yes, of course. I wouldn't want to keep the Lieutenant waiting." He moved closer to Berg, his lips almost on his ear. His breath stunk and he hoped it was offensive to the private. "Do you suck his cock?" he growled. "Or does he stick it in your thin ass?"

Private Berg didn't respond, just adjusted his glasses and turned.

"Follow me," he said.

Josef did, but not before he heard the meaty slap of a baton striking flesh. Someone else had taken his punishment. He didn't want to see any of them beaten, but as he followed the private, he was glad it wasn't him.

---

Private Berg stood outside of the office and tapped his knuckles on the door. Nothing more than a dainty rap, but it was enough to get a response from the other side.

"Come," Lt. Kollmer's voice was muffled beyond the door, but clear enough.

Private Berg opened the door and took a few steps in. He stood in front of the desk, clicked his heels, and saluted.

"Sir, the requested prisoner."

Lt. Kollmer didn't look up, rather kept his nose in a book. He had a thin pair of glasses on the tip of his nose. They gave him a wizened look. More like a scholar, rather than a killer. He grabbed a bookmark, slid it in and closed the book.

"Thank you," Kollmer said, placing the book on the desk. He pulled his glasses off and put them into a soft case.

Private Berg turned to leave.

"Private," Kollmer said, stopping the man.

"Yes, sir?" He looked back.

"Bring the professor a glass of water." He looked at Josef, who was standing in front of him, his eyes locked on the desk. "He looks thirsty and we have a lot to talk about."

Berg nodded and walked out, leaving the door ajar.

"Sit," Kollmer ordered, pointing to a chair in front of the desk.

"Thank you, sir," Josef said, easing himself into the chair. His stomach was still rolling, but his bowels seemed under control.

Berg walked back in with a glass of water.

"Thank you," Josef said, extending his hand.

Berg ignored the outstretched hand and placed the cup on the desk. He left the room, shutting the door behind him.

Josef looked at Kollmer for reassurance and when he nodded at the glass, Josef grabbed it and drank. The water was cool and almost sweet. A far cry from the warm water in the tanks delivered to the prisoners. It was almost as good as food. Almost.

"Have you ever read this?" Kollmer asked, sliding the book he was reading towards Josef.

When Josef walked in, he recognized the book immediately. It was *Kirchliche Dogmatik* Volume 1, by Swiss author, Karl Barth. The book and the ones following it were staples amongst the theological world. Josef had written many papers on the works of Barth, so needless to say, he was familiar.

"Ah, yes sir, I'm quite familiar with it." He took another sweet sip of water.

Kollmer smiled a wide, childlike smile. "Excellent," he said. He opened his desk drawer and pulled another copy. He handed it to Josef. "You'll see I've underlined certain sections in this volume. I was hoping you could clarify some of my questions."

Josef opened the book, the pages felt like shaking hands with an old friend. The copy was well worn and as Kollmer said, there were underlined passages.

Josef scanned the text, and for a moment he wasn't in a death camp. Rather, he was sitting at his desk in the University, planning his upcoming lesson plans. At work, when his stomach would growl, he'd have Ola's cooking to look forward to. Now, he only had thin soup and moldy bread to satisfy his gnawing appetite.

Lt. Kollmer cleared his throat, yanking Josef from his daydream.

"Where should we start?" he asked.

Josef flipped back to the first chapter, noticing the underlines. "How about the beginning?" He hoped the Nazi didn't take it as an insult.

Kollmer smirked, letting out a small laugh. "Yes, that makes sense. Let's begin at the beginning."

---

THE LUNCH HOUR FLEW BY. The two men speaking freely about Barth's take on theology.

Josef, as much as he hated Kollmer, was impressed with his knowledge on the subject. His questions were precise and thought-provoking. Josef, to his dismay, actually enjoyed his time with the Nazi lieutenant.

A light knock on the door cut them off mid-sentence.

Kollmer took his glasses off and looked at his watch. He knew he was over his time and was needed elsewhere. Even though he was of a high rank, he couldn't shirk his duties.

"Come," he said.

Private Berg opened the door. He stepped in, clicked his heels, and saluted.

"Sir, you're needed outside." He looked at Josef and back to Kollmer. "At the wall."

Kollmer stood. He adjusted his uniform and grabbed his hat from the rack. He opened his desk and motioned Josef to give him his book.

Josef handed it over and stood.

"Good talk today. We'll finish tomorrow." Then to Berg, "Take him back. I'm sure Sgt. Kurtz is waiting on him. Make sure he knows he's late because he was with me."

"Yes, sir," said Berg.

Kollmer walked out, leaving Berg and Josef alone. Once the sound of his boots started down the stairs, Berg spoke.

"He likes you, Jew, but don't confuse yourself. He'll shoot you as soon as you're used up. That is how he is." Berg's thin face was almost pinched, like he smelled something sour. "Enjoy the rest of your miserable life while you can."

Josef didn't speak. His pulse was throbbing in his ears. Even though he was weak from malnourishment, he knew he could kill Berg with his bare hands. It might even be worth it just to see the life drain from his face before more guards killed him. He would picture Kurtz's face though. The real tormenter in his life.

The idea disappeared like a feather in the wind. Nothing but a fantasy.

Berg turned and walked, gesturing for him to follow.

Gunfire echoed from the side of the building. Berg walked towards it, a grin on his face. Lined against the wall were two men, one was crying like a baby, the other shocked into stoicism. They stared ahead at the blood and brain matter of the two previous prisoners.

Lt. Kollmer held his gun in his hand, along with a few other Nazis.

Josef saw him raise his gun. It bucked, spitting death into the skull of the crying man.

"Next!" Kollmer yelled, a smile on his face. Two more men were led out.

## 10

THE NEXT WEEK continued the same.

Every day Josef was taken just before lunch and led to Kollmer's office. They would talk for the hour and he was sent back. Even though the soup wasn't much, Josef missed it every day. His weight was dropping faster than he ever expected, leaving him weak and gaunt. His dinner seemed to just ease the pain of hunger, but it was always there, gnawing at the muscle in his body.

Josef and Marvin, a new addition to their work crew, threw the corpse of another lost soul onto the pile. He thought it was a woman, but at this point, he didn't even look anymore. The first time Josef realized he was treating the dead bodies as cargo instead of corpses, he felt ill. It was almost as if he were one of them, the Nazis, and treating the dead like nothing. He knew that wasn't true, but he couldn't help but think of it. If he wept for every one of them, he'd be next in the pile.

The day was blessedly cool, with a heavy overcast of clouds above. It had rained in the morning, making the ground slick. Fat thunderheads rumbled in the distance, flashes of lightning dancing inside of them.

Josef heard the growl of the water truck. Without the sun, he couldn't tell what time it was, but was praying it was close. He was starting to shake from hunger.

Without realizing it, Josef was watching Private Berg approach and had a wide smile on his face. Abe was watching too, but not the Nazi; no, he watched Josef.

The intellectual stimulation Kollmer gave him was almost as good as food. It felt like nourishment for his soul, and sometimes that's more important. They had gone over a couple of volumes of Barth's works. Josef had clarified some questions Kollmer had about the relationship of God and his angels. They spoke for the whole hour, sometimes even sharing a laugh.

Sgt. Kurtz didn't bother with Josef anymore. He knew it was still within his rights to maim or kill him, but he liked his job. If he messed with Lt. Kollmer's pet Jew, he could be removed from his service and have to work a new post.

The prisoners watched the water truck bounce over, still working, but at an anticipated pace. The truck slowed to a halt.

"Get a drink, you rats," Kurtz bellowed.

Josef was always led to the front of the line. The other prisoners didn't know he was getting water when he visited with Kollmer and felt bad he was missing lunch. None of them, not even Abe, felt bad enough to share their rations though.

Josef sipped the warm water, just to make a show of it. He knew the ice-cold water awaited him. He wiped his mouth with his crusty sleeve and walked towards Private Berg.

Abe's eyes followed him.

---

IN THE DEATH CAMP, there were many forms of torture. One of the worst was starvation. It was a deceptive thing, starving to death, but it cut deeply. Every stage seemed like the worst and then your body hit a new low. It continued on this path until you were too weak to move and then sweet death.

Josef could smell the food in Kollmer's office from the hallway. His stomach growled painfully and twisted. Saliva pooled in his mouth, praying for just a bite of something, anything of nutrition.

Berg tapped on the door.

A muffled, "Come," replied.

Lt. Kollmer sat at his desk, like usual. In one hand he held open a new book and in the other was a fork hovering over a plate of food.

Josef couldn't take his eyes off the plate. Sausages, beans, cheese, and a chunk of bread. It looked like heaven. He had to stop himself from jumping onto the desk and stuffing his mouth. He would probably choke, but it would be worth it.

Kollmer didn't look up at Berg and the snappy private left without a salute, sneering at the superior officer.

Josef stood, while Kollmer read.

Without looking up, he said, "Take a seat, Professor."

He was only inches away from the plate, less than a foot. Josef stilled his hand before it betrayed him and sat.

Slowly, as if calculating something, Kollmer shut the book. He placed it on the desk and removed his thin glasses. He rested the tines of the fork on the plate and pushed it away, closer to Josef.

"I am a simple man, Professor," he began. "But I am an observant man. I see everything before it happens. My strategies are flawless and mind sharp. I leave emotion out of my decisions and plan my moves six steps in advance."

Josef fought to keep his eyes on him, but he kept looking at the food in his periphery. He swallowed his spit.

"For weeks you've been sitting down with me and have never asked for anything. Not even to use the pisser." He opened a hard case and removed a cigarette, taking his time. He lit it, closing the lighter with a metallic click. "Now, I know this place can be intimidating, to say the least."

Josef was nearly in shock at the statement. He'd watched this man kill people in cold blood for no reason. Every day he would pull corpses of men, women, and children from a gas chamber and load them into a truck. He'd seen men he worked with shot for nothing more than stretching an aching back. Yes, the camp was intimidating.

"I notice things." He smoked. "Do you realize I could summon you at any hour I'd like? It doesn't have to be your lunchtime. I could have the men rouse you in the middle of the night if I wanted to," he said matter-of-factly. "I needed to see what kind of man I was dealing with." He stubbed the cigarette out in an ashtray, a finger of smoke clawing at the air. "You're nothing but bones right now and it's only getting worse, yet you've never complained. I know the mind and how it works. I know it needs nourishment to fire and without, your thoughts become muddled and mush." He looked at the food in front of him. The number of calories it contained was more than Josef would consume in one week if he were on full rations.

He sat stunned, looking at the Nazi, who had his fingers tented with a smug glance. It was a test the entire time, to see if he would beg or ask for something, anything.

"I need your mind, Professor. There are things at work in this camp beyond my abilities, sad to say. A good general knows how to wield his army, to keep his blades sharp and guns loaded. Dogs, Professor, are beneath us, but if we want them to work, they must be fed." He pushed the plate of food towards Josef, careful to remove the fork first. "I am giving you this food, not because I like you, no. Actually, I despise you. The knowledge wasted on Jews makes me cringe. What kind of a tactician would I be to throw away a powerful weapon just for my prejudices? Make no mistake, one day I will kill you, but that is not today." He sat silent, pulling his cigarettes out again. He took one out, twirling it in his fingers. The strain on Josef's face was evident. The food was so close and he could smell it even better. "Do you understand?"

Josef looked at him. He couldn't speak for fear of drool running from his mouth. At that moment, he was a dog and didn't care. His body was screaming for food, willing him to pounce on the plate, ripping into the meal. He nodded.

"Good," said Kollmer. He gestured to the food. "Eat," he said, putting the cigarette into his mouth. He smiled as the starving man ate with his filthy hands, trying to keep hold of any shred of decency he had left.

## CHAPTER 10 | 83

JOSEF RETURNED to his work group later in the day. Later then he usually would. His stomach, for the first time in a long time, was almost full. The rich food almost made him vomit, but he was able to keep it down. He felt good, refreshed…and hated himself for it.

In the office, he ate his food like an animal. Sure, he'd eaten with his hands before—corn on the cob, spare ribs, chicken legs—but this was different. Kollmer, knowing his hands had been used all morning to move soiled corpses, didn't even offer him a napkin, let alone wash them. No, he made him eat like a dog.

After Josef finished what was arguably one of the best meals of his life, the two men sat and talked.

Kollmer talked more about the works of Barth, but then, as if shy, began switching the topics. His normal discussions had been basic, Theology 101, but Josef sensed a slight shift in him. He began asking questions about Hell and the denizens residing there.

Josef didn't much care about the topic, especially when it came to Hell. He knew every bastard in the camp with the SS lightning bolts would spend eternity there.

Josef walked over to Abe, who was helping another new man, who still stunk of the pesticide he was sprayed with, load a corpse.

"Let me help," he said, with a renewed energy from the food he'd eaten. It was almost as if he were helping them load lumber instead of the corpse of an obese woman. Her body, still warm and pliable, shifted like a bag of sand as the men heaved her into the truck. Slick vomit on the front of her chest made the ordeal even more difficult.

"Thanks," the new guy said. His face was tear-streaked, but he didn't let that stop him. He must've seen or heard someone die for not working. "I'm Aleks," he said, extending his hand.

"No problem," Josef said, quickly shaking the man's hand. He turned, walking towards Abe, who was already grabbing the ankles of an old man. "Here, I'll grab the arms." He reached down to grab the old man's thin wrists.

"It's ok," said Abe, yanking the man free. The corpse's head lolled back, his jaw opening like he was yawning. A toothless maw stared back at him.

The new guy, Aleks, took the old man's wrists.

"I got it," he told Josef, who was moving away from the pair as they maneuvered the corpse around him.

He stood dumbfounded at the opening of the gas chamber, watching them walk away.

Sgt. Kurtz, who was leaning in the shade, smoking and joking with another man, saw him standing idle.

Josef pretended to be stretching and picked up the body of a child. Unceremoniously, he walked out of the chamber and threw the body into the truck. It made a resounding thump as it hit the back.

## 11

IN THE FOLLOWING MONTH, summer faded away, welcoming in the cooler temperatures of fall. For the workers at Auschwitz, this was a Godsend. Heat exhaustion in the camp was killing almost as many as bullets. With sub-standard food, little water, and almost no rest, prisoners would die at their jobs and be sent right to the crematorium.

Mild temperatures and a cool breeze helped boost the morale of some of them. All except those who'd been at the camp the longest. Those who had experienced a winter in the camp dreaded the fall. They knew within another month or two, those cool breezes would be Arctic blasts, cutting through threadbare clothing. Fingers, toes, and noses would be lost to frostbite and turn black with rot. Sometimes the rot would kill them faster than the cold. If you were lucky, you were able to stay in the first stage of frostbite and only have the tips turn white. This was still bad, but not as bad as when it went to black. Once the rot set in, there was no turning back.

The men in Josef's work detail didn't think far enough ahead to worry about winter. Many were just trying to survive each day.

Two weeks prior, five men in another workgroup were caught planning a revolt. It was nothing that worried the guards; the men were so emaciated and their only weapon was a thin piece of metal.

No, the physical threat wasn't much, but the psychological effects were great.

The guards in the camp were vastly outnumbered. Even with their health and guns, they would have a hard time stopping a massive insurrection. An example had to be made of them.

The five men and the 125 others who shared their barracks, were detained. They were all stripped naked and beaten. Some were attacked by dogs, a fear of any prisoner. The five men responsible were taken to Block 11, where their torture increased to legendary stature. The rest of them were marched out to the gravel pit and executed.

The day of the mass execution was almost treated like a holiday. Most of the camp, at least on the men's side, followed the doomed men to the feared area of the camp: the gravel pit. The men, all 125 of them, naked and weeping, stood in front of the piles of stone.

The Nazis, nearly 200 of them, were all armed with submachine guns. They even brought four small trucks, equipped with the dreaded MG 42, also known as Hitler's Buzzsaw. At the command of the lieutenant in charge, the men opened fire, cutting all of the prisoners down in a wave of bullets.

The crowd watched in horror as bodies twitched with each bullet impact. Within the horror and revulsion was also part gratitude. Gratitude, it wasn't them out there.

Two weeks later, they all had the images of the pile of corpses etched into their minds, motivating them to work harder.

Josef did his share and then some. With him now getting a full meal once a day, he was able to put a little weight back on. He was nowhere near his original, pre-camp size, but he was maintaining what he had. His energy was up too. The food and actual good conversation fueled him to work harder. As if he had a purpose.

This didn't bode well with the other men.

It was nearly lunchtime and the chamber had just been cleaned out. The last bit of bodily fluid was pushed out with a rough broom.

The day was unseasonably warm, but nowhere near the sweltering heat of summer. The prisoners all huddled in a small piece of shade near the side of the building.

Sgt. Kurtz and his men didn't care. The lunch hour was their break time too. Besides, the next train had been delayed by a munitions train heading to the Soviet front.

Josef approached a crowd of prisoners, Abe and Aleks among them. All of the faces looked familiar and he'd gotten to know a few at the card games. He tried not to befriend too many, as often as they were executed, died, or were relocated to another struggling workgroup. New people were brought in daily, so the amount of work was consistent and tiring.

Abe and Aleks had been telling a joke, the other men stifling their laughs as not to attract the ire of the guards.

Josef stepped in, a smile on his face as if he'd been listening all along. If he had heard the joke, he wouldn't have smiled at all.

"Ah, Professor Lazerowitz," one of the men, who Josef thought was named Daniel, said. The other men around chuckled. Daniel wasn't at all physically imposing, but his reputation for a quick tongue had spread. He could sling insults better than anyone and often would. "Maybe you could settle a small debate we were having." He pointed to the other men in the circle. "When you suck Lt. Kollmer's cock, does he make you swallow his seed or are you allowed to spit it out?" The rest of the men burst out laughing, drawing looks from Kurtz and his men. The Nazi guards didn't leave their shade, but were now staring at them. If they did walk over, it wouldn't end well.

Josef wasn't the type to fight with people and wasn't easily offended, but life was different inside the camp. Yes, the Nazis were demons in human form, but some of the other men were just as bad. He'd personally witnessed two men fight to the death over a piece of bread. One man had taken it from dinner and the other stole it. In the end, they both died; one of a broken skull, the other with a gunshot to the head.

Josef knew he was being watched by everyone, the guards included, so there wasn't much he could do. He was easily half a foot taller than Daniel and thanks to his extra meal, outweighed him by twenty-five pounds. He took a step towards the smaller man, who stood his ground.

"What the fuck did you say, you little fucking troll?"

Daniel, ever the defiant one, crossed his arms over his chest. "Oh, I'm sorry, Professor. Maybe I wasn't clear. When Lt. Erich Kollmer, the man you see every day, the man who is rumored to fuck his private's ass, is jamming his Nazi cock in your throat, do you swallow his children or spit them out?" He leaned in, knowing he had the support of the crowd. "There, was that clear enough?"

Josef clenched his fist, but a strong hand grabbed him. A strong familiar hand.

Abe whispered in his ear. "Your ride is here, Pet Jew."

Josef heard the sound of the water truck arrive. He turned, pain masking his face, and looked at Abe.

Abe stared at him in the eyes, unwavering. The friendliness and compassion he felt for Josef was gone. It was replaced with disgust and scorn and jealousy. His weight, like all of the other men in the entire camp, had been dropping fast. The last remaining physical attribute he maintained was his grip, and even that was starting to wane.

"Hey, Pet Jew," said Kurtz from his shade, "let's go."

Josef shrugged Abe's hand from his arm, keeping eye contact with the man he once considered his friend. He walked away and joined Private Berg.

"Pet Jew," one of the men said, under his breath as Josef joined the other man.

He looked at Private Berg to see if he'd heard. The young man had a smile on his face.

"Let's not keep him waiting," he told Josef, as they walked away.

---

The attack came a week later.

Josef knew it was coming, but didn't know when. Since the stare down and insults at the gas chamber, things had only gotten worse.

He was moving corpses by himself, trying to load them into the trucks. Unless it was a child or small, elderly person, this was a back-breaking task. The other men, even the new guys, would just watch and laugh as he put the soiled corpse on his shoulder to hoist them over the pile. His clothes were wet with sweat and human excrement from the bodies.

Kurtz and the other guards did nothing and would laugh too, as he'd fumble with a corpse.

Abe approached him when they were both at the truck.

"Since you're eating more than any two men, we all figured you should do the work of two men." He smiled with bleeding gums and loose teeth. One of which had already fallen out.

When they were in the chamber, shuffling through corpses, some of the men would push him, claiming accidents. Josef could feel their feet when they'd kick him in the ass, once knocking him onto the pile of gassed bodies.

He wanted to fight them, to scream at them. They were all in this together. They were surviving together and he was just doing it better. Any of them would have traded places with him in a heartbeat and knew it. No, it wasn't anger at him meeting with Lt. Kollmer, it was jealousy. They were jealous of his semi-full belly, his slight muscle tone, and even the fact he had solid shit. Josef, having been bullied in grade school, didn't feed into their taunts. He took the name-calling; Pet Jew seemed to be their favorite. Even some of the physical abuse, which didn't amount to more than a few rough bumps here and there.

Then, one day it all stopped. There was a new look in their eyes now: hatred. He knew the moment it happened.

For one of their lunches, Josef and Lt. Kollmer ate meatballs smothered in a rich brown gravy. It was one step above dog food, but to a starving man, it was delectable. A small drop of gravy fell on Josef's shirt, staining it. His clothes were rarely clean, but to someone dealing with bodily fluids, it was easy to tell the difference between shit and gravy.

Abe, always with a sharp mind and keen eye, saw the stain first.

"The lieutenant doesn't make you wear a bib in his chambers?" he asked, pointing at the stain.

Josef wasn't sure what he was talking about until he looked down. He brushed at it and walked past Abe.

"I hope your four-course lunch was delicious," Abe said, loud enough for the others to hear.

Josef went straight to work, looking for child corpses to move. He watched Abe slither among the other men, his hands pointing at his shirt where the stain had been.

That was the last day anyone spoke to him. Now, they just glared, as they did at the guards when their backs were turned.

The day had ended as every other day had. They all lined up and were counted, being given their free time.

Josef didn't feel like playing cards and he doubted he'd even be allowed in. He just wanted to lay down and think of what he and Kollmer were going to discuss tomorrow.

The Nazi lieutenant had grown more curious about the war between the angels and demons. His thoughts of theory and opinion had started to wane and his lust for angelic battles had increased. They would talk of many things, but it would always come back to Lucifer's betrayal and his and the seven Princes of Hell being cast out of Heaven.

Josef walked over to his mattress and went to crawl in, but stopped. A large wet stain spread throughout the middle of it. He put his hand on it and smelled. Someone or many people had urinated in his bed.

"Who the fuc—" his words cut off as a disgusting piece of fabric was pulled over his head. Something hard hit his face and then he was on the ground. Kicks from bony feet and legs rained down on him. He couldn't see, but it wouldn't have mattered, they were coming from every angle. Josef curled into the fetal position, trying to protect himself. Blood poured from his nose and mouth, wetting the fabric, making breathing nearly impossible. Hisses of 'Pet Jew' and 'Nazi fucker' were said with each blow.

Finally, it stopped. He dare not move, fearing another attack. His entire body ached and screamed in pain. The labored breathing of the assaulters was all around him. One man spit on him, followed by a few more. He felt every glob of saliva like they were bee stings. Each one a psychological blow. Footsteps shuffled away and the door closed.

Josef pulled the cloth from his head. He was alone. His fingers, one of which was sprained from a kick, touched his face. He knew his nose was broken, but luckily he could still breathe and it didn't feel too crooked. On shaky legs, he rose. Pains from his abdomen spasmed and he prayed he didn't have any internal bleeding. His right eyebrow was cut and swollen, but the bone felt intact. The only good thing about the beating was the fact the men were so malnourished, they couldn't inflict serious damage. At least physically.

He needed to lay down and crouched to get into his bunk. The urine from the other men soaked into his clothing, but he didn't care. Josef lay on his back, forearm draped over his face, and wept.

---

JOSEF AWOKE the next day with the rest of the men. His body, which would ache from the constant loading of corpses, now hurt for another reason. His eye was swollen and he could see the top of his brow in his periphery. The body aches came not from labor, but vicious blows by men whom he once considered friends.

None of them looked at him, hobbling to the bathroom. There were whispers as he walked, but no one would speak directly to him.

Josef saw a few busted knuckles here and there, but that was it. It was as if nothing had changed between them. As if they hadn't taken a man, who had lost everything and was just trying to survive, and beaten him senseless. Abe was the worst one of all. From the first day in the camp, he'd been there. He'd always helped Josef, kept his spirit up when he could. Josef didn't know for sure if his former friend was involved in the attack, but he had to believe so. Every hiss sounded like him. Sounded like betrayal and hate. He didn't know if the men truly hated him or were jealous of him. While they ate weak soup and sat in the sun, he was eating officer's meals inside. He was able to read books which he'd never thought to see again. Even the conversation with Kollmer was surprisingly good.

Josef shuffled into the bathroom and urinated. His urine was tinged red and his kidneys hurt when he pissed. He didn't make a sound, just aimed his stream and prayed it would end soon.

---

NOTHING CHANGED at the gas chamber, except for the fact the guards were constantly making jokes. It didn't bother Josef, as long as they hit him with words and not batons.

"Even the Jews hate other Jews," laughed Kurtz, cigarette smoke puffing out of his mouth. The other guards laughed as well when Josef shuffled by, dragging an old woman by her armpits.

Josef maneuvered her corpse into the truck and started back.

The days were getting colder, but not nearly cold yet. It was a perfect fall day, with just a slight eastward breeze to cool you off. Even so, Josef was sweating. His body aches made work slower and harder. He was taking more time and effort to move one corpse than it used to take him and Abe to move four.

"Maybe the Pet Jew tried to suck their cocks as he does with you know who," one of the guards said. He was stupid, but not stupid enough to degrade Lt. Kollmer in front of other men. You never knew who was listening. One stupid mistake which was taken for treason would end you up against the wall or out in the gravel pits.

The other guards chuckled at the crude joke.

"Here comes his fag-boy now," said Kurtz, pointing with a cigarette towards Private Berg in the driver's seat. He looked for Josef, who was near the truck, trying to get the legs of a deformed-looking teenage boy into the back. "Pet Jew," he said to Josef, "your ride is here."

Josef used to hate when Kurtz would say that, but now it was a godsend. With a final push, he was able to get the boy's legs into the truck. He wiped his hands on his pants and walked towards the waiting vehicle.

Private Berg recoiled slightly when he saw Josef's swollen face, but didn't say anything. It wasn't uncommon for the guards to beat the men. Usually, any indiscretion was solved with a gunshot, not a beating, so the man was lucky in that sense.

"Get in," Berg said to Josef after the men had drunk from the tank.

The ride wasn't long, but he felt every bump in the road along the way. He was trying to clear his mind of the assault. Lt. Kollmer wouldn't care about his excuses. If Josef was no longer helping him in whatever he was trying to accomplish, he would be taken to the Death Wall and shot.

They walked upstairs, Berg hitting the door with a dainty knock.

"Come," the voice said.

Both men entered and Berg smiled at Kollmer.

"Lieutenant," he clicked and saluted.

"Private," grinned Kollmer. He hadn't yet noticed the damage to Josef's face or if he had, didn't care.

Berg turned and walked out, closing the door behind him.

"Take a seat, Professor," said Kollmer. "I see you have felt the wrath of Sgt. Kurtz." He pointed to Josef's face. With a laugh, he said, "Consider yourself lucky. That man is a sadist who is quick to shoot. If he just gave you a few punches, well, that's a blessing."

Josef knew all too well how quick Kurtz was on the trigger.

"It wasn't Sgt. Kurtz, sir," mumbled Josef through a swollen lip.

Kollmer, who was pulling a book from his desk, stopped. He pulled his glasses off, a storm brewing on his face.

"What did you say?" he asked—no, demanded. "And speak up this time."

"It wasn't Sgt. Kurtz who beat me." With every word, he felt like a traitor. Like a man who sells out his neighbor to save his skin. Like a Pet Jew. "It was the other men."

"The other prisoners?" Kollmer asked, a little confused.

Yes, prisoners did attack or rape each other from time to time, but it was so rare. They had worse things to worry about besides each other.

Josef nodded. "They said I'm your Pet Jew." He didn't tell him Kurtz had started the name. No good could come of that. He glanced up at the man.

Kollmer was able to visibly calm down, but inside, he was a tempest. These rats wouldn't dare take something from him. He owned them and if he wanted to speak with them, kill them, light them on fire, whatever, he would. They were not in control, he was.

He leaned forward, his fingers resting tip to tip. "Tell me everything."

---

THE NIGHT WAS COOL, which for the prisoners was a blessing. Those that had been there for the previous winter knew what was to come. Heavy snow, gusting winds, and ice would torment the camp in the coming months. But, for the time being, the cooler night air felt like a treat. Most of the men, who were mere shadows of their former selves, were wrapped in thin blankets.

Josef was one of them. He lay on his straw mattress, which was no longer wet, but still had the smell of urine. His face was still sore, which kept him from sleeping on his stomach. He didn't mind, he wasn't much of a stomach sleeper anyhow. Besides, he didn't want to be reminded of the other men using his bed as a toilet.

His dreams were disjointed and random, almost like the synapses in his brain were firing with different ones each. None were particularly good, but nothing as bad as a nightmare. No, it was a relaxed and uneventful sleep. So he thought.

---

SGT. KURTZ SLEPT on his bunk, one leg hanging over the side. He and two other soldiers had finished a bottle of Russian Vodka after dinner. The Soviets were terrible people, but could make a hell of a drink. He wore his uniform pants and undershirt, his uniform shirt in a heap on the floor.

Private Fischer, one of the men he'd drank with, was asleep in his bunk next to Kurtz. He let out a deep, baritone fart, said something in his sleep, and rolled over. He was a lightweight when it came to drinking and had almost puked, but kept it down.

Both men, dead to the world, didn't hear the sound of heavy boots approaching their room.

A meaty fist banged on the door, violently rousing both men from their drunken stupor.

Kurtz nearly fell out of bed, his hand instinctively reaching for his P38 pistol, which was hanging on a peg in the wall. His eyes flew open, but his vision swam, some from lack of sleep, but mostly from the alcohol. For a second, he thought he was dreaming when he saw Lt. Kollmer standing in his room.

Kollmer was dressed, wearing a pressed, clean, and polished uniform. He'd even shaven. The man looked like he was ready to accept the Fuhrer himself.

"Sgt. Kurtz," Kollmer said, his judging eyes taking in the state and smell of the room.

Kurtz rubbed his face, the stubble rough on his hands.

"Yes, Lieutenant," the light was assaulting his eyes. He held one hand up, not in salute, but to block the light bulb.

"You and Private Fischer get dressed." He looked at his watch. "Be outside in fifteen minutes and please be presentable." He didn't say another word, just turned and walked away.

Kurtz thought he'd overslept and missed his morning line-up, but it was pitch black outside. The only light came from the pole lights in the camp and constantly roving spotlights on the outer perimeter. He grabbed his pocket watch, a gift from his father upon completing his basic training, and checked the time. It was 3 am.

Private Fischer, who was still quite drunk, was laying back down. He had his pillow doubled up and was hugging it like a lover.

Kurtz stood, his legs betraying him for a moment, but he didn't fall back down.

"Get up, you little shit," he said to Fischer, who was snoring again. The young man probably thought he'd dreamt the whole encounter with the lieutenant. Luckily for him, Kurtz was a man who was used to functioning drunk.

"Get the fuck up," Kurtz said, this time slapping the young Private. The man's eyes sprung open, his face stinging from the slap. "Get dressed," Kurtz said, walking back to his uniform trunk, "we have work to do."

---

ABE'S DREAMS were a little more coherent than Josef's. He dreamt of his childhood spent on his family farm. The days of hard work, harvesting crops, raising animals, patching roofs, all of it rewarding. As a boy, he wanted to run and play in the woods, but his father needed the help. When his family, in which he was the only son out of six children, would sit down to dinner, the day's work was worth it. His young muscles ached, but not in a painful throb; no, they hurt in a rewarding way. They let you know you've accomplished something and the evening meal was the reward for that. Whether it was fresh meat, eggs, vegetables, or any other crop, it tasted like hard work.

He tossed and turned in his straw bunk. His muscles in his dream and in real life ached. Rather than farm work, his body ached now from throwing corpses of his countrymen and women into the bed of a truck. No longer did the fatigue feel good and rewarding; no, now it was painful and full of disgust.

The sound of dozens of boots woke him. His eyes snapped to the door.

With one, unnecessary kick, the door was flung open.

Dozens of Nazis armed with heavy clubs stormed in, screaming and swinging.

"On your fucking feet!" they yelled, almost as one. "Get the fuck outside!" was shouted, but ended with the sound of flesh being struck. A man let out a scream of pain as the club broke his elbow.

The entire barracks was in chaos. Men roused from their sleep not by a gentle mother telling them it was time for school, but by madmen armed with clubs. They bumped into each other, each one desperate to avoid the wrath of the rampaging guards.

Outside more Nazis waited. Four of them had snarling German Shepherds. The big dogs were at the end of their leashes, their handlers shouting commands. Spit flew from their fanged mouths, which were only inches from some of the men. One unlucky prisoner was bumped forward, into the waiting maw of a dog. He screamed as the powerful jaws clamped down on his arm. The dog thrashed and pulled, tearing muscle and breaking bone. The handler smiled and told the dog he was a good boy. With a command from the handler, the dog released the crying man, who crawled away, cradling his wounded arm.

Abe made it out of the barracks without a club strike, which he could deal with. It was the dogs that scared him.

When he was a boy on the farm, the family had a herding dog, Lundy. Lundy would kill rats, and chase the other animals around. He was a good dog and a part of the family until he went rabid. They hadn't realized it until it was too late. Lundy had bit Abe on the leg, but not in a playful manner like always. The small dog clamped down with all of its might, large teeth digging deep into the flesh. Abe screamed in fear and pain, getting the attention of his father. The short, yet powerfully built man, ran over to Abe with a piece of wood in his hand. With one swing, he broke the dog's back, making Lundy release its grip on the boy. Lundy's muzzle was stained red with blood and he bared his teeth at Abe's father. Abe watched his father beat the dog into a bloody mess until it was dead.

Seeing the man bit brought back memories and he shuddered.

The barracks were empty, all of the men standing in somewhat neat rows. No one said a word.

Josef stood with his fellow prisoners, and stared straight ahead. He wanted to make eye contact with Kollmer, but didn't dare push his luck.

Lt. Kollmer stood in front of a Kubelwagen, a small truck-like vehicle, similar to the American Jeep. A Nazi stood in the back of the Kubelwagen, his hands on the dreaded MG42 machine gun.

The MG42, which was nicknamed Hitler's Buzzsaw, had an impressive rate of fire. It fired so fast, it was hard to hear individual shots, rather it sounded like a buzzsaw, hence the name.

Lt. Kollmer paced in front of the prisoners. He was crisp and clean and eerily silent. He found Sgt. Kurtz and gave him a nod.

"All right, you dogs." The prisoners, without moving their heads, looked at him. "Right face," he said.

They all turned right, as if it were a normal day heading to the gas chamber.

"March," he said.

Nearly one hundred feet marched in unison, not knowing where they were headed.

They marched through the camp, past the empty gas chamber. It was cold and dark now, but in a few hours, it would be full of screaming, and dying. Thousands of scared people took their last breath in that room. Their fresh air was replaced with the almond smell of Zyklon-B.

Abe looked around as much as he could without moving his head. They were moving towards the outer perimeter fence and he suddenly knew where they were headed: the gravel pits.

The gravel pits were one of the most feared areas of the camp. Even worse than Block 11 or 10, the gravel pits were an area no one returned from.

Other men noticed their destination and began to panic. A low murmur passed along the men, some weeping. One man fled, hoping to get into the tree line hundreds of yards from the camp.

"Stop!" One of the guards shouted at the fleeing man.

Kollmer watched the man run and smiled. He heard the gunner on the MG42 begin to swivel the gun.

"No," Kollmer said to him, keeping the gun silent. "The dogs," he said to the canine handlers.

The two dog handlers nearest the fleeing man smiled. Each of them got their dog's attention, focusing them on the running man. The dogs began barking, straining at their restraints.

"*Fass,*" both men said the command for their dogs to attack. The dogs, finally released from their bonds, shot off into the night.

The man was being followed by the spotlights, making it much easier for the dogs to find their mark. He screamed as they leaped.

As trained, the dogs attacked with a primitive ferocity. One dog bit the man in the arm, staggering him. The other dog took him in the leg, bringing him to the ground. The man kicked and screamed, but there was no fight for the dogs. With brutal efficiency, the dogs ripped and snapped, blood flying from arterial wounds. The first dog, a sable-colored Shepherd, let go of the arm and began searching for the man's neck.

The man dug at the dog's face with his good arm, but it was no use. Within seconds, the dog's powerful jaws were around his throat, ripping his windpipe out. He gargled, drowning in his blood, as the dogs continued to attack.

Flesh ripped with the sound of tearing fabric. The dogs snarled, snapping at one another in their bloodlust. Their snouts were soaked with gore and they panted. They bared their teeth at each other, before setting back to the corpse. A tug of war was fought, and chunks of bloody meat came off in their jaws.

"*Hier,*" yelled the handlers, ordering the dogs to return.

Both dogs, reluctantly, released the bloody corpse. Lolling tongues dripped blood as they ran back. Each returned to their handlers, getting a 'good boy' and scratch behind the ears.

The column of men had stopped, each one had watched the scene in front of them. They knew they were headed for certain death, but a flurry of bullets seemed like a gift compared to being mauled by dogs.

"March," Kurtz shouted, prompting them to get moving again.

In front of the high gravel pit, was a deep and long trench. Mass graves weren't uncommon. This one was already partially occupied. The stench of rotting corpses rose from the hole in the ground. The men were lined up, facing the Nazi guards.

The Nazis stood shoulder to shoulder, with the Kubelwagen in the center. Each man was armed with a submachine gun. Lt. Kollmer broke through the ranks, standing in between the men.

"It has come to my attention, some of you do not like my preference in company," he said, voice echoing in the cool night air. He walked up and down the line of prisoners, looking into the eyes of every man. "Some of you have even gone as far as to mock me, and even farther still, to strike someone I deem my property."

No one had any doubt of who the man was talking about.

Josef shivered at the speech, yet he was still in line with the prisoners. When he'd first met Kollmer, the man told him he would eventually kill him. Josef figured this was his time.

"My actions are my own and no one, especially a gang of rat Jews, will undermine me," he sneered, still pacing. His hands were behind his back. "Professor Lazerowitz, step forward."

Josef nearly vomited, but put one foot in front of the other. He broke the ranks, feeling the eyes of the other prisoners on him.

"Yes, sir?" he stammered, trying to find his voice. He hadn't been this scared since the day his family was ripped from him.

"Come," Lt. Kollmer said.

Josef walked to him, feeling as if he were in a dream. Kollmer put a hand on his shoulder. Josef winced, still sore from the beating he'd taken at the hands of his fellow prisoners. Kollmer looked him in the eyes and smiled. Not a friendly smile, but a smile of a predator about to strike.

"David Ableson," Kollmer said.

Abe took a deep breath and stepped forward.

Kollmer turned his head towards Abe, the smile still plastered on his face.

"Yes, please step forward." He put his hand on Josef and spun him around, so he was facing Abe, who was approaching them.

Abe stopped a few feet from the men. He could feel the eyes and muzzles of the guns, trained on him. Not to mention the attentive eyes of the dogs, two of which were red-faced with blood.

"This is the man, yes?" asked Kollmer. "The man who taunted you, who led the others against you, who led the assault on you?"

Josef locked eyes with Abe. The two men stared at each other for a few seconds.

"Yes, Lt. Kollmer. This is the man," Josef said without breaking eye contact. The old part of him, the part still friendly with Abe, wanted to weep.

Kollmer nodded, pulling his pistol from its holster. "Now, I'm feeling generous this early morning," he said, the gun at his side. "His life is over, so do not get that wrong, but I'm willing to let you choose his death." Kollmer held up the black pistol, its finish looking oily in the headlights of the Kubelwagen. "The gun…or," he pointed to the waiting dogs, "the dogs?"

Josef watched the fear wash over Abe's face. He didn't fear death, none of them did. Living in the camp was temporary and death would come for them all. No, it was the thought of being killed by the dogs that caused Abe to tremble. He didn't know his former friend was fighting to control his bladder at that moment.

Josef looked Abe in the eyes again, seeing the fear. He knew what it was like to fear something, but he also thought of the compassion the man showed him in the first few weeks of imprisonment. He truly owed him his life and decided to grant him an easy death.

"The gun, sir. In the back of the head, if you'd please."

Kollmer looked at him, the maniacal grin widening. He nodded.

"Bring the dogs," he said.

Josef looked at him, but he wasn't shocked by the decision, nor would he try and stop it. That would only sign his death warrant along with Abe's.

"No, no," Abe cried, backing away from the approaching handlers and their dogs. All four had stepped forward and the dogs could sense his fear. They were growling and snapping, spit flying as they strained at their leashes. He put his hands up, pleading with them. The fight with his bladder was over and a torrent of hot piss poured down his leg.

"*Fass,*" the handlers said, releasing their dogs.

Abe fell under the weight of a mountain of fur and teeth. His screams were muffled, when one of the dogs bit him in the face, covering his mouth. Grunts, growls, and the sound of flesh ripping were the only noises. The night was still, the other men, Nazi and Jew, watching the brutal kill. His death was savage, but over in seconds. The dogs were slick with blood and the handlers had to separate them before they turned on each other. Their bloodlust was high and when they were in a killing frenzy, it was nearly impossible to stop them.

Kollmer grabbed Josef, who was staring at the mangled corpse of Abe. He pulled him behind the line of Nazis.

"Sgt. Kurtz," Kollmer said.

Kurtz smiled and yelled, "Ready!" Dozens of guns clicked as rounds were chambered and safeties disengaged. "Aim!" The guns were shouldered and the MG42 gunner was on his site. "Fire!" he screamed. The sound of rapid gunfire pierced the quiet night. Muzzle flashes lit Nazi faces, many with joyful smiles on them.

The prisoners fell, bullets riddling their bodies. Gunfire continued as they were on the ground, bullets gouging the earth and flesh. The MG42 chattered, ripping fully automatic gunfire into the line of men. Its barrel glowed red as it ran out of ammunition.

Josef didn't watch, he didn't need to. They were all dead and he was alive. That was all that mattered to him.

Lt. Kollmer jumped into the Kubelwagen, kicking spent shell casings out of his way. He looked at Josef and nodded before the vehicle sped away.

"Get walking," Kurtz said from behind him. He prodded him in the back with a still-warm submachine gun.

Josef walked, but to where he didn't know.

# III

# LIBERATION AND A WILD STORY

## 12

## YONKERS, NY 1952

Josef carried his one bag of groceries down the sidewalk.

The day was beautiful, one of those perfect fall days he'd come to love living in New York. In Poland, the winter months were downright brutal; so compared to them, the New York seasons were a breeze. Summers were just a bit hotter, but it was something he could deal with. Besides, at age fifty, the heat kept his muscles limber and loose.

He reached the front steps of his apartment building and adjusted the paper bag into his left arm so he could fish out his keys.

His apartment was modest, to say the least. It was a one-bedroom in a four-story building, which was nearly thirty years old. The pipes rattled, but all of the plumbing worked and the heat was strong. His living room window and bedroom window were on opposite sides of the apartment, so when left open he'd get a nice cross breeze.

Josef walked in and set the groceries on the counter. There wasn't much and it was put away in moments.

He took two steps into his living room and sat on his chair. Just like he always did, he picked up the last picture ever taken of his family, which sat next to him.

It was one of his favorite possessions and he hoped to take it to the grave. The picture was of all of them: him, Ola, Piotr, and Michal just after Hanukkah services. The boys were so excited for the rest of the day, which included playing with their new toys, eating a delicious meal, and sleeping with dreams of doing it again and again. Josef and Ola were happy too, as was common.

They had a great marriage that was the envy of many of their friends. Fights were very rare in their household and were never physical. Money wasn't abundant, but they lived well. Both of their boys were healthy, smart, and kind. They even had sex multiple times a week. Life was good until the bombs started to fall.

Josef stared at the picture and closed his eyes. He could almost smell Ola's Hannukah meal, hear the laughter of the boys and feel the touch of Ola's skin, flushed with too much wine. Occasionally, he wept when thinking of them. This was one of those times. Silent tears rolled down his cheeks, catching the newly formed wrinkles he'd acquired, and dripping onto his shirt.

Thoughts of them, of course, brought back memories of the camp. The last time he'd seen them on the train platform, to his eventual liberation by the Soviets.

Part of him wished they all could've died together, right on the platform. Then they would all be joined together in death. Another part of him was grateful for the fact he'd survived the war, unlike millions of others. Survival was the deepest human instinct; one would do anything to stay alive.

After the slaughter at the gravel pits, Josef's stay in the camp became quite uneventful. He was moved to a special dorm, which was much smaller, only holding eight beds. The conditions were improved, and even the food was better. There was a stipulation, just like working at the gas chambers: if you didn't work, you died.

Josef roomed with other intellectual men, all whom had specific talents and were recruited by high-ranking Nazis. Most were accountants, helping the Nazis set up untraceable bank accounts. One was an art dealer, who would appraise certain pieces and give advice on what to look for. Another man was a jeweler, who had the worst job of having to melt down gold stolen from other Jews. Then, there was Josef.

Josef would essentially read for most of the day from whatever books Lt. Kollmer had given him. At night, he and the Nazi would meet in the office and discuss random theological points.

Like many of the high-ranking members of the Third Reich, Erich Kollmer had a deep fascination with the occult. But his approach was different from the others. Rather than try and translate obscure text and meanings, he had someone help him. In the year and a half he and Josef spent together, he'd learned more about angels, demons, God and Satan, than in his years at University.

Josef took advantage of his time. Usually, the 'assignments' given to him were easy and short to read. He finished reading and making notes just after lunch. Then it was his turn to learn. He was never great with numbers, but his roommate, Myer, was. Myer taught him how to balance accounts and shift money around. They discussed stocks and trading and when and where to invest. In 1945 when the camp was liberated, Josef had more accounting skills than half of the accountants in the world.

Towards the end of the war, with the sound of artillery thundering in the background, Lt. Kollmer was more and more frantic. He would often meet with Josef in a disheveled state, although many of the Nazis were starting to crumble.

The Soviet war machine was bulldozing a path through the heart of Nazi Germany. The rage and savagery of their army was something to be feared, knowing the atrocities committed by Germany on Soviet people.

Josef and the other prisoners couldn't help but smile, internally, of course, at the duress their captors were under. To watch them scurry as rats brought them immense pleasure. They didn't relax though. No, those last few weeks in the camp were the most stressful. Some of the Nazis would just start shooting, killing as many Jews as they could. Even some of the higher-ranking Nazis would take part, often leading groups of their prisoners to the gas chambers. The ground around the gravel pit became a mass of churned earth. There was no more room to bury bodies and they were in the process of digging more mass graves in the tree line by the pits. What was once a well-oiled, death machine, was descending into chaos.

Towards the middle of January 1945, the Soviets were so close, they could be heard if the wind blew just right. Not just their guns, but their actual voices.

On the final night he saw Lt. Kollmer, Josef was lying in bed, not quite asleep. The sound of not-so-distant artillery was keeping him awake. Not only that, but the frantic shouting and sometimes gunfire around the camp. His two remaining bunkmates (Myer ended up with dysentery and was moved to the medical ward, so they were told) were fast asleep. They had a gift for sleep he would've killed for and would drift away with ease. Josef looked out the window across the room. In the distance, he could see lightning but knew there were no clouds in the sky. It was shell-bursts or screaming Soviet rockets; they were coming. His breath caught as the door creaked open. Light footsteps crossed the room, heading towards him. He thought back to the early days of meeting Lt. Kollmer. He never forgot the man telling him he'd kill him one day. Was he there to make good on his promise? If so, Josef would face him like a man.

He rolled over, looking up at the man looming over him, his Death's Head emblem shone in the moonlight. Lt. Kollmer held a pistol in his hand, but it wasn't pointed at Josef.

Josef wasn't scared. He was waiting to die since the day his family was taken from him. He took it all in, looking at the shadowy face of the man above him.

He knew the only reason he survived the camp, until that point, was thanks to Kollmer. Eventually, someone else would've found out a professor had slipped through the gaps and he would've been tortured and executed. Even though he'd kept him alive, Josef loathed the man. In a year and a half, he witnessed him murder dozens of people, some with a big smile on his face. Kollmer only saved him because he was using him, needing him for some diabolical plan he was hatching.

Kollmer raised the gun, pointing it at Josef's face. His expression was blank and calm as if chiseled from stone. For the first time in a while, he looked put together. His uniform was pressed and clean, face shaved and eyes blank, yet alert. He looked every part of a Nazi executioner.

Josef stared at him, his eyes doing everything possible to ignore the black maw of the gun muzzle. Neither of them spoke or blinked, just stared at each other. Josef felt if he blinked, that would be it. The gun would go off, a shot never heard and he'd be dead. The thought of that wasn't such a bad idea if he could see his family again. No, survival is the base human instinct and he'd made it this far.

Kollmer reached up with his thumb and de-cocked the pistol, lowering it back to his side.

"The Soviets are on our doorstep. I am leaving tonight. Best of luck." He didn't say anything else, just holstered the gun and walked away. He stopped at the doorway and looked over his shoulder. "You'll never know the curse you've given to me." With that he walked out, leaving the door open. His boots, which were so quiet moments ago, thundered down the steps.

Three days later, Soviet troops liberated the camp.

He sniffled, returning his mind to the present. A line of snot ran down his face, which he wiped with the back of his hand. Carefully, as if handling a live bomb, he set the picture back down. He composed himself, letting the memories of his slaughtered family drift from his mind.

After the war, Josef, like many of his countrymen, fled Europe. Some of the Jews went East, in hopes of reestablishing their ancient homeland of Israel. He knew that task would be a hard one, rife with conflict and war, two things he'd had quite enough of. No, he decided to head to the savior of the free world: America.

To the Nazis, the Americans were the worst kind of people. Their rights and freedoms made them weak and undisciplined. The world saw that was a bald-faced lie. The American industry and economy were one of the biggest deciding factors in ending World War 2. Not to mention the fighting spirit of her men.

Josef never believed the rumors about the streets being made of gold, but he knew there was money to be earned. During the rebuilding of Europe, he was able to learn enough English to feel comfortable. Once he had saved enough money, he was on the first ship headed West.

Within the first few months, his English was nearly fluent and he began looking for education work as opposed to labor jobs he was taking to pay the bills. He would tutor here and there, mostly Polish immigrants or their children, but it was money. Eventually, he landed a paying job doing what he loved. He taught night classes at a small college, which was a satellite building for a larger school in Manhattan.

Josef stood, walking over to his counter. He grabbed two slices of rye bread and opened the fridge, where he pulled out wax paper-wrapped meats and cheese. He wasn't much of a cook and almost lived on just sandwiches. As he concocted his meal, he thought about his lesson plan for the night class he had to teach in an hour. It wasn't what he wanted to teach, but the school made the rules and he wanted to keep getting paid.

He bit into the sandwich, thinking of angels and demons.

## 13

Josef didn't mind teaching at night. He preferred them to the early morning classes, which was fine by his colleagues. Ever since being liberated from the camps, he found sleep hard to come by. This would be no shock to anyone, especially considering the atrocities he'd seen. He loved the night; it was the rare time when the city shed its skin in preparation for the new day. Also, he did his best work and felt more refreshed in the inky blackness.

Josef had a driver's license but didn't have a car. It didn't seem like something worth spending his money on. Where he lived, everything, including the school, was within walking distance. If the weather was really bad (not just a little rain, but a downpour) he hopped on one of the many city buses. The air, even though it had the smell of a city, was different, more vibrant than that of Poland. Nothing could ever replace his native land, but he was growing accustomed to the Land of the Free and Home of the Brave.

His class ended at 10 pm and the walk home was less than a half-hour. The beautiful fall day had given way to a rather crisp fall night.

This didn't bother him. Less than seven years earlier, he'd been wearing threadbare clothing (and he was issued 'good stuff' by camp standards) standing outside for a line-up. He was lucky enough to work indoors, but still felt the bite of a Polish winter.

At least now, he was prepared. He wore a tan Fedora, with a black ribbon around it, and a light jacket, with a wool sweater underneath. He'd bought a second-hand pea coat, but the weather was still too warm for that. His briefcase, also used, was soft leather and swung from his left hand.

Crime in the city wasn't horrible, but there was bound to be some. Americans, he found out, were very possessive people. They liked the big and flashy and expensive. Unfortunately for them, work could be scarce, especially if you didn't have any discernible skills. Many GIs returning from the war found themselves fighting for jobs. Most of them were able to find work, but those who had mental health issues (shell shock) were often cast aside to fend for themselves.

Josef was cautious, but not afraid. He took a direct path home, keeping his head up and alert. He was a tall man and since moving to the US, he'd gained a little weight over his pre-war size. Even though he was fifty, he was still in decent shape. All things considered, he wasn't an ideal victim for a mugger.

He reached his building and pulled his keys out. In the distance, he heard a train whistle. For a second he flashed back to the fateful ride to Auschwitz. Feeling the sweaty hands of his family, hearing their cries and screams. The smell of the train car, unwashed bodies, and human filth. It was nearly ten years since they'd been taken, but to him, it felt like yesterday.

Josef climbed the steps to his apartment.

He walked in, setting his briefcase on the table by the door and hanging his jacket on the coat rack. The apartment was dark, except for a small lamp he always kept on in the living room. He navigated his way through the dim apartment and turned on the radio. He didn't care what it was tuned to, as long as it wasn't static. After flipping on the kitchen light, he went back and grabbed his briefcase.

It wasn't too heavy, just a few thin books on his subject matter and a couple of late papers from some students. There was also a letter from the college president. Josef hadn't opened it yet, but he was almost certain he knew what it was. Once every month, the college president would call a faculty meeting at the main campus, which was located in Manhattan.

Josef didn't have any issues with the city itself. Actually, he rather liked it. The hustle and bustle, the different foods and shops, and just the entire atmosphere. There was always something to do. He didn't know if he could live there, especially in Manhattan, but it was nice to be close by.

No, his issue wasn't with the city, but the transportation. He didn't have a car and had no intentions of getting one anytime soon. The only way he could get to Manhattan was either by bus or train. A taxi was an option, but it was too much money to justify using one. He would face his discomforts and take mass transit.

When he went to his first meeting by train, it was only the second time he'd been on a train since being liberated from Auschwitz. The passenger train was nothing compared to the cramped, dark and disgusting livestock car he and his family had been transported in, but there were similarities. When the train would rock, or brakes squealed, Josef had flashbacks. If someone had a crying child, he could only think of the small corpses he'd loaded into hundreds of trucks.

The buses were better, but not by much. He was still crowded, surrounded by bodies. Granted, these people were on their way to work and not a death camp, but the feeling of despair always crept up.

Once he was out into the city, he felt better, but the dread of the return trip home always loomed.

Josef put the letter on the table and opened the fridge. He grabbed a squat bottle of beer and popped the top off of it. It was cold and hit the spot, just enough to satisfy. Even before the war, he was never much of a drinker. He'd have a few beers here and there, but was rarely drunk. Ola hardly drank, so it was easier for him to abstain at parties and such.

He sat down at the table, putting his beer next to his briefcase. He pulled the letter out, opened it, and did a quick scan. Just as he'd expected. The letter fell from his hand back to the table. He picked up his beer and drained it. The rapid flood of alcohol made him feel light and went straight to his head, which was the plan. Hopefully, it would help him sleep and possibly suppress any nightmares.

Josef got ready for bed and set his alarm. He knew he probably wouldn't need it, but it was always better to be safe.

He drifted off to sleep. Unfortunately, the beer didn't work and nightmares came. Many didn't stick with him, but one did. It wasn't a nightmare that stuck with him, but a face.

The face of Lt. Kollmer.

## 14

THE TRAIN RIDE into the city was uneventful...for the most part. Josef was up earlier than his alarm and decided to try and get into the city before the rush of workers. He left his apartment before the sun was up and hopped on the train. The car was nearly empty and he was able to relax and even read a little.

He brought along his briefcase and papers and, of course, his red grading pencil. Motion sickness was never an issue for him and the short trip from Yonkers to Manhattan was the perfect time to catch up on work.

The train rocked back and forth ever so gently. Almost like a mother soothing a baby. His body moved with it, but his eyes stayed locked on the paper he was grading.

The paper was pretty good, written by a promising young woman, Mary Sutherland. Even though he'd only read a few of her writings, Josef knew she'd be one of his easier students. She was always engaging and paid attention to his sometimes dry lectures.

The brakes on the train squealed. Josef pulled his nose up from the paper, pencil still in hand. The tip remained sharp, as Mary's paper was the first in the stack and he'd yet to mark anything. He must've been lost in reading, not realizing the train was at the first of its two stops before hitting the city.

The doors opened and a couple of rougher-looking men boarded the train. He was used to seeing men dressed for business, wearing expensive suits. He'd also never been on the train this early in the morning. Different hours for different folks. They wore stained denim overalls, which covered muscular bodies. Each of them also had a sturdy-looking metal lunch pail. Their hands were clean, but Josef could see the grit under their nails. He'd heard about these men, which some people referred to as sandhogs. They were the ones who did the excavating for all of the city, including the water tunnels and subway tunnels. A handful more followed, moving to another car ahead of him.

The train lurched ahead and he got back to reading Mary's paper.

He finished it, with only one mark (a minor grammatical error, but he couldn't let her think her work was perfect). Josef was circling the 'A+' he scrawled on the front of the paper when the train slowed down again. The second and final stop.

He was putting her paper away and grabbing another when the train doors opened.

More people boarded this time and when he glanced up, his heart nearly stopped. Ola, Michal, and Piotr stepped on the train.

They were beautiful. Ola was in her favorite blue dress, which accented her creamy skin perfectly. She would only wear it on special occasions, but when she did, Josef's heart would stop. The tops of her breasts poked out, just enough to give a hint of sexuality, but not nearly enough to be trashy. Josef would often have to be reminded by his wife her eyes were on her face, not her chest. They would both smile and laugh, the perfect laugh she had. She always said she wanted to be buried in that dress.

Michal and Piotr were dressed identical, as Ola would often do. They were in navy blue slacks, with an eggshell shirt. Both of them had fresh haircuts and big smiles. Each boy held one of their mother's hands, looking up at her lovingly.

Josef began to rise, keeping an eye on them in the small crowd.

They were coming towards him now, so close he could almost touch them. It felt like he'd been here before. They were just out of reach, their fingertips sliding through his hands. The day on the train came back to him, a repressed memory that never died. The taste of his wife's lips, the touch of his boys sweaty and scared hands.

They were all looking at him, smiling.

"Daddy?" Piotr said. Smoke came out of his mouth.

The smell of almonds, the Zyklon-B, flooded Josef's nostrils. He recoiled, the odor assaulting him.

"Why did you let us die?" Michal said, getting closer, his little hand outstretched, almost to its limit. "They did awful things to us, Daddy. Terrible things and you let it happen."

Josef stood frozen, staring at his babies, his sons, the ones who he swore to protect. His mouth was agape and tears hung in his eyes. A croak came from his throat, but he couldn't form words.

"Yes, Josef," Ola said, her face shifting before his eyes, "why didn't you save us?" Her skin was blackening as if she were covered in invisible fire. Her dress began to pull away, the invisible flames licking at it. Ola's breasts were freed from the restraint of the dress, but they were no longer milk-white and supple. Rather they were charred nubs of flesh, glistening with globs of melted fat. "Save us, Josef," she said, her hair completely gone. Her eyelids had burned off, leaving a shocked look on her face, as she lumbered forward.

Josef collapsed in the seat. Piotr, who was just as burned as his mother and brother, reached out for him.

"Save us." His blackened hand grabbed Josef's paralyzed shoulder.

Josef jumped, reaching for the charred hand, only to find that of the conductor.

The conductor, a man in his late sixties, pulled away from the sleeping passenger, thinking maybe he was a drunk who'd fallen asleep on the train.

"End of the line, sir," said the conductor, his majestic white mustache twitching.

Josef looked around, noticing they were the only two left in the car. A paper was in his hand, but his pencil was on the floor. His heart was pounding, but the fear of the dream was starting to ebb away.

"Sorry about that, boring term paper," he joked, holding up Mary's report. His forced smile was thinly veiled and the conductor didn't seem to care about his excuse. The man had a schedule to keep and wanted him off the train.

Without another word, the conductor nodded and walked away.

Josef grabbed his pencil from the floor and stuffed everything into his bag. He shuffled off the train and onto the platform. The doors closed behind him and he swore he could smell smoke...smoke and almonds.

---

Josef didn't mind the board meeting. It wasn't his favorite thing in the world, but it got him away from his everyday life. Plus it was nice to see the main campus of the school. After a few hours of discussion, an early lunch was called.

Many of his colleagues decided to stick around the school and grab lunch in the cafeteria. Josef didn't get many opportunities to expand on the variety of his food, so he took the time to explore the city.

When he moved to America and saw the towering skyscrapers of the city, he was in awe. Back in Poland, there was nothing like them, not even the biggest church was as close. He was always afraid the giant buildings were going to collapse, crushing everyone underneath. Luckily, smarter men than him had engineered and built them. Some of the city was still old, with a few smaller buildings here and there, but they weren't long for this booming metropolis.

Cars were another thing that took getting used to. In Europe, cars were not nearly as plentiful. They were around, but the gas rations of the war made them rare at times. Even in some of the bigger Polish cities, horses were the main form of transportation. Not in the US. Cars, buses, and trucks belched their way up and down the street, shrill horns blaring.

Foot traffic was still the main mode of transportation. The sidewalks, especially at lunchtime, were packed with workers. People walked and didn't stop. There were no, 'sorrys' for bumped shoulders, or an 'excuse me' for a stepped-on foot. No, the people of Manhattan had places to be and wouldn't let anything stop them.

Josef, having visited the big city many times, adopted the customs of the people. He would still mutter his apologies out of habit, but didn't expect anything in return. Today, he barely said anything; he was on a mission.

Poland was a country of rich tradition and comforting food. Especially their sausages. Some of the finest meats came from the country and Josef had had his share. To him, they all paled in comparison to the boiled, American hotdog. He didn't know why the mass-produced, blended meat sticks were so good, but he loved them, especially with yellow mustard and raw onions.

Almost all of the hotdog carts were the same, but he had one he loved. Aaron was the owner and he too was a war refugee from Poland. He wasn't Jewish, but he was still a fellow countryman.

Josef could see his red and white umbrella in the distance, as he swam in the sea of people. He could smell the steam from the cart and could almost taste the hotdogs in his mouth.

The sidewalk was a cacophony of conversations and voices, but one, in particular, stopped him in his tracks. He strained his ears, trying to pick it out from the crowd. People pushed around him, sneering at him as he stood still. A silly older man who was lost, possibly.

"Come," someone said in perfect German.

Josef's testicles retracted against his body. His heart slammed into his ribcage, fighting to get out. The smell of hotdogs and bodies made him want to vomit and he fought with every fiber in his being to hold his gorge. He scanned the crowd, looking at faces, trying to find the man to whom the voice belonged.

"Schatzi, come," the man said again.

Josef was able to find him, but briefly. The man had black hair, which looked dyed. He was tugging on a leash connected to a small dachshund, who was sniffing a garbage can.

Josef was frozen. People started walking around him, instead of into him. He stared, just catching a glimpse of the man's face before he walked into a building. Even though it was only a fraction of a second, he would know that face anywhere. It haunted his nightmares. It was the face of the lieutenant of the SS, Erich Kollmer.

Kollmer walked into a building and disappeared from Josef's sight.

Slowly, as if in a dream, Josef looked up at the building. *EK and Son Antiques* was written at the top above the door.

Josef was in a fog. Kollmer was gone, but had he ever really been there? After his vivid nightmare on the train, Josef didn't know what to believe. Could that have been just another German man talking to his dog? No, Josef was sure it was him. But was he? It had been over seven years since he'd last seen him. When he was in the camp, Josef was in his early forties and Kollmer had been at least ten years his senior. That man he'd just watched had thick black hair and a fairly youthful build. But did he? Or was that what Josef wanted to tell himself? He needed answers and he wasn't getting them by standing on the sidewalk. Robotically, his feet began moving towards the store. He stopped as if waking from a dream.

*What am I going to do?* he thought. *Barge into this man's store and ask him if he was a vicious, Nazi death dealer?* No, Josef couldn't do that, could he? He needed proof, something solid, or at least a better look at his face. That would be enough for him. Just a full-face look and then he could figure out a plan to confront him. After that, he didn't know.

All those years he wanted to kill every Nazi and vowed if ever given the chance, he would avenge his family and the millions of others killed by them. This may be his opportunity, but could he take it? Did he have to take it? There were rumors amongst the other survivors whom he'd met, some of the Nazis were being hunted. The newly reclaimed Jewish nation of Israel had mercenaries to hunt and capture (or sometimes kill) Nazi war criminals. A high-ranking leader of the Auschwitz death camp would be a nice target for this group, but Josef had no idea how to find them or who to even contact.

His head was starting to hurt. The adrenaline dump of possibly seeing a man who was a devil and at the same time a savior to Josef, was overwhelming. First things first: find out for sure who the man was and go from there. Until then, Josef couldn't do anything.

He looked at his watch and realized he needed to start walking back to the school. His stomach was in no shape for lunch, his hunger flying away like smoke on a strong breeze.

Josef turned around, wading through the sea of people as he walked back to the school.

---

JOSEF'S MIND wandered through the rest of the meeting. He kept thinking about Kollmer and couldn't seem to get him out of his mind. The worst part was he wasn't even sure if it was him. Since dozing off on the train and having his vivid nightmare, he wasn't so sure if the after effects of the terror were still lingering. It would make perfect sense for his wounded mind to see Kollmer, the man he had witnessed murder hundreds of people. There was no other choice; he needed to see him again to be certain.

The meeting ended at 3 pm, giving Josef plenty of time to get back home and relax. Josef wasn't going home; he was going to the store he'd seen Kollmer head into.

He had a gut feeling the store was his, but it wasn't a guarantee. For one, it was doubtful he used his real name to open a business. More than likely he'd just been a customer. Also doubtful, because he'd brought a dog in with him. Not many antique stores allowed animals.

Josef walked. The crowd was still ever-present, but not nearly what it was. His stomach was growling since missing lunch and he decided on getting some hotdogs after all.

He found a bench and sat. Each hotdog (he'd gotten 3) went down in a few bites. He knew they were delicious, but his mind was elsewhere. His eyes were focused on the storefront. The door would open and close periodically, but no man with a dog would come out.

Josef wadded up his garbage and set it next to him on the bench. He sipped from his coffee, which wasn't the best beverage to wash down hotdogs, but he was tired.

He sat for an hour, watching, but seeing nothing.

*What the hell am I doing?* he asked himself. *What if it isn't him? Well, that would be great. I'd rather it not be him.* He told himself this, but deep down the seed of vengeance was growing. Part of him wanted it to be Kollmer. What he would do after that was another decision. *And if it is him, what then? Am I going to attack him in the street or scream him a murderer in the crowd?*

The sun was dipping below the horizon. Long shadows of tall buildings spread out on the streets. A once refreshing fall breeze now carried a slight chill. Josef, now sitting for nearly two hours, was starting to get cold. His coffee was long gone. The cup now contained the wrappers from his hotdogs. He was just about to stand when the door to the shop opened.

Josef's heart raced. He stood to get a better look at the man, who was locking the door to the shop. His back was still to Josef, the little dog sniffing at passers-by. The crowd was heavy, but Josef didn't need much, just a look at his full face. Even for an instant.

The man turned and in the ever-changing kaleidoscope of bodies, Josef saw him. People walked around the man, none knowing he was a mass murderer.

Josef's mouth went dry. He kept his eyes locked on Kollmer, which was easy. He was walking up a set of stairs on the side of the building. With a quick motion, he walked into an apartment above the store and was gone.

Josef was numb. He stared for a few more seconds until he finally snapped out of his trance.

It was him, he was sure of it. One of the most feared Nazi killers was living a comfortable life in America. A wave of emotions flooded his senses. Hatred, loathing, disgust, and fear. Yes, deep down he still feared the man. Josef had to realize he was no longer in the camp, but free.

Josef walked towards the train station. He was able to collect his thoughts.

*I want to kill him,* he thought, bumping into people as he walked. *You're not a killer though.* This voice was his, but he could hear Ola creeping in. He wasn't a killer, but if he were to become one, this was the perfect person to start with. Josef didn't know what he was going to do, but he knew he'd have to wait. Not long, but at least sleep on it.

Josef boarded the train. He was able to get a window seat as the powerful engine began to pull. He stared outside, not focusing on anything. The scenery was a blur, a smudge in time. A plan began to form in his mind. It wasn't a very good one, but it was a plan. By tomorrow night, either he or Kollmer would be dead.

## 15

Josef barely slept. The terrified faces of countless corpses haunted him. Thankfully none were of his family, but the thousands of strangers he loaded into trucks.

When the sun began to rise, Josef was already on his second cup of coffee.

He sipped from the mug, the black coffee almost too hot to drink. It tasted amazing as if he were in the roasting room and the beans were pulled fresh and ground just for him. At first, when he had his first cup, he was confused. He checked the bag, thinking he'd bought a more expensive brand, but he didn't. It was the same bargain brand of American coffee he'd always had. Then it hit him. This pot of coffee could very well be his last. After tonight he'd be a changed man or a dead man.

Josef sipped again, the silky, dark coffee tasting like ambrosia. He made a mental checklist of everything he wanted to get situated before heading back to Manhattan. Luckily, he had no classes to teach that day, so there was no awkward sick call-out.

He took his time, savoring the drink, and got to work.

NEW YORK IS COMMONLY REFERRED to as the city that never sleeps, and that night Josef found out why.

He got off the train around 5 pm, hoping to catch another glimpse of Kollmer at his store. He figured by the time it was getting darker, the street traffic would be clearing out. Josef was wrong.

The sidewalks were just as congested as earlier times of the day. Cars, trucks, and buses leaned on their horns and belched fumes into the air. People, many of whom still wore business attire, moved like the tide. They pushed and jostled each other, not a word of apology anywhere.

Josef was relieved to see his favorite hotdog vendor was still open when he reached the bench. He was also relieved to see Kollmer still in his store, helping a woman with an ugly-looking lamp.

Before walking over to the hotdog cart, he had to get a closer look at the man he was there for. The street traffic was busy, he didn't worry about being seen. The last time Kollmer had seen him he'd been seven years younger and sixty pounds lighter. Josef's hair was much longer than the Auschwitz haircut he had. Plus it was mostly grey and thinning now. He carried the weight well, but the American diet was trying his waistline. His belly was just a little round, but at just over fifty, this didn't bother him too much.

When he passed the store, he took a moment to linger. Nothing out of the ordinary, just a potential customer browsing. He was careful to keep his eyes low and wished he had a hat. Kollmer never looked his way, probably used to the passersby.

Josef watched him mingle with customers, smiling, laughing. How many people would never smile or laugh again thanks to that man? How many families were ripped apart by his hands? Tonight they would get their vengeance.

"What can I get you?" someone said.

Josef snapped out of his trance, his mind coming back to the present.

"Oh, sorry," he said to Aaron, the hotdog vendor. The trays of hotdogs leaked steam from the edges. "I'll take two with mustard and onions."

With deft hands that served thousands of hotdogs, Aaron handed him his order.

Josef sat on the bench, eating and watching.

The minutes and hours ticked by, but surprisingly the street traffic stayed consistent. A steady flow meant more people walking into Kollmer's store.

Josef didn't know if the store had set hours or if Kollmer just closed when he felt like it. He hoped it closed sooner than later. Once the sun had gone down the temperature dropped significantly. He wasn't shivering, but was getting uncomfortable.

It was nearing 8 pm when he finally got his break.

Kollmer walked over and flipped the sign from 'Open' to 'Closed.' He then went back behind the counter and grabbed a few things, put his jacket on, and headed towards the door.

Josef's heart began racing. Suddenly, he was no longer cold. In fact, he'd broken out in a sweat. He touched the hammer in his coat pocket as if it were a talisman to keep him safe.

Kollmer walked out of the store. Schatzi followed right behind him. He locked the door, giving it a confirmatory tug. The Nazi and his dog rounded the corner and walked up the stairs to the apartment.

Once inside, Kollmer moved over to the windows, shutting the blinds.

Josef wanted to race up the stairs, kick in the door and start swinging, but he knew he had to wait. He needed to calm his rapid heartbeat and get his breathing under control. He had a plan, albeit not a great one, and he was going to stick to it. Josef checked his watch and waited.

A half-hour later, in the dark of the night, he stood and walked across the street. He felt like everyone was watching him, knowing what he was about to do. He kept his head low to conceal his face and protect his ears from the cold breeze.

Silently, he walked up the steps. His heart was racing again, but he felt calm. It was as if he were taking an important test, but he had all the answers.

Josef knocked.

At first, there was nothing, no reply from the other side.

*Maybe he's in the shower or on the toilet,* he thought. His resolve was fading; fear and doubt were insidious, crawling through his mind. As if on auto-pilot, he knocked again. Harder this time.

"Yes?" asked a voice Josef had heard so many times before. "Who's there?"

Josef could hear Kollmer's footsteps and the sound of Schatzi's nails coming towards the door. He cleared his throat.

"Delivery, sir. For *EK and son*." He hoped he didn't waver when he spoke. The footsteps were closer now.

"What? I didn't have a delivery," Kollmer said, sounding aggravated at being disturbed.

Josef's heart slammed into his chest like it was trying to escape. The locks rattled. He clenched the hammer in his pocket, praying it wouldn't get snagged when he pulled it out.

The door opened and time seemed to stand still.

For a moment, Josef thought he was wrong. This man wasn't Kollmer, but some poor guy who vaguely looked like him. He wanted to be wrong, yet wanted to be right. He'd never truly hurt anyone in his life and if it was Kollmer, that would be changing in the next few heartbeats.

The two men stared at each other, which seemed like an eternity. Josef watched the series of emotions change on the older man's face. First, he was annoyed at being disturbed. Second, the look of confusion at seeing a delivery man not in uniform and with no package. The final few were a blend of each other. His confusion shifted from the lack of packages to vague recognition. Fear and hatred rounded out the wheel of emotions when he realized the man in front of him was a former death camp prisoner...who was holding a hammer.

Josef swung the hammer, but took a little off the swing at the very end.

Kollmer put his hands up, but just a fraction late. The dimpled head of the tool smacked him in the forehead with a resounding crack. His skin split as he stumbled backward into the apartment. He stepped on his dog, who let out a squeal and ran away. Kollmer lost his balance and fell. He tried to get up, but was dazed. Blood ran down his face, pooling in the corners of his eyes.

Josef stood over him, his breath coming in ragged gulps. The hammer was clenched tight in his sweaty hand. It felt good to hit him. Actually, it felt great. The look of fear when the hammer was in descent was one of the best moments in Josef's life. He'd seen that look countless times on the faces of innocent people murdered by the man on the floor.

Kollmer was starting to try and stand.

"Don't you fucking dare," said Josef, holding the hammer in front of him as if it were a gun. He fished around his pocket, feeling cold steel. "Put these on." He took a pair of semi-rusted handcuffs he bought from a pawn shop and threw them to Kollmer.

The cuffs smacked him in the chest, but he made no move to put them on. Kollmer, still hurt, but regaining his senses, stared.

"I should've fucking killed you when I had the chance," he sneered, blood running freely down his face. "I should've let the other rat Jews tear you apart like they wanted."

Josef wasn't hearing what was said, rather just watching him. He wished the other prisoners, especially Ola, could see him now. A Nazi, lieutenant, battered and bloody at his feet.

"Put them on now, or I start swinging again." He shook the hammer to make sure the man knew he was serious. Josef's nerves had calmed. Something he didn't think would be possible in this situation. Walking up the stairs, he thought he would either piss himself or puke, but he was able to control it. Now, he felt fine, besides the red-hot rage building in him. Could he murder this man in cold blood? Could he beat him to a bloody pulp with a hammer while the man begged and screamed for his life? He didn't know yet, but that was a decision for later. Right now, he needed the man secured before he got any ideas.

Kollmer, who was sitting up now, stared at Josef. He didn't think Josef was a killer, but he already hit him once and Kollmer didn't want to get hit again. The handcuffs were rusty, but recently oiled. They closed around his wrists, but he left them loose enough to get out of.

"There," he said, holding his hands up.

Josef wasn't stupid and could see the obvious gaps in the cuffs. He reached forward, closing them tightly. The metal bit down onto Kollmer's wrists.

"Ah, what the fuck?"

"There, now they're tight."

Kollmer's hands were already turning red from the slow circulation. He flexed his fingers a few times.

"Get up," Josef motioned with the hammer.

Kollmer was still in good shape even though he was older. He wiggled around a little, but was able to get off the floor.

"Ok, what now?"

That was an excellent question. Josef didn't know. He had a grand plan to walk in and subdue the man. After that, it was up in the air. Part of him wanted to beat him or stab him to death and leave his rotting corpse in the living room. Another part wanted to march him to the police station and turn him in for the war criminal he was. Right now, he just wanted to sit down.

"Walk," he ordered, gesturing towards the kitchen.

Kollmer listened, reaching up with his hands to wipe the blood from his face.

"What is it that you want?" He looked over his shoulder. "Money, art, gold? Whatever it is I can give you. What about some books? You loved to read. I've acquired some rare pieces in my line of work. You can have whatever you'd like." He pulled a chair out and sat. His head was throbbing from the hammer blow. He'd give Josef whatever he wanted to get him out of his life. His art could be replaced, but he wasn't ready to die.

Josef sat across from him, the hammer resting on the table next to an ashtray and pack of cigarettes.

"How about you hand me one of them?" asked Kollmer, pointing at the smokes.

Josef stared at him, almost not wanting to give him anything. Finally, he slid the pack and matches towards him.

"Ah, *danke*," Kollmer said, pulling a cigarette from the pack. He lit it, breathing deep and blowing out. He looked like a chimney. "So," he said, smoke coming from his mouth, "what are we doing here?"

Josef felt the tide turn. Suddenly, he was back in Kollmer's office. He was the authoritarian and Josef was the prisoner. There was an unspoken power struggle happening across that table and Josef wasn't going to lose. He took a deep breath, careful not to say anything he couldn't stick to. Death threats wouldn't work against a man like Kollmer. He'd see right through them.

"I'm not sure yet," he said. The truth felt good. His defense had no chinks in it. "When I decide, I'll let you know."

Kollmer was surprised at the answer. He expected threats and screaming, but the calm demeanor was a shock to him. His turn to battle back.

"You know," he said, putting his cigarette out in the ashtray, "I'm actually glad you're here. Except for this," he touched his head, which had stopped bleeding, but was a furious shade of purple. "I wanted to thank you for what you did for me."

It was Josef's turn to be surprised. He stared at the man, the mental battle in full fury.

"And what was that? Be your puppet, your Pet Jew." Josef hoped he sounded angry, but in fact, he was scared.

Kollmer smiled that evil smile. "You really had no idea what I was doing, did you? All of the questions and translations I had you figure out." He stared at Josef, who stared back.

"Sorry if my concerns weren't about you. I was more focused on not getting a bullet in the head, and when I would eat next. I just did what you told me and kept my mouth shut."

Silence. Kollmer grabbed another cigarette. The handcuffs made lighting the match difficult, but he was able to get it lit. He waved his hand, extinguishing the match before setting it in the tray. He smiled.

"I caught one," he said, a predatory glare on his face.

"Caught what?"

Kollmer took an intentionally long drag on his cigarette. The smoke came out of his nostrils.

"A demon."

Josef didn't know whether to laugh or cry. This man was clearly delusional. That was to be expected from a man who followed Adolf Hitler and killed hundreds, if not thousands of people. The look on his face must've given away his thoughts, because the look on Kollmer's face changed.

"You don't believe me, but you will." He crushed the cigarette out and leaned forward. "You worked mainly at the gas chambers, yes?"

Josef nodded. "You know I did. So, what are you getting at?"

"Did you ever work the crematoriums? Loading bodies into the furnace. Making them crispy." He smirked.

It was rare, but sometimes his work group was sent to the crematoriums to feed corpses into the ever-hungry flames.

"Was there anything you noticed about any of the corpses? Any kind of weird damage on them?"

Josef didn't know what he was getting at. Most of the corpses were fresh from the gas chambers, the smell of Zyklon still on them. Others were killed in various ways, but mainly gunfire. If they were gunned down by firing squad, their bodies could be pretty torn up. Josef, early in his stay, would look at the bodies, still hoping to find his family. After a while, he didn't and just threw them into the flames. There had been a few, he remembered, that didn't look right. As if a bullet-ridden corpse could ever look 'right.' The bullet holes were in a pattern and large chunks were missing...as if they were partially eaten.

"The bite marks," Kollmer said. "You did see them, but your starved and fearful brain never noticed them. Until now."

Josef was flashing back to the camp. They were few and far between, but some of the more mangled corpses appeared to be chewed on.

"Who or what do you think made those marks? It surely wasn't any of us. Sure, some feral Jews might resort to cannibalism, but those bite marks weren't human and you know that. What about the shadows?" Kollmer was in his glory. He had Josef and knew it. "I know you were never out at night, but if you were, you would've seen them. Just outside of the lights were where they'd lurk. Most of my fellow Nazis didn't know what they saw and usually chalked it up to a trick of the light, but not me. No, I knew it when I saw them. It was in the book."

Josef felt like he was in a dream. He stared at Kollmer, each word feeling more and more surreal.

On autopilot, he asked, "What book?"

"This might take a while and I'm feeling parched. A glass of water, please."

Josef rose, keeping a side-eye on Kollmer.

"The cabinet on the left," he said.

Josef took two glasses and filled them with water. He set one down in front of Kollmer. Josef sat with his, sipping from it. It brought memories of his first meeting with the Nazi lieutenant.

"Ah," Kollmer said. "Now I can start." He set the glass down on the table and looked at Josef. "The ghettos were a pain in my ass. Clearing all of you rats from your nests was a full-time job. It became easier when we started killing whole families in the streets. Once you saw a child's head explode from a rifle round, it made surrender much more appealing. After my battlefield commission and before I was sent to the camps, I was on ghetto duty. Many people would hide their belongings, in the aim of one day returning. They seldom did, but that gave them the glimmer of hope.

It was a hot day when I found the book and stone. We routed a group of Jews out of a basement in an old building. They were shot in the street and left there to rot. That wasn't the best part. They were hiding some decent valuables. Art, furniture, jewelry. They were a band of thieves themselves. We were just taking it back. Everything was cleared out, but as luck would have it, I stumbled across the best treasure of all." He sipped from his glass. "A book and rock. The other men I was with saw no value in such mundane items, but like yourself, I'm somewhat of a scholar."

Josef almost laughed at this, but maintained his stoicism.

"The book was mostly in Polish, a language I'm more than familiar with. But, the second half was in Latin. I took it and the rock, which looked like obsidian but was flat black and not shiny, back to my room. I began reading, thinking it was garbage. It was more of a manual rather than a story or formal book. It talked of demons and how they lurk among people, hiding on earth. They were most prevalent in areas of great suffering as if pain and torment were a beacon for them. This led them closer to our realm, allowing them to transcend from Hell. There were crude pictures of them feasting on not only souls, but on flesh. Of course, I took this as absolute garbage, some gypsy ramblings of fearful zealots. Until I was transferred to Auschwitz." He lit another cigarette and stared off. Kollmer was silent for almost half a minute.

"They came as shadows," he whispered. "I thought I was seeing things, but I remembered the book. Fear, pain, death, were abundant in the camp. It must've been a bonfire for the denizens of Hell. The mass graves and piles of bodies were their feeding grounds. At night, when the camp was asleep, they would slip into our world. Shadows of liquid black would slink through the camp. They would crunch and slurp on corpses until they were sated, and slither back to the underworld. The other guards knew something prowled the camp at night, but no one would admit it. They didn't know what it was, but they all knew it was otherworldly. Some of them would fire shots into the corpse piles, giving themselves false bravado, but it wouldn't do a thing. The crunching would go on. I never got a good look at them, but I did see a corpse being carried away from the camp. Whatever was carrying it leaped the fence like it was not even there. What power did this beast have? I was in awe. I pulled the old book from my foot locker and began reading again, this time with a serious mind. There was a section on harnessing the power of a demon and how to trap one. I studied it and ensured there was plenty of torment and pain to keep them around. I requested the transfer of Dr. Mengele, who was making leaps and bounds in the advancement of medical practices." He grinned at Josef. He knew his sons ended up on Mengele's table, but he was saving that for later. "His methods were a little unorthodox, but created plenty of pain and suffering. For nights I studied, preparing my attempt to capture one of these beasts. Then, the night came. You were there."

Josef was watching him, hanging on his words. He didn't know what to believe. In his years of studying religion, he'd seen plenty of text concerning demons and angels. Every culture, regardless of religion, had them. They would be slightly different in some regions, but some things were always the same. Everyone couldn't be wrong, could they?

"The gravel pits," Josef muttered.

Kollmer nodded. "It was perfect. I could keep you loyal, show you my brutal side, eliminate dissidents and bring forth anguish. Why do you think I chose to kill them at night? Or why did I let the dogs kill some of them? The tables were set; that night was the best chance I had to get one and did I ever."

Kollmer finished his water and set the glass on the table. He studied Josef's face, looking to see if the man believed him. Honestly, he wouldn't believe himself if he didn't know what lurked below the building.

Josef needed a minute, but did not want to sit staring. He drank from his glass, taking each sip slowly. He was coming up with a response for the story when Kollmer spoke.

"I can show you if you'd like." He looked towards a door in the back of the kitchen. "That door is the back way to the store and will go into the basement." He stood. "Shall we?"

Josef rose, grabbing the hammer.

"Ah, no I don't think we'll need that," Kollmer looked at the hammer, which had a smear of brown blood on the face of it.

Josef pointed to the door with the tool. "Walk," he said, his voice sounding almost disembodied.

"You're the boss," Kollmer replied, venom in his words. He knew what they were walking into. Soon, he'd be free. He opened the door and flicked a light switch. The stairwell lit up. They walked down the stairs until they hit a large, metal door with an imposing industrial lock. Kollmer tried grabbing the keys out of his pocket, but the handcuffs were making it difficult. "Do you mind?" He asked.

Josef did mind, but he was curious and knew this had to be done.

"Put your hands on the wall above your head."

Kollmer stalled. "Is this necessary? I'm an old man, older than you, and I'm handcuffed."

Josef just stared, not saying a word.

"Fine." Kollmer put his hands up as Josef quickly fished a keyring from his pocket. He took it when offered and shuffled through the keys. He unlocked the door. It swung in silently, the hinges were well oiled.

He flipped a light switch and Josef stood shocked.

The first thing Josef noticed was the smell. It assaulted him almost before the lights were turned on. It was the smell of animals in an enclosed space. Urine and feces, mixed with wood shavings were almost nauseating. Josef's sense of smell had gotten weak since leaving the camp. The room was small, much smaller than Josef thought it would be. The wall to the right was filled with shelves holding cages of animals. Some were filled with cats, mice, birds, snakes and one even had an emaciated dog.

The wall on the left had a single shelf with a bottle of what looked like holy water, a few unburned candles, chalk, and paint.

Josef took this all in in a glance, but his eyes settled on the center of the room and the far wall.

In the center of the room was a pentagram painted in what looked like blood, but was probably paint. It was surrounded by a circle of faded chalk and stumps of candles. Phrases written in a cryptic language were all over the wall. In the center of the pentagram sat a stone.

It looked like obsidian, but it wasn't shiny, rather it was flat black. The edges looked sinister and even sharper than regular obsidian. One touch of the stone looked like it would flay your flesh.

In front of the pentagram sat the book. It rested on a plain, wooden pedestal and was closed.

The animals began shrieking seeing Kollmer walk towards the book.

"Now, when I trapped the demon, I thought I captured an under-demon. You know, one of the minions of the greater beasts." He flipped through the book under the watchful eyes of Josef. He turned and faced him. "I didn't. I caught something much greater than that. A being more powerful than I could've imagined." He laughed. "How else would I have escaped that war-torn continent. Or be able to open a successful business in a country where I barely spoke the language."

Josef watched him walk over to one of the cages with a bird. It beat its wings furiously, trying to escape, but it was no use. Kollmer grabbed the bird, feeling the sting of the little beak peck at him. He snapped its neck with an audible crack and instantly stopped its thrashing. He pulled the head from the bird, dripping blood on the stone. Kollmer dropped the corpse on the floor in the center of the pentagram.

"This demon thrives on greed, fulfilling your wildest dreams. Wealth, women, health. It all comes with a price and that price is blood." He grabbed a box of matches, lighting each of the candle stumps on the ground. He retraced some of the lines with chalk, checking each of them. When he was satisfied, he walked back, standing in front of the book.

Josef stood back and watched, the hammer hanging limp at his side.

The ritual took mere seconds, but to Josef, it seemed a lifetime.

Kollmer began chanting as he read from the book. There was no wind, yet the candle's flames flickered. The animals began to howl and scream, many of them voiding bladder and bowels.

A black slime oozed from the rock, spreading over the ground like an oil spill. It began to take shape, rising and changing colors. The black tar took the hue of blood the higher it rose. The shape was vaguely humanoid, but nowhere near what a human should look like. A new stench spread into the room; the smell of burnt hair, sulfur and shit.

Josef thought the odor of Zyklon-B was the worst thing he'd ever smelled; he was wrong.

The shape solidified and Josef nearly screamed.

In all the years of studying demons and seeing pictures of them, Josef had never been prepared for what stood in front of him. He knew Kollmer wasn't lying when he said he'd captured something strong, not just a minor beast.

The demon was short, much shorter than the average man. He had a pot belly, that oozed pus and was covered in boils and lesions. His skin was cracked and bleeding, looking like fissures of gore. He had a long face resembling a crescent moon and a pointed beard. His eyes were jet black, the same flatness as the stone it was trapped in. Horns sprouted from his head; their bases were raw and bloody. His hands were three-fingered and tipped with cracked claws and his feet were long and calloused. He was nude and his penis was grotesquely fat and covered in sores. Pus dripped from an open wound, hitting the ground with an acidic hiss. He squatted, as if ready to attack. And he did.

The demon launched itself forward, its body striking an invisible barrier on the outside of the pentagram. He recoiled off the barrier and smirked at Kollmer. A black snake crawled from his mouth, which was filled with rows of sharp teeth.

"Ah, I see your bonds are still good, filth," the demon grumbled. Its voice almost had a machine-like sound to it. "Have you brought me a snack?"

Josef walked trance-like, towards the demon. The hammer fell, clanging on the ground.

Kollmer slid behind him, his cuffed hands ready to strike.

"Yes, Belphegor, I have."

Josef snapped out of his trance at the name. He was looking at Belphegor, one of the seven Princes of Hell. A chief demon on the level of Beelzebub and Lucifer. This was madness and he was about to be fed to the beast. Josef felt Kollmer's hands on his back and he turned. Kollmer stumbled past him, trying to keep his balance as he approached the barrier of the demon's cell. The cuffs made it difficult, but he kept himself out of the demon's grasp.

Josef reacted with a level of fury and rage he didn't think possible. He punched Kollmer in the face. Teeth and bone cracked. Lips split, blood splattering. Off-balance, Kollmer was ever closer to the demon, who was running a forked tongue over his shark-like teeth. Josef kicked, aiming for Kollmer's stomach. His shoe sunk into soft flesh and Kollmer let out a rush of air. A look of panic set on the Nazi's face as he felt burning when he passed the barrier. He didn't even have time to scream.

Belphegor set on him like a ravenous beast. His claws sank into the side of Kollmer's arm, ripping flesh from bone in a rent of blood and meat. He pulled the doomed man close, like a lover. Instead of sensual kisses, the demon bit half of Kollmer's lower jaw off.

Kollmer's tongue wagged, a macabre grin staring at Josef, who watched in revulsion and a hint of delight.

Belphegor crunched on the bone and teeth, his maw making quick work of it. With supernatural strength, he pulled Kollmer's arm off. The severed limb tore, shreds of flesh dangled. White bone, fresh and clean, stuck out from the mangled stump.

Kollmer, in his last few moments of life, hit the ground, free from the demon. He dragged himself, the stump of his arm pumping his life blood onto the floor, towards the edge of the barrier.

Belphegor watched in glee. He knew the man would never make it, but he liked when they thought they had a chance. The theft of their salvation was a delectable taste. He grabbed Kollmer by the ankle and pulled him back.

Kollmer tried to scream, but without a lower jaw, it was impossible. Rather he gargled blood from his ruined face. Thick blood frothed from his throat.

Belphegor bit Kollmer in the thigh, severing his femoral artery. A fan of blood washed over the demon, making his pus-covered flesh glisten. He grabbed Kollmer by the head, bringing him nose to nose.

A final look of complete fear and despair was plastered on Kollmer's ruined face.

Belphegor smiled, smelled the fear and pain coming from this morsel of man flesh. He bit, his jaw extending inhumanly wide. With one chomp, he took the rest of Kollmer's face off, leaving half of his brain exposed.

Kollmer was finally dead, but his torment was far from over. The demon knew the soul was his to play with. He threw the corpse on the ground and began to feed in earnest.

Josef watched the demon tear open Kollmer's gut. His evil mouth dripped with bodily fluids. Loops of intestines were gobbled down like spaghetti. Stomach matter, bile, and shit oozed from the hellish maw of the demon. Within moments, Kollmer was nothing more than bloody pulp and scraps of cloth.

"Mmm, that was a meal long overdue," the demon said. His potbelly had a piece of liver stuck to it. His once flaccid penis was fully erect and covered in blood.

Josef couldn't take his eyes off him. The gore-soaked monster licked its claws, the forked tongue getting every bit it could.

Belphegor smiled at him. It was one of the worst things Josef had ever seen in his life. Rows of shark-like teeth covered in blood, with bits of flesh stuck in the many crevasses.

"He was right, you know. I can give you whatever you want. If you just erase the wards and free me, I can grant you anything." That predatory smile again. He flexed his claws, the drying blood starting to crack. His penis was softening, which was a relief for Josef for some reason.

"Ah." Josef's throat felt like sand. There was no moisture and he tasted the sourness of bile in the back of his mouth. He watched a bloated maggot crawl out of Belphegor's nose. His tongue flicked up and grabbed it. The bug popped in between his teeth, oozing down his chin.

"Just erase a line and you can have whatever you'd like. What do you want? Money, women, men, power? Fuck, I can give it all to you." He stared at Josef, their eyes locking. Belphegor smiled. "Oh, I know what you want." His voice changed. He was no longer speaking as a demon, but as Ola. "Josef," he said in Ola's voice. "Please, do what he says," she begged. "They are torturing me, Josef. They rape me constantly, putting things in every hole. Disgusting, foul beasts, they use me in the vilest of ways, Josef. Please, do what he says and save me. Josef, my love, it hurts so bad." He paused, letting the conversation seep into Josef's brain. "Josef!" Ola wailed. "They're coming back! No, no, God no!" The screams nearly ripped out his eardrums.

Josef cried and took a step towards the ward.

"Leave her alone, you motherfuckers!" he screamed. "Leave her the fuck alone!"

Belphegor smiled.

"Ok, ok," the demon said, the tortured voice of Ola was no more. "That was low, even for me. What about this?" He looked at Josef and spoke. "Daddy." It was Piotr. "Daddy, are you there?" Michal and Piotr's voices interchanged. "Daddy, there are monsters here. They hurt us, Daddy. Why did you let this happen?" One of them cried. "Why are we here? They bite us. Their teeth, their teeth are sharp, Daddy. Oh God, it hurts!" Josef cried freely, stepping closer to the ward. Belphegor tensed, ready to grab him when he entered the circle of protection. "Daddy! They're coming back."

"Run!" he yelled to the voices of his dead sons. "Run and hide, boys."

"Daddy, we're lost. It's dark and there are dead people everywhere. We lost Mommy. We're sorry, Daddy."

Snot ran down Josef's face. He stepped closer, his toes nearly at the edge of the ward.

"God, fucking dammit!" he screamed. Somehow, he regained his wits, knowing it wasn't his family coming from the mouth of the demon. His family was in the kingdom of Heaven, not the bowels of Hell. He stepped back from the line and walked to the book.

Belphegor upped the screaming, trying to entice him to come closer, but Josef was able to fight it.

Josef flipped through the book as the demon paced in his invisible cell. He didn't look up at the monster, who was yelling every obscenity he could. Finally, he found a way to banish the demon.

Josef grabbed the jar of holy water and opened it. He dipped the silver wand into the holy fluid, watching the excess drip from it.

Belphegor smiled, knowing he was about to be dismissed into the stone, but also knowing the holy water couldn't kill him.

"See you soon, Josef Lazerowitz."

Josef splashed the water on the demon. It hissed when it hit his flesh, which blackened. The darkness spread as he began to fold up onto himself. He became a puddle of tar, finally getting sucked back into the stone.

The animals were silent and Josef noticed one of the cats and three mice had died.

There was nothing left of the mess that was once Lieutenant Erich Kollmer. Not even a drop of blood.

The room spun, but Josef didn't faint. He leaned on the wall, which was cool to the touch. The smell of sulfur still lingered, but was fading. The spinning stopped and he was starting to feel better. Without warning, he puked on his shoes, vomit splashing onto his pants. He continued to dry heave, tears blurring his vision. Finally, when there was nothing left and the dry heaves stopped, he walked out of the room.

The keys still dangled from the lock. He pushed it shut, gave a tug, and put the keys in his pocket. He started up the stairs. Josef wasn't sure what he was going to do with his new "friend", but whatever he decided, he knew life just got more interesting.

# IV

## WILL YOU EAT?

## 16

Robert stared at his elderly friend, his mouth slightly agape. What he'd just heard throughout what felt like an eternity, was the most insane story ever. He reached over, grabbing the half-empty bottle of bourbon, and poured himself another shot. He'd had two during the course of the story, but now he felt as if he needed more. It was fiery, but good.

Josef stared at pictures of his family. God, did he miss them. Finally, he looked up at Robert.

"It's true, all of it. I swear on the souls of my children and wife." He poured himself another shot. His doctor would certainly not approve. Without a grimace, he tossed it back.

Robert was swaying slightly. He didn't drink often and the three shots of alcohol were hitting him. Plus, he'd only eaten half a slice of pizza. Josef's story wasn't the most appetite-inducing tale.

"How?" That was all he said, his fingers absently touching some of the pictures. He broke his gaze and looked up at Josef.

"I know, it all sounds crazy, and by God it is, but it doesn't make it any less true." His eyes were watery, mostly from unearthing old memories, but partially from the bourbon.

"So," Robert pointed to the father in the picture, "this is you?"

Josef nodded. "Yes, I was forty-one when that was taken. It was nearly one year before we were sent to the camp."

Robert wasn't the best with math, but even he could do simple equations.

"You're telling me you're 118 years old." It almost came out as a question, but formed as a statement.

Josef, who barely looked a day over eighty, nodded. Granted, cancer had aged him rapidly, but the sacrifice of Molly, the old lab, helped maintain his looks.

"That would make you one of the oldest people in the world. They would've done articles on you and news reports."

"Yes, of course they would've if they knew my real age. You see, in the fifties we didn't have the technology of today. The country was overrun with war refugees like me and paperwork was often mishandled. My original documents were lost in Poland and I had nothing to go off for proof." He waved a dismissive hand. "It didn't matter. The clerk at one of the many offices I went to messed up my date of birth anyway. Instead of 1901, they typed 1920. So yes, I'm old, bordering a hundred according to my records, but far older than that."

Robert looked at him, stunned. Nothing was making sense.

"But how?" He asked, fearing the answer.

Josef leaned in, putting his old, gnarled hand on Robert's shoulder.

"You have to believe me, Robert. This, " he paused, looking for the word, "*beast* can help you, but don't listen to his lies. If you believe his lies, he will take your soul." He was starting to cry silent tears.

Robert didn't believe him. Did he? Part of him thought it was the ramblings of an old man who was lonely and dying. Another part of him believed. He believed because it was so outlandish it had to be true.

"He did this to me," Josef said, backing away from Robert. "He gave me life, but there were sacrifices. Horrible sacrifices." He looked off, as if something were in the corner. "Each one was necessary. I couldn't let myself die and leave that thing to no one. No, it needed a master, or preferably, someone to kill it."

They sat in silence for a moment. Josef tried to read Robert's expression, but didn't know what was written on the young man's face.

"Mr. Lazer, I—" He stood.

Josef grabbed his hand. His old grip was iron-like.

"No, please. I need you to see it first. I will show you and if you don't believe me, you can go. Never speak with me again. Hell, you could put a bullet in my head. God knows I deserve it after all these years."

Robert had his hands on the back of the chair. Josef's trembled on his. Robert sighed.

"Ok, show me. But quickly. I really need to get home and check on my mother."

Josef flashed a quivering smile and patted Robert's hand.

"Thank you, Robert." He nodded his head, walking towards the basement door. "Follow me." Josef felt like he was having an out-of-body experience. For over sixty-five years, he'd kept Belphegor locked in the stone. He knew the day would come when he'd have to pass his curse on to another. He was relieved, yet saddened it had to fall to Robert. Josef could only hope the young man would be able to control his emotions and use the demon to his benefit. Hopefully, he could deal with the burden of the sacrifices.

Josef opened the basement door, flicking on the light.

Robert stood at the top of the stairs, but couldn't see much beyond the bottom. Except for one thing: a rubber dog toy in the shape of a duck lay at the foot of the steps.

"Did you get a dog?" Robert asked.

Josef looked at the dog toy, remembering Molly, his last sacrifice.

"Come on," Josef said, ignoring the question. He started down the stairs. Robert followed.

The basement was like any other: water heater, boiler, assorted boxes stacked high, and an old rocking chair. It did have one quality Robert had never seen before. Towards the far wall, there was a drawing of a pentagram on the floor. The star was surrounded by a circle and nubs of black candles. A shelf containing chalk, paint, water, and fresh candles sat off to the side. On the back wall, cryptic words were scrawled in rough handwriting. The writing was cramped, but each character was clear, even though Robert had no idea what it meant. A book sat closed on a small stand. It was bound in black and looked old, but Robert couldn't see any writing on it. He saw the final thing in the room: a piece of black stone in the center of the pentagram.

"What the fuck?" Robert whispered to himself, looking around the room. He figured he was going to walk down and see an old plastic statue of Satan and let Mr. Lazer talk to it and leave. He only came down to entertain the old man, who he considered a friend. This setup was a little more extravagant than that.

Josef looked a little ashamed and yet proud at the same time. He hadn't shown this to anyone—well, anyone still alive. This was his burden, his secret and his to leave to who he chose.

"I felt the same way you did the first time I saw Kollmer's basement." Josef seemed to have a second wind. He was walking around, touching the stuff on the shelves. "Although I don't keep animals down here as he did in his basement." He smiled at Robert, whose mouth was still agape.

"This is ridiculous," Robert said, looking at the pentagram. He didn't walk into the center of it though. He didn't believe Mr. Lazer, but wasn't taking any chances. He had grown up Catholic after all.

Josef didn't immediately respond, rather let the young man take it all in. Giving him time to process what he was seeing.

"I know this is overwhelming, but I swear on the lives and souls of my family, it's true. Every word of it."

Robert looked at a jar of holy water. A metal wand sat next to it. He'd seen them in church plenty of times, but could never remember what they were called. The priest would use it to splash holy water on the parishioners. He thought about the conversation they'd just had upstairs, and tried to remember little parts. Something brutal clicked.

"You would perform sacrifices down here?" His voice cracked, something that hadn't happened since puberty.

Josef turned away from him, took a deep breath, and turned back.

"Yes, in the long and short of it, yes. Animals for the smaller things, but if it was something larger…" He let the rest die on his lips. Josef didn't want to think of the screams.

Robert started backing towards the door.

"It's not what you think," Josef said, stopping Robert from leaving. "I had to and you will too. You need this as much as I do, that's why it's being left to you."

Robert began to speak, but Josef held up a hand, silencing him.

"Before you condemn me, listen." Josef was starting to feel weak again and sat in the rocking chair. "If you had the opportunity to save your mother, would you?"

Robert paused. His mind skipping back to his mother, who was at home dying of cancer. His eyes welled up with tears. He used the back of his hand to wipe his face.

"I would do anything for her," he said, taking a deep breath, hoping to stem the flow of tears.

"I'm giving you that freedom. I'm giving you something to keep her alive, to save her. It's the vilest thing I've ever seen, but it can help you."

*Would I kill an innocent person or animal just to save mom?* he thought. Deep down, he knew he would. It might be difficult to do, but knowing he'd keep her alive was the biggest thing to him.

Robert's mind was made up the minute he was told he could save his mother. Whatever trick Mr. Lazer had, he was willing to try. He moved back towards the old man in the rocking chair.

"Show me," he said.

Josef's face was scared and relieved at the same time. He hated summoning the demon, especially since the last time was so recent. On the other hand, he was relieved Robert believed him. He stood up, the chair rocking at the release of his weight. Josef felt like he'd aged ten years since sitting down. His bowels cramped with fire, but he kept going.

"Don't listen to his lies," Josef said, standing in front of the book. He turned to a well-used page. "He will say the most horrific things to you, but never trust him. And above all, never enter the circle." He pointed to the solid chalk circle around the pentagram. "When you are done, splash him with holy water to dismiss him back to the stone."

Robert nodded as if this were a normal conversation. This old man was giving him advice on dealing with a demon in a way he'd give directions to the store.

"Will the holy water kill it?"

Josef looked up at him. "No, I've only found one possible way to kill a demon, but I'm not even sure if it's true."

Robert looked at him, signaling him to go on. If he was going to have something as vile as a demon under his control, he wanted to know how to kill it.

"The legends and books I've read say the only way to truly kill a being of Hell is with a Seraph Blade. During the battle of Heaven and Hell, the angels discovered something very powerful about their holy blood. When it was used to craft a weapon, that weapon could kill a demon, not just banish it. This changed the tide of the war, forcing the denizens of Hell into the abyss where they belong. That is here nor there, since I've never heard of one being found. More than likely they are myths, but until five minutes ago, you didn't think I had a demon in my basement." Josef rubbed his hands on the page in the book. "Ready?"

Robert nodded, whether he was ready or not. His pulse raced and his armpits were damp with a cold and fearful sweat. It was the same perspiration he'd get when he was in trouble or had to see the principal as a kid.

Josef lit the candles around the circle and walked back to the book. He began reading.

Robert stared in awe as black slime oozed from the solid stone. The goo poured out, taking shape as it rose. It changed color, shifting to blood-red as it took a humanoid form. Within seconds, Belphegor stood before them. His stench of shit and sulfur polluted the room.

"Why have you summoned me?" the demon growled.

Robert hadn't pissed his pants since he was a young boy, but at that second, he thought he was going to.

Before him stood a creature of nightmares, a demon. The

disgusting beast was short, fat, and slick with pus. His wooden-like horns curl back almost like a ram but were jagged and rough. Their bases were raw and weeping blood. He flexed his three-clawed hands, the knuckles cracking. His black eyes bored holes into the two men in front of him.

"Oh, I see now," the demon said, his many rows of crooked, yet razor-sharp teeth on display. "Another plaything." Without warning, he rushed the wards. In a flash of light, his body bounced off the protective circle. "Ah, still drawing well I see."

Josef, for as scared as he was, smiled at the beast.

"Yes, my drawing skills are just as good as always." He looked back at Robert, the smile sliding from his face. "This is not a sacrifice though."

Robert stared at him, wondering how many people met their fate down here, sacrificed to a demon.

"Besides, I doubt you can help me any longer. Not that I want it. Nor do I deserve it."

Belphegor dug something wriggling from his nose and ate it. It crunched like popcorn and brought a revolting smile to his face.

"So why have you brought me out of my sleep if not to feed me? The dog was delicious and I hope you're feeling well from her pain, but you know I love man-flesh the best."

Josef knew, oh he knew.

"I've brought you here to let you know he," Josef pointed back at Robert, who was watching the exchange, "is your new master."

The demon screamed, "I have no master and if I did, it wouldn't be a flesh bag! Your kind is fucking meat, nothing more. You are a pet who happened to get lucky." His eyes began to smoke, the smell of hellfire burned the men's nostrils.

Robert was almost in a trance, his mind not quite comprehending the entire situation. Before him stood a demon, something he didn't fully think was even real. Not only was it standing before him, even more grotesque than imaginable, but he was just told he'd be its master.

Josef looked away from the angry hell-spawn and back at Robert.

"I'm sorry to leave this to you, but you must realize it's the only option. I cannot risk him getting loose on the world." He was starting to cry, his already watery eyes leaking tears.

Robert was crying too, but he didn't quite know why. He nodded, as if on auto-pilot.

Josef squeezed his shoulders. "Thank you," he mumbled. "Don't forget about the holy water." It was the last intelligible word he said.

Without warning, Josef turned and ran at the demon. The lights dimmed as he passed the invisible barrier and into the realm of the beast.

Belphegor wasted no time at all and fell on the old man like a lion on a sick gazelle. His powerful, clawed hands pulled Josef to the ground with such force, his left leg snapped backward. The old man would've screamed, but his throat was already ripped out by multiple serrated teeth. A gout of blood hit the barrier, running down it as if it were glass.

Robert wanted to scream, his throat burned for it, but he couldn't. His bladder finally let go and hot urine ran down his leg. He didn't care. His eyes were locked on the scene in front of him.

When Josef told him about the demon eating Kollmer, he wasn't yet convinced it was even real. It had sounded so far-fetched, like a bad horror movie. What was happening in front of him was certainly real.

The demon's hands ripped chunks of meat and organs from Josef's corpse and greedily stuffed them into his blood-stained mouth. He was slick with blood and the pustules on his body began to weep, mixing the fluids together. Bugs, some of which were not of this world, crawled from the open sores. They'd move over the repulsive flesh on innumerable legs, or segmented bodies, only to find another oozing hole to disappear into. Throughout the grisly meal, Belphegor would look at Robert and smile. His grin extended to unnatural heights as if his face was going to split. He stopped eating, all of the best pieces having been consumed, and walked to the edge of the ward. Ichor, which was red, black, and even a tinge of green, dripped from his wicked claws. Steady drops hit the floor, leaving a tiny trail as he walked.

"Come closer, boy. I can't see you well," the demon demanded.

Robert took a step forward, as if in a trance. Silent tears ran down his face. His shoes squished, as they were now full of urine. Robert's pants clung to him also, chilling him as his piss cooled. If his genitals weren't already shrunken from fear, they certainly would've been from the coolness of his waste. He stopped, the realization of what he was doing hit him.

Belphegor smiled again. "Do it for Mommy," he said, using his mother's voice.

The urge to go forward was there, but Robert resisted, backing up.

"Fuck you." Robert's voice sounded like it was a million miles away.

Belphegor laughed, pieces of Josef's flesh caught in his teeth.

"Now, that is fucking rude," he said. "And, my oh my, did you piss yourself?" The demon put his clawed hands to his face, feigning shock.

Robert absently touched the cooling urine on the front of his pants. That was the least of his worries. He grabbed the bottle of holy water and dipped the metal wand into it.

"I can save her, you know," Belphegor said. "I know she's dying." He looked at his arm as if he were wearing a watch. "Any day now." That wicked smile was back. "I can't wait. She'll be such a good plaything." He reached down and grabbed his oozing penis. "Maybe I'll start her with this." He waggled it towards Robert, drips of pus and thin worms falling from the sores. "I know my brothers will have fun too."

"Fuck you." Robert wanted to argue, to tell him his mother was a good person deserving of Heaven.

"Awe, you probably think Mommy is a saint, but let me tell you, she's not. When she dies, and that'll be soon, she'll be in the beautiful, wretched, grotesque kingdom of Hell."

Holy water dripped from the wand as Robert prepared to dismiss the demon.

"I can save her, though. She can be as old as my last meal. You too, as long as you bring me food." His forked tongue flicked out like a snake. The way it moved was repulsive. "Think about it, but don't take too long, Bobby boy."

Robert struck, flinging the holy water on the demon.

Belphegor smiled as he turned into black and red slime and slithered back into the rock.

## 17

Robert pulled into his driveway. He killed the engine and just sat there. Esther's car was gone and the only light on inside the house was a dim lamp coming from his mother's room.

The car cooled, ticking away its last bit of life. Was his mother's life ticking away too? That was a stupid question. Of course, it was. Hell, she might be dead inside the house.

One thing was certain, Josef was dead. That was without question. Robert had mixed emotions about the last few hours. He felt terrible for the things Mr. Lazer had to deal with in his life, yet he was angry for leaving him such a burden. It was the last thing Robert needed at this point. Part of him also wondered about the gifts of the demon. Could it be used for good if he was careful? Could that foul beast heal his mother, extending her life beyond the natural timeline? He had no idea, but he did know a few things. One thing was certain, he needed a shower and fresh clothes. Also, he needed to sleep.

Robert opened the car door, the overhead lights and chime letting him know the keys were still in the ignition. He took them out, shutting the door gently.

The house was quiet and dark, but he didn't need lights to find his way around. He stripped down, peeling his sticky pants off, and put them in the washing machine. He left his underwear on just in case his mother decided to get up, which was doubtful. The last thing he needed was for his mother to see him naked.

He showered fast and threw on shorts and t-shirt. With the hall lights off, he peeked in on her.

She was asleep, the shallow rise and fall of her chest gave him some relief. How many times would her chest rise and fall? At birth, we have a finite number of breaths and heartbeats. What number was Helen Sinclair on?

Robert shut the door and walked into his room. He fell onto his bed and stared at the ceiling. His phone, which he'd neglected over the last few hours, vibrated on his nightstand. Sarah Denbrough, his co-worker, friend, and at one time could've been girlfriend, had texted him. It was nothing of importance, just checking in.

He often wished things could've been different for them. Seeing the pain his mother felt and knowing no one knows when their end will come, made him think about the kiss he and Sarah shared. Maybe they could give it a shot.

It was late and he didn't want to text her back. Besides, he was drained, physically and mentally, and didn't want to get into a long text conversation. He clicked off his light and rolled over. His mind raced, seeing the brutal death of Mr. Lazer, but sleep was coming, even if it was going to be filled with nightmares.

As he drifted off, Robert smelled sulfur.

---

A GOLDEN RAY of spring sunshine burned into Robert's eyelid.

His eye fluttered, confused by the sun. He was usually up in the dark, helping his mother with something or another. He was working the closing shift at L-Mart and wouldn't have to go in until later that evening.

A sound brought him fully out of his slumber; pots and pans banging around. He sat up like a shot and threw the blankets off him. He ran out of his room and saw his mother's door was open. He looked in and saw an empty bed that had been expertly made. Taking the steps two at a time, he flew down the stairs and into the kitchen.

Helen stood at the stove, with a frying pan in her hand. She was shaking it back and forth, sliding around an omelet.

Robert watched in awe and happiness, which faded when he thought about what the doctor told them. A dying wind, he called it. Some terminally ill people will get a second wind just before death, as if their body is expending all energy before their end, leaving nothing behind. He started crying.

"Mom?" his voice cracked.

Helen turned. Her face was not the face of a healed woman. It was sunken and skeletal, looking like she'd aged twenty-five years overnight. She wore a robe, which concealed most of her cancer-ravaged body, except her shoulders. They pressed against the fabric like two jagged points.

"Oh, good you're up." She slid the omelet onto a waiting plate. "Go on, sit down." She put the plate where he usually sat. She pulled a fork from the drawer and set it down. "Coffee?" she asked, already pouring him a cup.

He stood there dumbfounded and half asleep. Steam rose from his plate and cup, beckoning him to sit.

She mixed a small pot on the stove. It looked like she was just finishing up a pot of grits.

"Will you eat?" she asked, spooning the thick cereal into a bowl. She put a healthy slab of butter and salt into the mush.

Robert pulled his chair out, wiping the tears from his eyes.

She sat next to him, putting her hand on his. It was cold and felt like a bundle of flesh-wrapped twigs. She smiled, no life left in her fading eyes.

"Eat up, we have a lot to do today," she said as if they were getting ready to run errands like when he was a boy. She blew on a spoonful of her food and put it to her tongue, testing the temperature. Gingerly, she ate.

"Mom, are you ok?"

She sipped her coffee, which was more milk and sugar than actual coffee.

"No, but I'm ready," she said, mixing her food. "After Cardinal Carafa gave me my Last Rites, I've been ready to go. I've been blessed with this final burst of energy, which will allow me to plan my eternal rest."

Robert thought back to what Belphegor had said about her going to Hell. He said she'd done things, horrible things, that would land her soul in the lake of fire.

"I need you to call Mr. Gray at the funeral home. Tell him I don't want my wake to be in the back room, I want the front room. I always liked that spot. It lets a lot of God's light in." She took another small bite. "It shouldn't be long now, maybe tonight. Just let him know that."

Robert was sobbing, head in hands. He couldn't listen to her so easily talk about her imminent death. It was too much for him.

"Mom," he said, wiping his nose with his napkin, "you're talking like you're already dead."

"Honey, I was dead the day I was diagnosed. It's ok, I'll be in the Kingdom of Heaven. I'm thankful for the life I've had. Even with the ups and downs. I'm thankful God has let me live this long and to have you as my son." She smiled with tears in her eyes.

They hugged each other. Robert's shoulders heaving as he cried. He tried not to hold her too tight, for fear of cracking a bone.

She broke the embrace, wiping her face with the heel of her hand.

"Now come on, and finish up eating. We have a lot to do today before you go to work."

Robert did as she asked, making some of the hardest calls he's ever made. He arranged his mother's funeral while she sat in her favorite chair.

She did her part too. She called Cardinal Carafa, who was delighted to hear from her. She told him it was almost time and he promised to be there to officiate her mass.

Robert moved like a ghost, careful not to disturb his mother as she napped in the chair. He cleaned up the house and made himself a sandwich. It was almost time to go to work. Esther would be showing up soon.

"Mom," he whispered, as not to surprise her.

Helen moved a little, her eyelids cracking open.

"I have to get ready for work, but there's a can of soup heating on the stove. Please eat something." After she'd taken the time to make herself a nice bowl of grits, she'd barely touched it. Her dying wind petered out faster than expected and left her drained.

"Mmmhmm," she moaned, eyes closing again.

Robert stood under the hot water in the shower. He wanted to cry, but he was cried out. When he got out of the shower, he could hear Esther downstairs. Her voice was bassy and carried. Robert couldn't hear words, but knew she was talking.

He dressed and headed downstairs.

"Robert," Esther said, giving him an angry look. "Why is your mother out of bed?" She put her purse on the table, next to the pile of old bills. She draped her coat over the chair and walked towards Helen, who was sound asleep in the chair. She pulled a thin blanket from the couch and covered the sick woman.

"Can I talk to you?" Robert asked as he walked into the kitchen. He turned off the stove, which had a boiling pot of uneaten soup on it.

Esther followed.

He told her about the earlier part of the day. His mother's second wind, arranging the funeral home and mass, and calling a few of her distant friends.

Esther didn't speak, only nodded. She hadn't seen it a lot, but it wasn't unheard of. One of her first patients had the second wind, an 82-year-old man named Reynold Parton. He was dying of colon cancer and one day felt great. So great in fact, he decided to go chop wood. Well, he missed a log, burying the ax into his ankle. The wound had been too much for his already frail body and he died on the way to the hospital.

"I'll watch over her," she said.

"I know." He looked at his phone, checking the time. "I have to run, but please call me if there are any issues." *Like if she dies,* he thought.

"Don't you worry. Let me take care of her."

Robert walked over and kissed his mother on the forehead. He leaned in close, his lips almost on her ear, and whispered, "I love you."

She mumbled back, but he couldn't understand it.

---

ROBERT SHUT his locker in the back of L-Mart. Work was the last place he wanted to be, but the bills were piling up at an alarming rate. As much stress as he was under, especially having witnessed the brutal and insane death of Mr. Lazer, there were still things that needed to be done. He couldn't exactly call the bank and tell them to forgive their bills because his mother was sick and he'd witnessed a demon eat his friend.

He tied his apron around his waist and made sure his name tag was properly displayed. An improperly displayed name tag was one of Mike's pet peeves. The last thing Robert needed was his douchebag assistant manager giving him a hard time.

Robert turned the corner, almost crashing into Sarah.

"Oh shit," he said, putting his hands out. They hovered over her breasts.

Just before he put his hands down, she inched closer, brushing her tight apron against his fingertips.

"Sorry," they both said at the same time.

Robert, for just a split second, felt the firmness of her chest. It had been a while since he'd had a pair of tits in his hands. He blushed at the thought of her naked. Absently, he ran a hand through his hair, looking away from her. If he'd paid attention, he would've seen her blush too.

"Hey, I text you last night," she said, her redness fading away but the feeling of his touch lingering.

"Yeah, sorry about that. I had something to deal with." *Yeah, my friend was ripped apart by a fucking demon right before my eyes.*

"No problem. I was just checking in." She let it linger and realized she kind of sounded like a psycho. "I mean, I wanted to see how your mom was doing. That's all." It wasn't the whole truth but again, not wanting to look like a psycho.

"I was going to text you back, but it got a little hectic and I fell asleep." He hoped she didn't press the issue. He felt his grasp on reality slipping and didn't need any more stress.

"That's understandable," she said, twirling her foot. She was looking for the courage to continue. "I know things are rough for you right now, but if you ever need someone to talk to or if you want to hang out, I'd totally be ok with that." She hoped she didn't come across as desperate, but hoped she was forward enough. Some guys had to be led by the nose.

Robert looked at her. She really was quite attractive, which made things much more difficult. He wanted to do vile, filthy things to her, but he knew the time for that wasn't right. Maybe after his mother... He pushed his mind away from that.

"Listen, Sarah, I like you. I really do," he said, watching her smile but remain apprehensive. "It's just with my mom the way she is and with me trying to save some cash, I just don't think getting serious right now is the best idea."

She smiled, but it didn't reach her eyes. It wasn't quite a rejection, but it was enough for her to take the hint. She had one more trick up her sleeve; a little bait to dangle from the sexual hook.

"I completely understand and wouldn't want you to divide your attention from your mother." She moved in close, her breasts pushing against his chest. Her lips tickled his ear as she spoke. "If you ever just need someone to, I don't know, help you release some tension, give me a call." She tried to sound seductive, but she'd never really been the slutty, seductive type. As a matter of fact, this was the first time she was even putting the booty call out there.

Robert felt himself stiffen and thanked the L-Mart gods for giving him an apron. He cleared his throat, the smell of her in his nose.

"Ah, thanks," he said, as she backed away. "I'll be sure to keep that in mind."

She gave him another smile as she walked towards her locker.

"Sinclair?" A voice called out.

Robert already knew who it was. "Back here, Mike," he replied, trying to keep the scorn from dripping from his tongue.

The assistant manager, Mike, walked over to him with a list in hand. He smiled, meaning he had something shitty for him to do.

"Here, if you could take care of this before your meal break." He handed him the list. The first item was bathroom duty. Usually, this was reserved for maintenance, but recent budget cuts led to fewer hours for them, meaning another employee was left picking up the slack.

Robert was looking at the list when Sarah walked by.

"Good night, Robert." She never called him by a nickname and loved his full name. "And please, think about what I said"

Robert didn't know what part, but had an idea.

"Goodnight, Sarah. Great job today," Mike said, flashing her his dumpster smile.

She looked at him like a mouse.

"G'night." She didn't even dignify her response with his name.

Mike's eyes were glued to her ass as she walked around the corner and towards the exit. He looked back at Robert, the pang of jealousy in his eyes.

"Yeah, I don't want to keep you," he said, tapping on his clipboard. "Oh, and I hear the ladies' room is pretty bad, so I'd start there." Mike whistled something obscure as he walked away.

Robert went to the janitor's closet and grabbed a mop and gloves. He wasn't happy about cleaning the bathrooms, but his short interaction with Sarah took his mind off the pitfalls in his life. At least he had that.

---

THE WARM SPRING air had given way to a chilly night.

Robert walked to his car thankful he'd remembered his jacket. The parking lot lamps bathed the area in pools of yellow light. In a few weeks, they would be buzzing with bugs, but now they were clear.

"Oh, what the fuck?" he asked, walking up to his car. A ticket was slid under his windshield. For what, he didn't know. It could've been a host of things: the registration was expired, it wasn't inspected and his tires were bald. He plucked the ticket from the windshield and looked at it, ready to blow his lid.

"Huh?" he said aloud. It wasn't a traffic summons, it was an old lottery ticket. He looked around, thinking maybe someone had put it there, but his car was the only one in the area. The ticket didn't say if it was a winner, but it was from a few days ago, so the numbers had already been drawn. "Fuck it," he said and got in the car.

Minutes later he pulled into an all-night gas station. The clerk, a forty-something, balding man who looked like every stereotypical child molester ever, sat reading a sports magazine. At least the sports magazine was on the outside. The inside magazine, Robert could see, was some kind of porno mag. He couldn't believe people still bought porn magazines.

"Hey, can you check this ticket for me?" he asked the clerk.

The clerk, his name tag labeled him as Ron, looked up. He rubbed his wispy, weird-looking mustache with the back of his hand.

"Just scan it there," he pointed to the lottery scanner near the penis enlargement pills.

"Thank you," Robert said, briefly reading the info on the pills.

"They don't work," Ron said without looking up from his magazine. "They do give you a raging hard-on if you're having trouble in that area."

Robert didn't answer, just scanned his ticket.

The machine read the bar code and immediately started beeping. Robert looked at the small screen.

"Winner, $1000," he read. "Holy shit, I won," he said walking over to the register.

Ron put down his magazines and reached out for the ticket.

"Let me just verify," he said, taking the stub of paper. "13-15-18, yup, you're the lucky winner," he said. He wrote a few things on the ticket and stuck it in the drawer. "I'll be right back."

Robert couldn't believe it. He knew the money wasn't life-changing, but at least he could keep the lights on for another month and pay off a few other small bills.

"Here you go." Ron handed him an official lottery envelope stuffed with cash.

Robert opened it and quickly counted before putting it in his pocket.

The last few days, especially the last twenty-four hours, had been the worst in his life, but the conversation with Sarah and now the cash were highlights for sure.

He jumped back in his car, half expecting it not to start. It started on the first turn. He drove home, a smile on his face.

---

Robert peeked in on his mother. She was asleep, but her breathing was shallow and labored. Not only that, but each breath seemed to take longer and longer. He closed the door and walked into his room.

Surprisingly sleep came fast for him. His mind was so taxed recently, it needed a shutdown.

"You like it?" a familiar voice said in his dream. It was one he'd had often as a kid, but hadn't had in years. He and his mother were at a local carnival. He won a game and it kept spitting out tickets.

"Like what?" Robert asked, reeling in his tickets. He looked at them in surprise. Rather than normal carnival tickets, which were redeemable for prizes, these were lottery tickets.

"The ticket," the phantom voice said.

Robert shuddered as the stream of paper continued to flow. He knew the voice: Belphegor.

"What are you doing in my head?"

The demon laughed. "I am everywhere, stupid boy." He still didn't show himself, but his voice surrounded Robert. "That measly lottery ticket is my thanks for the meal the other night." He was talking about eating Josef. "That is but a mere fraction of my power. Bring me more meat and I'll give you everything you've ever wanted. Unless you want your mother to be my plaything."

"Shut the fuck up," Robert said.

Belphegor laughed again.

"Soon, she'll be mine for eternity. We're going to have so much fun."

Robert tried to block it out, but he knew it was true. She was dying and her day was coming sooner than later.

"It's simple, boy.

"Bring.

"Me.

"Meat.

"If not, your mother will be dead soon and in my grasp and that of my brothers." The phantom voice let out a wet laugh. "Trust me, they are much, much worse."

The tickets continued to fly out, but they began to change. Tickets of bloody flesh flew, overwhelming Robert. He tried to back away, but was stuck. The wet skin tickets began to surround him, climbing up his body like a constrictor. He struggled against them, but couldn't move. Each breath was a fight as they wound around him. His last gasp was agony and before he went to black he heard a single word echo through the area.

"Meat!"

Robert woke in a panic, his blanket wrapped around him. He fought it as if his life depended on it. His struggle lasted for a few seconds before he realized he was safe in bed and not wrapped in inhuman flesh.

His heart was thudding, but he was starting to get himself under control. He fixed his blanket and laid back down, staring at the ceiling. He closed his eyes, but this time, sleep was slow to come.

## 18

ROBERT DIDN'T SLEEP AGAIN. As a matter of fact, he was up most of the night. His dreams were disturbing to say the least. The death of his mother, depraved sex acts, images of Mr. Lazer being ripped apart and other vile things, haunted his slumber. He awoke in the darkness of the early morning and went into his mother's room.

Every time he opened the door he said a prayer. He wasn't the best of Catholics, but in the last couple of days his faith in God had grown. If there was evil in the world such as the demon, there had to be a God.

He had oiled the hinges on the door so they wouldn't squeak as he pushed it open. The hall light crept by, but only a sliver, and it did not reach the bed.

Helen lay on her back, as if she were in a casket already. Her face was sunken, eyelids looking thin as tissue paper. Her hair hadn't fallen out completely, but it was thin. She had her left arm across her chest, which was nearly the width of two of Robert's fingers.

Robert stood at the door and stared. He waited a few agonizing seconds, the tears built in his eyes. She breathed, barely. He let out a sigh of relief as one of her last remaining breaths escaped her dry lips. Like a specter, he moved into the room.

Robert knelt by the bed, just his forearms on the edge of the mattress. He interlocked his fingers as if in prayer and looked at the shell of his once powerful mother. The emotions of the past few days washed over him. A torrent of silent tears poured from his eyes, eyes that hadn't been dry in a while. He felt like a baby, crying all the time over things he couldn't change.

But could he change this? Could he save his mother's life? According to Mr. Lazer and the Hell-cursed demon, he could. At what cost though? He'd need to give someone to that beast. And then what? His soul would be damned for all eternity. Not to mention, he'd have to live with the fact he killed another human being in the worst possible way.

His mother began choking, but didn't wake up. Wet coughs racked her frail body, but even that wasn't enough to wake her.

Robert stood up in a panic, watching her body fight to stay alive. Finally, it stopped and she started breathing again. Another breath gone.

At that moment, he knew he could do it. He could give someone to Belphegor in exchange for just a few more years with her.

It was as if a weight had been lifted from his chest. He knew he could do it and knew it had to be sooner than later. She didn't have much time. Now, he just needed to figure out how he was going to do it.

Did he dare move the stone and try to redraw the circle? The demon seemed to test the bonds when summoned. If his drawing wasn't perfect that beast could be released. No, that was too risky. He had to capture someone and bring them there. It was the only way.

"I'm going to save you, Mom. I swear to God I will." His tears made small circles on her blanket as they fell from his wet cheeks.

He knelt there, just staring at her. He knew he could kill for her and knew he would.

When Robert was in high school, he would smoke cigarettes with his friends. At first he did it just to be cool and hang out with his buddies. He never really liked smoking, and at first was repulsed by it. He never grew up around smokers and when he was a kid, would go out of his way to avoid it. His habit grew in school and he found himself smoking alone. Most of his friends quit, the allure growing old. Not him. He kept puffing away. It wasn't a big deal because his girlfriend smoked and a cigarette after sex was a great thing indeed. Eventually, when that bitter break-up came, he kicked the habit, knowing most girls didn't like it. He liked sex more than smoking, and quit for good. Or so he thought.

Robert sat on a small chair in the backyard of their house and unwrapped his first pack of cigarettes in over two years. With deft hands he pulled the foil from the box and took one out. The flame sucked lovingly into the tip, crackling the dry tobacco and paper. He inhaled hard, as if he'd never quit, and coughed. And coughed again, and again until his lungs hurt. His head swam with the flood of chemicals into his bloodstream. He put it back up to his lips and pulled again, this one much smoother.

After sitting with his mother for another hour, he knew he needed to get things in motion. She didn't have long, and if he was going to save her it had to be tonight.

Robert wanted to start with an animal, maybe a cat or dog, but he couldn't chance it. His mother's time was running out, and running out fast. It had to be a person.

Countless times he scrolled through his phone looking for someone he could not only sacrifice, but who he would be able to follow through with. He couldn't think of anyone he wanted to suffer that fate. No one deserved it, but did his mother deserve to be dying? Life, he realized, was far from fair. From the moment he made the decision to give someone to the demon, he knew who it had to be. He just didn't want to admit it and wasted time scrolling through contacts in his phone.

His nerves were shot and he couldn't get the courage to make the call or even text. The cigarettes helped...and the fact his mother was knocking on death's door and he was answering.

Robert inhaled on the cigarette, his fresh lungs burning through a hefty chunk of tobacco and paper. He picked up his phone and unlocked it. He went through his messages and settled on Sarah's name. He opened his text messages and typed.

'Hey, what are you doing later tonight?'

---

SARAH'S PHONE chimed with the familiar sound of a new text message. She was just waking up and rolled over to find her phone. It was a message from Robert. At first she thought the worst, that his mother had finally passed away and he needed her to cover his shift. When she read his message, her heart started beating faster.

She unplugged her phone and sat up in bed. She brushed the few stray hairs from her face and re-read the message.

*Did he want to hang out?* she thought. *Maybe this is a booty call.* She wanted a relationship with Robert, but she, like him, had been lacking in the sex department. If he just wanted to fuck, at least to start with, she would be more than ok with that. She started writing back immediately and stopped. She didn't want to seem desperate.

Sarah put her phone down and walked the three steps across her studio apartment to the bathroom.

She never shut the door when in there. Since she was seventeen, she'd been on her own. Her parents, like Robert's, had divorced when she was young, but unlike him, her mother was a raging drunk, who liked to hit. From a young age, she knew she wasn't sticking around her mother and the day she'd saved up enough money, she left. It was nearly six years since she'd last seen her mother.

Sarah slid back into bed, hoping to have some leftover body heat in the sheets. She picked her phone back up and wrote.

'Nothing. I was just going to order a pizza and watch a few corny movies. U?'

She hoped it sounded playful and not desperate. She was going to add the date she had with her vibrator, unless he wanted to fill the roll, but thought it was a bit forward. Suddenly, the blankets were a little too warm. She kept a sheet on her, but that was it. Her screen let her know Robert was typing. The bubble flashed as he wrote for a few seconds, much longer than normal. His message popped up.

'I was just thinking maybe we should give us a shot. With my mother being sick it made me realize you can't wait for life. I'm plant-sitting for a friend and figured we could have dinner there, since he's out of town.'

Sarah read the message over and over. She smiled a wide smile. After all of the missteps and failed relationships, she finally had the opportunity for something good.

'That sounds great. Just let me know when and where.'

She stared at her phone, hoping it wasn't a joke. His text bubble popped up.

'I'll pick you up at 8. OK?'

'Sounds good. See you then.' She re-read the messages over and over, giggling like a schoolgirl. She put her phone back on the charger and threw off her sheet. Her closet wasn't very big and her date was ten hours away, but she had to find something to wear, which for her, could be an all-day affair.

---

ROBERT LOOKED AT HIS PHONE, his hands still shaking. The first part was done and he felt like he was going to be sick. Sarah cared for him and he cared for her, but he would do anything for his mother. He just hoped he could carry through with it.

A wet, painful cough came from his mother's room. It was followed by a mournful, sad moaning. She was lucid, the medication keeping her somewhat sedated. Her pain would end tonight, one way or another.

---

## CHAPTER 18 | 171

SARAH HAD the day off from work, so she was able to stew over her date later that night. She spent the entire day cleaning her small apartment, which she kept pretty clean to begin with. She did some light grocery shopping and even swung by the mall to kill some time. It had been years since she had been this excited for a date and couldn't get it off her mind.

Once it hit 5 pm, she was able to officially get ready. She showered, shaved, and waxed everything that needed it. Normally she didn't wear a lot of makeup, so she didn't want to slather it on. With a deft hand she applied just enough to accent her natural features, but didn't leave her looking like a clown. She stood in front of her full-length mirror in just a bra and underwear. Her selection in that department was lacking too, but she didn't have the extra cash to spend on fancy lingerie. Besides, her large breasts needed support, something most fancy bras couldn't provide. She wore a clean, white bra and a white thong (that she had splurged on earlier at the mall). Sarah didn't know if Robert would be seeing either of them later, but she wanted to be prepared.

She put on a light red lip stain, something that wouldn't come off during dinner or making out. With a pouty, teasing look, she blew a kiss at the mirror. Satisfied with her makeup, she dressed.

Earlier, after a few hours of deliberation, she decided on her outfit. She wanted to wear something nice, but also something that accented her figure. She also wanted to wear a skirt for easy access, but not something she'd wear in a club. Sarah slid into a tan skirt, which flared past her knees. The turtleneck she picked was snug, more than enough to show off her chest, but was long-sleeved and showed no skin. She thought it was a nice combo that should get Robert's attention. Considering she'd caught him checking her out in her L-Mart apron, she didn't think this would be an issue.

She looked out the window just as his car pulled up in front of her building. She put on a pair of high boots, grabbed her purse and jacket and ran out the door.

ROBERT SPENT the day in turmoil.

After getting off the phone with Sarah, his mother's coughing fit became worse. He went into her room as she began vomiting. There wasn't much in her system, but chunks of bloody bile splashed on the floor. He kept her calm as she gasped for air, the fit passing. Slowly, as if drowning, she fell back asleep. Robert cleaned the floor and wiped up her blanket. He could smell urine coming from her, but couldn't wake her back up to clean it. After straightening up her room, he went back to his own.

He stared at his phone, re-reading the text messages from Sarah. She was the last person he wanted this to happen to, but she was the only logical choice. Sure, he could try and lure someone else over, but that wasn't guaranteed. He thought about kidnapping someone, but again there were serious risks involved that may get him caught before he could complete the sacrifice.

Throughout the day Robert cleaned and fed his mother. He would tell her it would be better, but she was so far gone she didn't seem to understand. The only thing helping with the pain and easing her towards death was her medication.

Before she'd gotten sick Robert had only seen Fentanyl on the news. The high-powered narcotic was responsible for millions of overdose deaths throughout the world. It was also a useful tool for those in chronic pain. When taking pills hadn't been a chore, Helen's doctor had prescribed her a massive bottle. She didn't like taking them, but always kept them near her bed.

He didn't eat anything until closer to 5 pm. The same time Sarah was singing in the shower, he was eating a bland grilled cheese. He sat at the kitchen table, picking through the mound of bills.

The money from the lottery ticket was a help, but it was a band-aid on a bullet hole. He would never catch up with all of them. Eventually, he'd lose the house.

Robert went back upstairs to check on his mother. She was cleaned and seemed to be resting comfortably. His cell phone said it was 7:30 and time for him to go pick up Sarah. It felt like he was going to an execution, which he technically was.

It was chilly outside after the sun had set. Robert was sweating a nervous sweat. Not the athletic, good workout sweat, but the sour sweat that seemed to come out cold. His crotch and armpits were wet and chilly. On a normal date this would be a problem, but this was far from a normal date.

He got in the car and left. Just before he turned onto Sarah's street, he felt it; he was going to puke. He pulled over and flung open the door, as the torrent of half-digested grilled cheese came spewing out. He snorted, cleared his sinuses and spat the last few bits onto the pavement.

"What the fuck am I doing?" he asked himself, as he closed the door and looked at the rearview mirror. Robert found a half-empty bottle of water under the seat. He rinsed his rancid mouth with it and spit it out of the window, his reflection looking back at him, but not answering the question. He knew what he was doing. It was the right decision. Hell, it was the only decision. He popped a few pieces of gum in his mouth and drove on.

---

ROBERT MADE small talk with Sarah for the entire ride. He kept his mouth moving and ears open, listening to her answers. He did anything possible to take his mind off the task at hand. He kept stealing glances at her, trying not to crash the car. Her sweater was snug in all the right places and just a hint of her knee was showing.

Sarah knew he was looking at her. She and other women had that sixth sense when men were looking at them. She would stretch her back at just the right moment, pushing her breasts out. Robert even noticed her hiking her skirt up just a touch, revealing more of her milky skin.

Every glance he took was painful. One part of him wanted to ravage her, knowing her lust would meet his full force. The other part could hardly look at her knowing what fate awaited.

"Here we are," he said, pulling into Josef's driveway.

The lights were all off and he pulled the car close to the side door of the house. They got out and were immediately greeted with sensor lights.

Robert put his hand in front of his eyes, blocking the light as he fished the keys from his pocket.

"Come on in," he said, trying to maintain the facade of happiness. He flipped a switch, lighting up the kitchen area. "Make yourself at home," he told her, taking his coat off and putting it on a chair. The pictures Josef had left on the table were in a shoe box in the downstairs bedroom.

Sarah looked around, taking in the dated decor and appliances.

"Is your friend an old man?" she asked, touching a tasseled dish towel.

Robert smiled. "Yeah, he's an old timer, but he's a good guy." He thought of all the times he'd talked with Josef in the store and diner. Then his mind went to the mess and possible blessing he'd left to him. "Years ago he got into hydroponics."

Sarah raised an eyebrow and smiled. "Go on," she smirked.

Robert laughed, "No, not *that* kind of hydroponics." He paused for a second, thinking. "Well, I guess it is that kind, but he's not growing weed, I don't think. He grows his vegetables and herbs and what not down in the basement." He pointed to the door with his thumb. "It's pretty self-sufficient, but I need to check it daily and water the houseplants and outside garden." He wished he'd shut up. There wasn't a single houseplant in sight and if she looked outside, she'd only see an overgrown lawn and no garden. "I'll be right back up and then I'll start dinner." He started towards the basement door. "Oh, there's beer in the fridge, if you'd like one. Help yourself," he said, and opened the door to the basement.

Sarah wandered around the kitchen, floating in between there and the attached living room. She absently touched old pictures, all of which were of the Lazerowitz family before the war.

"Sarah," Robert shouted from the basement.

She walked to the top of the stairs and yelled down. "Yeah?"

There was a pause, as if Robert were thinking.

"Can you help me with something?"

She was starving. She wanted to have a snack before she left, but was too nervous. She was regretting that and her growling stomach was letting her know. If he needed help before dinner, she'd help. Anything to get to food...and then maybe some dessert on the rather large couch.

"I'm coming down." She started down the stairs and was assaulted with a vile odor. "Robert, what the fuck is that smell?" she asked, still walking down the stairs.

"Oh, that?" he said, matter-of-factly. "He uses some kind of odd fertilizer. It stinks like matches and shit."

She didn't disagree with that statement. Sarah was almost at the bottom of the stairs when she saw the circle.

"What the hel—" She stopped at the bottom of the stairs.

Belphegor stood in the protective circle. His black eyes, purulent skin and clawed hands, caused her to pause. Just enough time for Robert to wrap his arms around her.

"What the fuck?" she shouted, as he lifted her off the ground. She thrashed against him, but his muscles felt like cords of steel.

Belphegor paced, a wicked grin on his face. His serrated and jagged teeth were brown, some were missing. His forked tongue whipped around, seeming unnaturally long.

"Can you heal her?" Robert asked. His voice wavered and for a moment, he thought he was going to lose his resolve. Sarah still fought, kicking and thrashing, but Robert's grip was strong.

Sarah thought it was a strange question, considering she wasn't sick or injured.

"Yes," the demon hissed. His large penis was erect. The tightness of the skin caused the pustules to ooze different shades of liquid. "For this delicious morsel, I'll heal her and more." The demon put his clawed hands against the barrier, waiting for his prize to come to him.

"Robert, stop!" Sarah tried digging her heels into the floor, but they only slid. He pushed her towards the demon. "Please. Fucking stop!" Her screams turned into piercing shrieks. Every one of them made Belphegor smile wider. A stream of hot urine soaked her panties, and dripped down her leg, making the floor slick.

"I'm sorry," Robert said, he held her tight. His arms pinned hers to her sides.

"Yes, yes," the demon rejoiced

"No," she screamed as her arm broke the plane of the protective barrier.

Robert was sure to push her, keeping himself far from the beast. He backed away, grabbing the holy water.

Belphegor grabbed Sarah, his clawed hand tearing gouges in her flesh as he pulled her in. He was behind her, with one hand around her throat, the other probing her body.

"Mmm," he groaned, smelling her with his animal-like nose. "You're going to taste divine." His penis slid under her skirt, as if it had a mind of its own.

"Robert, please," she cried, her make-up running down her face. She shrieked and a snot bubble swelled in her nostril

Belphegor grinned, his smile unnaturally long. Suddenly he began bucking and thrusting.

Sarah's eyes went wide, but her scream was stifled from a strong hand around her throat.

The demon's forked tongue slithered around her neck like a snake and found her waiting mouth. Her eyes nearly bulged from her head as the tongue bore down her throat.

"Fucking stop!" Robert yelled. He'd had enough of the performance. This wasn't what he was looking for. He wanted a clean, quick kill and be done. This was over the top. "Just fucking end it already!" he yelled, crying now. The pangs of regret were almost physical. The fear in Sarah's eyes, the pain, the fucking betrayal. He wanted to look away, but couldn't. It was as if the performance was magnetic.

Belphegor stopped and looked at Robert over Sarah's shoulder. With a swipe, his unoccupied hand ripped down her chest. The sharp claws cut fabric and flesh like it was non-existent. Her sweater ripped open and bloody strips of her breast and shirt were dangling free. Blood mixed with her flesh, dripping from a severed nipple. The butter-yellow fat glistened in the light of the basement, adding to the grotesque colors of impending death. The demon's claw was red and he prepared for another strike.

"End it," Robert pleaded. He didn't have the energy to scream again. His knees were weak and felt like he was going to collapse. Through teary eyes, he watched Sarah's face, a pain-mask replacing the fear.

Belphegor held his attack, staring at Robert. He still had his other wicked hand around her soft throat. He could feel her panicked pulse raging away. Without breaking eye contact, Belphegor ripped. His claws, which were already buried in her flesh, tore a chunk of her throat out. Destroyed flesh, tattered blood vessels and a ribbed trachea, pulled off her body like overcooked meat. A spurt of blood sprayed against the barrier and finally, life faded from Sarah's eyes.

Robert threw the holy water on them, dismissing the demon and his prize back to the stone. His legs finally gave out and he collapsed to the floor. The smell of sulfur still hung in the air, but his nose was pouring snot. He watched Sarah's corpse suck into the stone, Belphegor smiling the entire time.

---

Robert drove home in silence. He was on auto-pilot, his subconscious doing the driving.

Before he left, he vomited twice. Vomited until his eyes felt like they were going to pop and then vomited a little more. He cried, some was from the pain of retching, but mostly it was from Sarah. He knew the depravity of the demon and knew what was going to happen to her, but it didn't make it any easier. When Josef died it was a shock to him, his brain shielding itself from some of the brutality. Also, Josef had given himself to the monster. This was different. Sarah was innocent. She'd never wronged him and actually liked him. Worse than that, she'd trusted him. In the fleeting moments of her life, that trust was still there. Robert knew he could never do it again. He had to find a way to get rid of the demon. Nothing was worth this.

Robert's headlights lit up his house, which was dark. He killed the engine, listening to it tick and cool. Part of him knew when he went inside, his mother would be dead. It was his penance for killing an innocent person. She wouldn't have died peacefully either. No, there would've been a freak accident or something. Maybe a stray dog got into the house and was feasting on her weakened body right now.

Robert's mouth was sour from the puke. He opened the car door, the interior lights bathing him in a buttery glow.

Inside the house it smelled the same: sick. He took his shoes off and walked upstairs.

Robert stood outside of his mother's room and listened for a second. There was no sound, but he didn't expect much. Her breathing was shallow at best, especially with one lung. Ever so gently, he opened the door.

Helen Sinclair lay asleep on her bed, still. A moment later, she took a breath. A much larger breath than Robert had seen in a while.

Robert backed out, not wanting to wake her. He wasn't concerned about her not getting back to sleep, but was concerned he'd break down about Sarah. Right then, he just needed to shower and go to bed.

After a burning hot cleansing, Robert dressed and got into bed. He was drained. Sleep came surprisingly fast, but didn't last long. His dreams were plagued by the smell of sulfur and the sound of screaming.

# 19

Robert never set an alarm when he had to work the early afternoon shift at L-Mart. His internal clock always had him up well before it was time to get ready. That morning, his clock was running a little behind, but luckily for him, his mother's was right on point.

The day was gloomy, which he noticed right away. Gray light filtered through his curtains and he could hear the sound of rain on the leaves. He could hear sounds coming from downstairs and thought it was Esther. He grabbed his cell phone and looked at the time. She wasn't due for another two hours. The memories of the previous night came flooding back to him.

"Sarah," he whispered. The pain of watching her violated and killed by the demon was rekindled. Her screams, the blood, the look of betrayal in her eyes, all hit him. But something else was invading his mind: music.

The song came from downstairs. It was Cyndy Lauper's "Girls just want to have fun." The sound of dishes clanking also followed the music.

Robert immediately thought back to the other day with his mother's dying second wind. This already seemed different. He didn't know how or why, but knew she was better. He smiled and threw back the blankets like a kid on Christmas morning, Sarah all but a memory.

He took the stairs by twos and ran into the kitchen.

Helen was just sitting down with two steaming plates of food in her hands. She looked at him, surprised.

"Oh, I'm sorry, I can make something for you too. Just give me a minute. I'm absolutely famished." She smiled at the plates of pancakes, eggs, bacon and potatoes, as if it was the first time she'd seen food.

Robert stared at the meal. He'd have a hard time eating all of that, but it was impossible to think his mother could. He watched her dig in, eating as if she hadn't in weeks. Well, the amount she was currently eating was far more than what she'd eat in two or three days combined. She was still thin, but there was a light in her eyes and glow to her skin. He was no doctor, but she looked much better.

Helen washed down her breakfast with a cup of coffee, which Robert had also helped himself to. She stifled a burp with the back of her hand and smiled at her son.

"Wow, I don't know what got into me." She sipped the coffee. "I woke up with energy like I've never had before. Even prior to the cancer, I didn't feel this great. I guess I should be dying every day," she joked.

Robert smirked, but it didn't reach his eyes.

"Well, let's not go too crazy. The other day you were like this and then comatose for the rest of the day."

Helen took her dishes to the sink. "I know," she said, "this just feels different." She put the plates in the sink and leaned on it, sobbing.

Robert got up and walked over to her. He put a hand on her back and gently rubbed. She still felt like skin and bones, but a warmth, that of a growing life-force, emanated from her.

"Hey, don't cry, mom." He felt tears forming. These last few days he'd cried more than in his entire life. "Take every day as special and enjoy what you have."

She turned and faced him, hugging her son. Her tears soaked his shirt, but he didn't care in the least.

"I know, but I almost hate being teased like this." She spoke into his chest. "I wake up feeling like a bear coming out of hibernation and by tonight, I'll be at death's door." She backed away, looking up at him. "The scary thing is I feel different than before. Last time I knew I was still sick, but having a good day." She paused, looking out the window. "Now, I feel healed," she croaked, as if saying it would take it away. "I feel better than ever and I hate it. I hate the carrot dangling in front of me. I hate knowing by tonight, hell may be in an hour. I'll be shitting myself in bed."

Robert was taken aback by the profanity. It was something he rarely heard from his mother. He took her face in his hands and kissed her forehead, the same way she used to do when tucking him in. She always told him a kiss on the head would give him good dreams. Right now, he felt like he was in a dream and it was going to end any second.

"Trust me," he said, looking at her misty eyes. "Take it for what it is. If you feel good, great, just don't overdo it."

Helen nodded, wiping her eyes with her hands.

"Will you eat?" she asked, looking at the mess in the kitchen.

"Yeah, let me get ready for work first."

She smiled, happy to take care of her son again. "Great, I'll have it ready when you come back down." Helen scraped the bits of leftover eggs into the garbage and opened the fridge.

---

THE JOY ROBERT felt at seeing his mother up and moving, dissipated when he pulled into the lot of L-Mart.

Memories of Sarah flooded over him. Not only that, but what if he was implicated in her disappearance. She was supposed to work the same shift as him today, so when they did roll call, everyone would know she was absent.

He walked into the store and got prepped for his shift. Jordan and a few others, one being Darren, who worked maintenance, were all getting ready too.

"What up?" asked Jordan, tying his apron behind his back.

Robert wasn't in the mood for small talk, especially seeing Sarah's empty locker. He knew if he seemed down most people would blame it on his mother's sickness. Still, he didn't want to raise any flags, especially if Sarah told anyone they were going out.

"Not much. Just another day and another dollar."

Jordan stopped and put on a mocked, shocked face. "You mean they pay you to be here?" He laughed at his own lame joke and straightened his name tag. He looked around and pulled out his phone. "Where's Sarah?" he asked, checking the time and any missed messages.

Robert mimicked him, looking around like she might be hiding somewhere in plain sight.

"I don't know," he lied. "Maybe she banged in." He closed his locker and started towards the break room, where Mike, the assistant manager took roll call.

Mike stood at a table with a clipboard in his hand. His skin was especially greasy, as if he used butter for lotion. His few fresh pimples looked extremely sore, as did his disposition. He stared at the clipboard, his pen wedged in-between his crooked teeth.

"He's so fucking nasty," Jordan whispered to Robert through the side of his mouth.

Robert huffed, acknowledging his friend. He couldn't believe Mike had actually tried to kiss Sarah. Well, his chance was over. Her last kiss had been a kiss of death. Robert pushed her from his mind, and tried to focus on the fact his mother was doing better. That was the whole point of sacrificing Sarah in the first place.

Mike began reading off names. Finally, he came to Sarah, who he already knew wasn't there.

"Sarah," Mike said, knowing he wouldn't get a response. He was doing it for effect, but no one really gave a shit about him. "Sarah Denbrough," he droned, trying to put authority in his voice. "Has anyone heard from her?" he asked the crowd of employees. A quiet murmur ran through the group. "How about you, Sinclair?" Mike pointed to Robert with his slobbery pen. "You and Sarah seem pretty," he grinned, "tight. Have you heard from her?"

Robert feigned innocence, but felt like everyone knew. He shrugged his shoulders, but could feel the leer of everyone staring at him.

"No, I haven't talked to her since the other day at work." He was starting to sweat, the heat of guilt overwhelming him. No one was looking at him anymore and it felt like a weight lifted off of his shoulders.

"Ok, well after roll call, give her a shout and see what's going on." Mike said, returning to the last few names.

Robert took his phone out and walked to a semi-private area. He knew she wasn't going to answer, but he dialed anyway.

The phone rang and rang, finally going to voicemail. He was going to hang up, feeling stupid for even dialing, but something kept the phone to his ear. Robert didn't know if it was the desire to hear her voice or something else, but he listened as the message played.

"Hi, this is Sarah. I can't come to the phone right now as I'm being fucked and mutilated by hellish beasts. Leave your name and number and I'll be sure to return your call. Wait for the beep."

Another voice came over the message, a gravelly, disgusting voice, and said, "Beep."

Robert looked at the phone and hit end. His heart was racing at the message, but the sound of Belphegor as her *beep* was too much.

"No luck?" asked Jordan. He looked at his friend, who was pale. "Hey, are you ok?"

Robert stared at him, trying to calm his nerves and will blood back to his face. He plastered on a fake smile.

"Yeah, I'm fine. Just a nasty burp. I thought I was going to puke for a second." He rubbed his stomach. Robert held up the phone, bringing the focus off his sick pallor. "Ah, yeah, no luck. I'll give her a shout later."

Jordan walked away, heading to check the stock list and find out what happened on the first shift.

The phone felt electric in Robert's hands. He wanted to call back, just to see if the message was the same, but he couldn't bring himself to hit send.

"Well?" asked Mike, waddling his chubby ass over to Robert. "Any luck with our girl?"

Robert wanted to smash Mike's teeth down his throat. Sarah was never and would never be Mike's girl. The only thing that pathetic slug would get is his hand or maybe a cheap whore.

"No answer," Robert said, picturing Mike's face bloodied from a solid punch.

"Ok, I'll try later, but for now this is an unexcused absence," he told Robert, as if it mattered. She was dead and gone.

Robert's shift had gone smooth from then on. He stocked shelves, moved products around and helped unload a delivery. He was just grabbing a drink from the water cooler when he saw Darren approaching.

Darren was one of the cool, older guys. He was nearly sixty, but didn't look a day over forty. He was one of those ageless black men, like Will Smith, who always seemed younger than they were. He had been working at L-Mart for years as a maintenance man, but he was a jack-of-all trades. For the better part of his life he was a super in an apartment building in NYC, but as he got older he left the hustle and bustle of the Big Apple and moved upstate.

"Hey, Bobby, can I talk to you?" Darren asked Robert. He kept his voice low and spoke close to him.

Robert crushed the little paper cup and threw it in the can next to the water cooler.

"Sure, man. What's up?"

Darren looked around, confirming they were the only two in the area.

"Did you clean the women's bathroom the other day?"

He did and did a piss poor job at it. He was aggravated with Mike, hell he was aggravated with life, and didn't put much effort into it.

"Yeah, my bad. I know I did a shitty job. I was just pissed at Mike…" he trailed off, looking at Darren.

"Nah, I don't care about that. I just want to know what you cleaned."

Robert thought back to it. He hadn't done much.

"Well, I wiped the counters and sinks. I refilled the paper towels and toilet paper. I didn't clean the floors or toilets."

Darren nodded. "That's what I thought. Besides, I didn't think you'd do this anyway."

"Do what?" Robert asked.

"Hide this," Darren pulled a small camera from his pocket. It was just a lens, wire, battery and memory card. "I found it earlier when I was wiping down the bowls. Some sick fuck hid this in there."

Robert had an idea of who it might be, as did Darren, but neither said it aloud.

"My nephew is a cop, so I'll give him a call and get this figured out."

Robert nodded his approval. "Yeah, hopefully it isn't an employee, but you never know anymore."

"Sick fucks," said Darren, pocketing the camera and walking away.

Robert walked back out of the batwing doors to the store and almost right into Mike. It was as if he summoned him by thinking what a dirtbag he was.

"Just the man I was looking for," Mike said, a shit-eating grin on his face. "I just got a call from Sarah."

Robert felt his heart race. He was no longer pale, but could feel his face getting red. "You did?" he was able to croak out, hoping it sounded genuine. It didn't matter anyway, Mike was gloating over the fact she called him and not Robert.

"Yeah, bad news, lover boy. She said she's moving to Oklahoma. Something about a job offer with an uncle of hers. It was hard to hear her, there was a lot of screaming and yelling. She must've been on a plane or something." He squinted, thinking about the conversation, which now seemed odd. "Anyway," he snapped back to reality, "sorry to break the news. She'll certainly be missed. Especially those fat tits of hers. Mmm, mmm, mmm, what I would've given to get smothered by them." He wasn't even looking at Robert anymore; he was lost in his own sick fantasy. Without another word, he walked away.

Robert was stunned and relieved. He didn't know what would happen with Sarah's disappearance, but it seemed to sort itself out. He felt a pang of regret, but deep down, he knew he'd made the right choice.

---

Robert walked in the front door of his house later that evening. He figured he would heat up something frozen or maybe have leftovers if Esther cooked. Sometimes she would make something small for herself, as his mother had barely eaten in days. Although Robert wasn't too sure, considering his mother devoured a trucker-sized breakfast earlier in the day.

The thoughts of Sarah weighed on his mind, but he did what he could to push them away. A regretful twinge of relief reverberated through his body when Mike told him about her phone call. It would definitely help clear him if anyone suspected foul play. Somehow, he didn't think that would happen.

His house, which normally had the odor of staleness and sickness, smelled clean and fresh. As soon as Robert walked in, the scent of floor cleaner and food hit him. It was an odd mixture, something he wasn't quite used to since his mother had gotten sick. He held out hope, but still kept his guard. The whole thing felt like a mean trick and he was going to be the butt of it.

Robert saw fresh vacuum lines in the living room carpet. He took his shoes off and walked towards the kitchen.

"Don't," his mother said, a mop in her hand. She pointed at his socked feet and the wet floor. "You'll get soaked."

Robert stared at her in near awe. Her skin, which days before looked like it was falling off her bones, was now firmer and healthier looking. She wasn't back to her pre-cancer look, but even from that morning she appeared better. Her hair, which hadn't fallen out, but was thinning, now looked thicker and fuller. Her clothes still hung off her gaunt body, but rather than seem emaciated, she now looked just skinny. A heavy, gold crucifix bobbed around her neck as she moved. It was a miracle...but Robert knew his prayers weren't answered by God.

CHAPTER 19 | 187

"I made a lasagna for dinner. It's still hot, if you want a piece," she said, resuming her mopping.

Robert watched her attack a stubborn spot with vigor. Two days ago a walk to the toilet was arduous.

"Mom, where's Esther?" The aide should've still been there at least for another half hour.

Without looking up, she said, "Oh, her daughter and granddaughter came into town for a visit. I told her she could have the rest of the night off and I'd keep her posted on my condition. I feel just great." Her hand went up to the crucifix around her neck. "Robert, I think our prayers have been answered." Her smile wavered and she began to cry. They started small, but broke into full-on sobs. The mop clattered to the floor as she used both hands to cover her face.

Wet socks be damned, he walked into the kitchen and hugged his mother. He kissed her head, which smelled clean with just a faint hint of sweat. He was careful not to hug her too tight; she still felt as thin as a bird.

Helen wept with tears of joy and faith, onto her son's chest.

"Oh, look at me," she said, backing away. She rubbed her eyes with the back of her hands. "Blubbering over a miracle."

Robert smiled at her. It was great to see her happy and healthy.

"Well, I guess you can't really call it a miracle until I see the doctors, but it sure feels like one." She wiped an errant tear. "It was as if I woke up and the cancer was gone." She held her hands up like a magician doing a trick. "Poof, into thin air." After a moment, she collected herself, sweeping away the final, errant tear and bent down to pick up the mop. "Shoo," she said, pushing him back out of the kitchen. "Let me finish up here."

Robert stripped off his wet socks and stood on the threshold of the kitchen.

"I was going to call Cardinal Carafa, but I need to hear from the doctors first. Then I can let him know a miracle has happened."

"Sounds good," he said. He knew exactly what the doctors would say. They would say they've never seen anything like it. In all of their X amount of years in medicine, they had never seen a late stage cancer patient completely clear of cancer. Even if they weren't religious, they would think it a miracle. None would admit it, but the thought would be there. "I'm going to take a shower. I have the breakfast shift tomorrow at the diner."

"Ok," she said, leaning on the mop. Her brow was sweaty, a few thin hairs clung to her forehead. "Hopefully I'm better and I can get another job. Help support this house too."

Robert loved her. At that moment, it had all been worth it. This time yesterday she had one foot through death's door and now she was talking about finding a job.

"One day at a time, Mom."

She nodded. "You're right. I'll make you a plate and leave it in the living room."

"That would be great," he said, walking upstairs. Seeing her like that, he felt as if he could float.

## 20

ROBERT DIDN'T MIND the breakfast shift at the diner. It was normally a regular crowd, easy food to serve, quick turnovers and decent tips. Plus, he was done by 10 am, giving him the rest of the day to himself.

Today, he was partnered with Everett.

Everett was the opposite of Kitty. He was in his mid-forties with a head of dyed black hair. He was as tall as Robert and had a pinched in face, with just a slight amount of pock marks. Like Kitty, he smoked like a chimney. Unlike Kitty, he hated getting small tables. He'd always forgo a one-top or two-top in the hopes the next couple would be bigger. He worked nights at a local Italian restaurant and this was side money.

It was hitting 6 am, the diner just opened. Robert was wrapping silverware and Everett was somewhere fucking off. He didn't mind if the older man didn't help. They never really got along anyway, so if they kept their distance it was fine by Robert.

He looked up as a brand new, monstrous pick-up truck pulled into the parking lot. A man hopped out and headed towards the door.

Robert grabbed a menu and walked to meet him as he entered.

"Good morning, sir." Robert said.

The customer was your average guy, average height and weight, blue jeans and flannel shirt. He had short, blondish hair and a couple days stubble to match.

"Morning," he replied with a clear southern accent.

Robert wasn't taken aback by it, even though they were in New York. Many travelers passed through the area on their way upstate, which had beautiful natural wonders.

"Just one today," the man said.

"Great, follow me." Robert walked the man to a booth in the back corner of the restaurant and seated him. "Can I get you a drink to start?"

The man looked at the menu and then up at Robert.

"Just a black coffee and water. No lemon, please."

"Sure thing," Robert said. He saw Everett come out of the kitchen. He must've heard the door and was just checking to see if he lost out on a bigger table.

Robert brought the customer his drinks and then the flood gates seemed to open.

Within the next ten minutes, almost half of the parking lot was full. It turned out there was a pretty big concert the previous night and all of the attendees were hitting the road at the same time.

Robert and Everett performed a delicate dance of seating, ordering and delivering food. It wasn't quite chaos, but it was busy. As busy as it was, Robert was able to keep up, delivering food to his first table, the solo customer and keeping the man's coffee hot.

Everett had a nine-top and was going to need help with the drinks, but Robert wanted to make sure he gave the first guy his bill before being caught up with helping.

He handed the man the black, bi-fold bill holder and said, "Sorry for the wait. We kind of got slammed all at once."

The man smiled a genuine smile. "Ah, don't worry. I worked in my uncle's restaurant when I was a boy. I know how it goes."

Robert looked at Everett, who was trying to balance a tray with steaming coffee.

"Let me go help him. Thanks again," Robert said, walking away.

Robert and Everett were able to successfully serve his large table, when the man walked out.

"Here," he said, handing the bill holder to Robert. "It's all you," meaning he left cash for the bill and tip.

"Thanks," Robert slid the bill holder into his apron pocket, hoping the guy didn't stiff him on the check.

Robert watched the man walk out towards his truck. A woman in the parking lot slapped her husband in the arm, pointing at the man. Robert couldn't hear what was being said, but the woman handed her phone to her husband and got next to the man for a picture. She smiled and shook his hand, reluctantly letting him go before walking into the diner.

"...believe he was here. That's crazy." She was still in conversation with her husband. Her chubby face was flushed with excitement. "Ah, two please," she said to Robert.

He started them towards a table and asked, "Ma'am, who was that guy in the lot?"

She looked at him like he was covered in snakes. "You mean, you don't know who that was?"

Robert shook his head, putting their placemats down as they took their seats.

"Huh, kids these days and their rap/crap music." She looked at her husband, who was searching the menu. "That was Clayton Gentry, the greatest country music singer ever. We just saw him last night." She opened her menu and without looking at him said, "I'll take chocolate milk and he'll have a coffee."

Robert didn't even acknowledge her, just walked away to get their drinks. He grabbed the bill holder in his apron, the one Clayton had given him. He opened it and smiled. Inside were five $100 bills.

Today was going to be a good day.

---

Robert was right, it was a good day and only getting better. His shift continued like normal. He had a few more tables and got decent tips, but nothing compared to the first one. It was more than he'd make in some months, let alone a day.

Kitty came in and relieved him at 10 am and he headed home.

Even the drive home was good. It was bright and sunny, the first hints of the approaching summer. He even seemed to hit every green light on the way back. His phone went off, but he couldn't afford a ticket, so he ignored the text message. Normally, he would've pulled over and checked it. Every message filled him with dread, but since his mother's condition seemed to be getting better, he waited.

Robert pulled into the driveway, taking his phone from the cupholder. It was from his mother.

'Feeling even better today. Called the doctor and he said he could get me in at 9:45. Call you later.'

Robert smiled reading the message and wrote back.

'That's great. I hope you have good news. Keep me posted.'

He walked into the house, which for the first time in a long time, was empty. He tossed his keys on the table and looked through the mail. The amount of outstanding bills was dwindling and with the big tip he'd gotten, he could knock out a few more. Robert opened the refrigerator and took out cold cuts. He was making a sandwich when his phone rang.

"Jordan?" he questioned himself, looking at his friend's name flashing on his cell phone screen. He could count on one hand the amount of times his friends called him. Text was their preferred method. "Hello," Robert said.

"Are you watching the fucking news? Or have you been on any social media at all?"

Robert had accounts on the big three in social media, but hadn't had time to check anything that morning. He wandered into the living room, his partially made sandwich sitting on the counter.

"No, why, what's up?" He could hear Jordan laughing on the other line.

"Dude, fucking Mike. Dirty little perv."

Robert grabbed the remote and turned on the TV.

"...an employee brought it to the attention of the police earlier," the

CHAPTER 20 | 193

news anchor said. "This morning, local and Federal agents executed a search warrant at the residence of Michael Talb." A picture of Mike, it looked like the one from his L-Mart ID, flashed on the screen. "An unidentified source stated numerous flash drives, computers and hard drives were recovered as evidence. They are believed to contain illicit images of child pornography and hidden camera photos of women and girls. This all stemming from an alert employee of L-Mart." The female anchor shuffled her notes, clearly looking disturbed. Her male counterpart, who looked like he was half plastic, jumped in.

"Yes, truly a disturbed individual and we're thankful the police were able to get him." He turned to another camera. "In other news—"

Robert flipped it off. When Darren showed him the camera he knew it was Mike's. Sure, it could've been a customer's or another employee, but deep down he knew the truth.

"What the fuck?" muttered Robert, smiling ear to ear.

"I know, right? I knew he wasn't getting any pussy, but to watch chicks piss and shit. Bleh, what a weirdo. Not to mention what they said about the kiddy porn. I hope someone kicks the fuck out of him in jail."

If Robert could get him in a particular basement his fate would be far worse.

"Yeah, seriously. No wonder Sarah always stayed away from him."

"And every other female on the planet. Oh well, I guess work will be quite interesting tomorrow," said Jordan.

"We'll see." Robert's phone beeped. He looked at the screen seeing his mother calling. "Hey, bro, my mom's calling me."

"No problem, I'll see you tomorrow."

Robert didn't reply as he hurriedly answered his mother's call.

"Mom, what's going on?"

"It's gone!" she yelled.

Robert, for the first time in a long time, shed tears of joy. He could feel them sliding down his face.

"Gone?" His voice cracked. "Gone, gone?"

"Gone, fucking gone!" she shouted. "The doctors have never seen anything like it. In fact, they want to do a study on me. This, will of course, be accompanied by more testing, but they said it would be a paid study. First, I have to go back for a few more minor tests, but right now, I'm in the clear," she was crying, almost choking on her words. "Robert, it's a miracle. God has given me a second chance at life."

He wept harder, knowing the truth, but not caring. He had her back from the brink of death.

"I hope you don't have any plans tonight because I'm cooking a big dinner. I'm going to call Cardinal Carafa and give him the news. Tell him how prayer saved me. Hopefully he'll be able to make it for dinner."

"Mom, that's great. I can't wait to hear all about it when you get home."

"I'm just leaving the office now and heading to the store. I'll be home in an hour or so."

"Ok. I love you and be careful," Robert said.

"Love you too." The line went dead.

---

When Helen said she was making a big dinner, she wasn't lying.

Robert watched her (she wouldn't let him help in the kitchen) float around like an angelic chef.

Every burner had a pot or pan on it. Delicious smells filled their house when only days ago it smelled like death.

With every meal, she gained a little weight and looked just a little healthier. It wasn't so much her appearance, but her attitude. She'd been given a new lease on life and wasn't wasting a second. As soon as she walked in the door from shopping and put the groceries away, Helen jumped right on the computer and started job hunting. Robert told her about the extra money he'd made that day and they'd be fine on bills for another month, but she insisted.

Robert sat on the couch, the TV volume low, holding a paperback in his hand. He loved to read, but since his mother had taken ill, his mind would wander. Now, he was able to focus just a little better, getting back to his first love of the written word. Headlights flashed through the window.

"Rob, the Cardinal is here," his mother yelled from the kitchen. "Can you let him in?"

"Sure, Mom," he said, already getting up. He slid a bookmark into the book and set it down.

Robert opened the door just as the Cardinal was preparing to knock.

"Cardinal, how nice to see you," said Robert, smiling.

"Hello, Robert," the holy man replied. He took a few sniffs. "Wow, it smells phenomenal." He walked in. "I'm glad I made the drive." He stepped by Robert and paused. He took another sniff, like a dog testing the air. His brow furrowed. "Were you burning matches?"

Robert smelled himself, checking to make sure he'd put deodorant on after his shower. He smelled fine, at least to his own nose.

"Nope, unless Mom's burning dinner."

"I heard that," she yelled from the kitchen.

"Hmm, maybe it was just a phantom smell." He smiled, but it looked forced. His eyes seemed to bore into Robert, searching. His gaze wasn't held long, but it was forceful. In an instant, it was over. "Oh, here," he said, handing him a bottle in a brown bag. "A little bit of the sacrament for dinner."

Robert took the wine from the bag, looking at the label like he had any idea if it was good or not. His choice of alcohol was cheap beer, when he actually drank.

"Cardinal." His mother glided out of the kitchen. Her hair was pulled back in a loose ponytail. She looked ten years younger. She hugged her old friend and kissed him on the cheek.

"Oh, Helen, you look wonderful," he said, holding her tight. "And the food," he rubbed his belly, "smells delicious." He backed away, holding her shoulders, taking her in.

She was starting to tear up.

"Dinner is ready and I don't want it to get cold," she said, wiping a tear from the corner of her eye. She floated back into the kitchen and began putting dishes on the table.

Dinner, as expected, was great. They ate and drank, sharing stories and updates.

"It's a miracle, Cardinal. It truly is." Helen's cheeks were flushed. She only had a half a glass of wine, but her tolerance was low.

Cardinal Carafa looked at her, smiling and said, "God and the power of prayer is the most powerful medicine there is."

Robert almost vomited, the image of Belphegor raping and butchering Sarah burst into his mind. The juice from his steak turned viscous, congealing into blood before his eyes. His gorge was rising.

"Robert, are you ok?" asked the Cardinal.

He snapped out of his gore-filled daydream and his stomach settled instantly. Quickly, he put a fist to his chest and stifled a burp.

"Yes, sorry. Just ate too fast."

`Carafa's eyes flashed to Robert's plate and back to his mother.

It was in that instant Robert knew the Cardinal had figured out his secret. He didn't know how, but somehow the man was on to him. Call it the power of God or whatever, but he knew. Robert just hoped he could make it through the rest of dinner and dessert without puking.

## 21

Robert made it through dinner without embarrassing himself. It turned out to be a pleasant evening. Cardinal Carafa left with hugs, kisses, and plenty of leftovers. He told them to call him with any news and he'd be in touch.

Robert slept like a baby, no nightmares, and woke up feeling refreshed. He even beat his alarm. He was sitting at the kitchen table eating breakfast and absently scrolling through social media.

Mike's arrest was still fresh and every other post was about him. Some people said they had a feeling, some girls saying what a creep he was to them.

A bowl of cereal never tasted so good as it did right then. He was just about to click on a link for some obscure product, when his phone started to ring. It was the L-Mart main line. Panicked, he looked at the clock above the stove. It was only 9 am and he didn't have to be in until 11 am, so he knew he wasn't late. He answered with his heart in his throat.

"Hello," he said.

"Is this Robert Sinclair?"

Robert had heard the voice before, but couldn't place it. "Yes, this is he."

"Hi, Robert. This is Frank Escala, the regional manager of your L-Mart store."

Robert hadn't seen their regional manager since he'd been hired. He came through for an inspection and they were briefly introduced. L-Mart's managerial ranks were a little odd. Each store had three assistant managers, one of which was the executive. The executive was the real boss of the store. The other two were shift managers, in charge of scheduling and so on. Every couple of stores had a regional manager, who oversaw them all. He was the head honcho and could hire and fire.

"Oh hello, sir," Robert said, taken aback.

Frank laughed on the phone. "No need for the sirs, especially over the phone. Mr. Escala or Frank will do." He paused, the sound of rustling paper in the background. "I see you're supposed to be in at eleven, is there any way you could come in an hour early?"

He had nothing else going on and just needed to take a quick shower.

"Sure, sir. I mean Mr. Escala."

"Great, meet me in the employee break room at ten."

"Sounds good," Robert said, hanging up.

Robert was on edge. The call seemed innocent enough and the man was pleasant, but with Sarah's abrupt departure and Mike's scandal, he couldn't be sure. Besides, he was the last one to clean the bathroom before the camera was found. Did they think he had anything to do with it?

He dumped the few remaining soggy bits of cereal down the drain and headed upstairs. He took a shower, got dressed and peeked in on his mother. She was asleep, a smile on her face. Robert smiled too and quietly walked down the stairs.

---

ROBERT WAS EARLY for the meeting. He made sure to wear the cleanest uniform he had and his name tag was straight. He even combed his usually messy hair.

## CHAPTER 21 | 199

The store was abuzz with chatter about Mike, some people saying they never saw it coming, others saying he should've been locked up a long time ago. Either way, the reign of Mike Talb was over.

When he walked into the employee locker room, he noticed Sarah's locker ajar. Absently, he pushed it open. Empty. Just like that, she was a memory. Another pass-through in the corporate world of retail like many before her.

Robert checked his hair and made sure he didn't have a cliffhanger in his nose with his small locker mirror. He took a deep, hopefully calming, breath and walked into the break room.

Mr. Escala and the other two assistant managers, Ryan and Kim, sat talking at a table. They stopped when he walked in. Ryan nodded to Mr. Escala.

"Hello, Robert," the manager said, standing to shake his hand. Frank Escala was short, with a horseshoe pattern baldness. His slight gut pressed against a white dress shirt that looked like it came from L-Mart. He was clean-shaven and almost had an ageless look about him. He was either a sloppy 25-year-old or fairly young 45-year-old.

"Hello, Mr. Escala." Robert would lay off calling him sir, but Frank was just too personal. They briefly shook hands. Robert turned and shook hands with the assistant managers as well.

"I'm sure you've heard about the scandal and arrest of the former assistant manager, Mike Talb." Of course Robert had. In 2019, news was at everyone's fingertips. Like it or not, it spread like fire.

Robert nodded. They all seemed jovial, but he couldn't gauge if it was happy smiles or 'we think you were part of the potty cam and you're fired too' smiles. His heart was thumping like an unbalanced engine. He hoped sweat wasn't coming through on his armpits. Subconsciously he pressed them down harder against his body.

Frank opened a folder in front of him and flipped through a few papers. Robert couldn't see what was on them, but didn't strain too hard to find out.

"I'll be brief. The last hire we had for assistant manager was a complete fuck up." The assistant managers looked at their boss for just a split second at the use of his vulgarity. "We, the L-Mart team, are not looking for a repeat."

Robert was nodding, hoping to keep the conversation away from him. Maybe they just wanted to ask about Mike.

"Are you dedicated to the L-Mart team, Robert?" Frank asked.

Robert nodded, "Absolutely, sir. I mean, Mr. Escala. I've been here for a year and this is my main source of income."

Frank smiled. "That's good to hear, because I'd like to offer you the assistant manager's position." He spread his hands open and asked. "Would you like to be the new assistant manager?"

Robert looked at Kim and Ryan, who were both smiling and nodding. He always wished they worked with him instead of asshole Mike, but he made due. He was taken aback by the question, his brain still processing it. He thought he was coming in to be raked over the coals and possibly fired, not promoted. He snapped back to reality.

"Yes," he blurted, his own smile reflecting back at them. "Of course, I'm interested."

Frank stood, as did Ryan and Kim. "Excellent," he said, extending his hand. "Welcome to the managerial team."

Robert was in a fog. He shook hands, but couldn't feel flesh. It was all just motion for him. This promotion meant more hours, a higher salary and a start to a retirement.

Frank looked at his watch. "Well, this has been great, but I have another appointment I need to get to." He packed up the folder and papers, sliding them into a leather briefcase. "These two will take care of you and show you the ropes." He pointed to Kim and Ryan. "Best of luck." He started walking away and stopped. "Oh, and if you have any weird, illegal fetishes, please don't explore them in my store." He didn't smile or laugh.

Robert had to fight from grinning. The thought of Mike sitting in a jail cell was comical to say the least.

"Yes, Mr. Escala. I'm sure that will not be an issue."

Escala nodded and walked out.

"So, newbie," Ryan said, patting him on the shoulder, "let's get started."

## CHAPTER 21 | 201

THE REST of Robert's day was one of the easiest he'd ever had at L-Mart. Ryan and Kim showed him his office, which was a desk in a cramped room they all shared. It was nothing major, but it was his. They showed him all of the scheduling information and software, which was pretty basic. The hardest part for him was the inventory ordering. There was a little learning curve, but if Mike could figure it out, he should have no issues.

Word traveled quickly in the big store. Robert walked around with a big grin on his face, getting 'congrats' and 'you deserve it' from his co-workers, who were now his employees. He tried to keep Sarah out of his mind, but couldn't. His feeling of accomplishment was tarnished by what he'd done to her. Deep down, he knew he didn't earn this position. Plenty of people had been there longer than him. For some reason the corporate office had chosen him and he knew why.

Robert wasn't one to look a gift horse in the mouth and would do the job to the best of his abilities.

His day ended two hours early. Ryan and Kim had thrown a lot at him and he already had come in early. He couldn't wait to let his mother know the news.

Robert sat in his car with the windows down. The warm spring air blew through the car. It was a little hotter than he preferred, but after breathing recycled air-conditioned air all day, this was what he needed. He took his phone out and called.

"Hey, Mom," he said.

"Hi, Robert," she replied, panting.

Panic set in. "Are you OK? You sound like you're having trouble breathing."

"Oh," she took a deep breath, "I'm fine. I was cleaning the house. The floors were absolutely disgusting and needed a hard scrubbing."

Robert breathed a sigh of relief. The gift from Belphegor didn't seem real still. He was waiting for it to be ripped out from underneath him any second.

"Oh, ok. Just take it easy, ok. I know what the doctors said, but you should still relax."

"Relax? I feel like I can fly to the moon with two feathers and a prayer," she laughed. "What's up? Did you need something or just checking in?"

Robert had forgotten why he'd called and then remembered the official assistant manager badge in his locker.

"Well, I have some good news." He let a second of silence hang over the phone line.

"You've met a girl and are getting married?" Helen asked, laughing. "You know, when I got sick I thought I'd never see my grandbabies. Well, now I have a chance so, chop, chop."

Robert's mind went back to Sarah. Could he have loved her? Could she him? He knew there was something between them, making her sacrifice all the more bitter. He could be the regional manager of L-Mart, providing for their growing family. They would've had a boy and a girl, who would've been beautiful and smart. They would take family vacations to the Jersey shore every summer and save up for a big vacation here and there. He shook the vision from his eyes.

"Not quite, Mom. I'm still on the prowl," he chuckled, but it sounded forced even to him. "No, I got a promotion today. I'm the new assistant manager at L-Mart."

"Oh, Robert, that's wonderful," she beamed over the phone line. "So no more stocking shelves?"

"Nope, mostly paperwork and supervision. Plus, a decent raise in pay. I won't have to work much at the diner. Just here and there if I want to." The money at L-Mart wasn't life-changing for most people. It was a solid income if you were single or had a partner with a second line of work. The assistant manager position was different. This was a legit living wage, albeit not an extravagant one, but livable. It also meant he could catch up on bills in no time.

"I'm proud of you," she said.

Robert knew she was, but it always felt good to hear it.

"Thanks, Mom. The other reason I called is because with this position I'll need some new clothes. Nothing crazy, but a couple of decent button-up shirts and ties. I was thinking about heading over to the mall and wanted to know if you wanted to go? Maybe grab something for dinner in celebration."

She laughed. "We've been doing a lot of celebrating lately."

Sarah.

"Yes, we have," he said. The warm air was getting uncomfortable now. Images of hellfire, burning flesh and torture flashed through his mind. It was quick, like lightning, but it was clear. He turned on the air conditioner and rolled up the windows. "I'll come by and pick you up, if you want to go."

"Ah," Helen paused, "yeah, that sounds good. I need to look at clothes too. Nothing fits anymore. Plus, it would do me some good to get out of the house. I'm going to get cleaned up first."

"Ok, see you soon," he said.

"Bye."

---

ROBERT WAS NEVER a huge fan of the mall. Sure, he'd go with friends, but he didn't have money like some of them. His mother usually bought his clothes from L-Mart or another discount store. He didn't wear name brand shoes until he was in high school and even then, he was expected to get at least a year from them. Luckily, he was pretty well liked, so no one really made fun of him, but from time to time, he'd see someone look at the name of his jeans and smile.

The mall was crowded, with it being a Friday night. A new horror movie was just released and all the teenage couples were flocking to see it. They all looked so young and fresh-faced. Robert was only a few years removed from high school, but felt like the old man.

He circled the lot a few times, looking for a close spot so his mother wouldn't have to walk too far.

"Oh, just pick a spot," she said from the passenger seat. She knew what he was doing, even though he didn't say it. "I feel great." She flipped down the visor mirror to check her hair. In the couple of days since she'd recovered, her hair had been filling out at a near alarming rate. Her scalp was no longer visible and hair shined with a new life.

Robert listened to his mother and picked a spot.

The long days of summer were still months away and even at 6 pm, it was getting dark. The lights were on in the parking lot, casting an ethereal glow.

They walked through the lot, alert for any texting teenagers zipping around.

"So, Hibachi then?" Robert asked.

"Yeah, that sounds good," Helen replied, putting a hand to her stomach. "I'm starving." She looked at him. "Maybe I'll treat you for ice cream when we're done."

Robert smiled. That was more of a treat for her; he didn't have the sweet tooth like she did.

"Sounds good." They stopped at the crosswalk to cross the road around the mall.

Helen walked forward.

The truck was barreling down, but Helen was oblivious. It may have been invisible for all she knew. The darkness in the cab obscured the driver, but for a split second the truck passed under a light.

Robert saw him then. Belphegor was behind the wheel, his black eyes staring, his shark-toothed mouth grinning. Then he was out of the light and gone in the blackness of the cab. Robert's feet were cement and his throat locked, but his eyes worked perfectly. Actually, his vision seemed to narrow and focus.

The grill of the pick-up took Helen full in the face.

Time slowed down. Robert's keen sight absorbed everything like instant replay. Her nose, which was facing the truck as she looked in the last seconds of her life, crunched. It flattened into her skull, meat, blood and bone rupturing. Her teeth exploded from her mouth like red and white confetti, bordering on comical. Her neck snapped back with such violence, Robert could see the soft flesh of her throat rip as she was partially decapitated. A burp of gore erupted from her, coating her neck in crimson. She was whipped to the pavement in a flash, the back of her skull fracturing like a watermelon. Before she was sucked under the truck, Robert could see the pink and grey of her brain mixed in with her thick, healthy hair. Helen was pulled lovingly into the hot metal under the truck and dragged. A smear of skin, fat, and blood was left where she stood. Finally, the squeal of brakes broke his trance.

"Ah!" Robert screamed, not forming any words. He collapsed in the parking lot, looking at his mother's tangled corpse wrapped around the driveshaft of the truck.

Helen was twisted. Her corpse was a mangled rope of meat and clothing. Blood and other bodily fluids mixed and dripped from the mush that was once Helen Sinclair. Her disfigured face hissed as it came to rest against an exhaust pipe. A subtle smell of cooking meat permeated the air.

A primal scream, one of undeniable anguish, erupted from Robert's throat. He screamed until he felt like his lungs would collapse and then he screamed some more.

A teenage boy and girl jumped out of the truck and looked underneath. The boy began vomiting immediately and his date collapsed, her head bouncing off the road with an audible thump.

A crowd started to form. Cell phones were out, some calling 911, others recording the grisly scene.

Sirens wailed in the night, but Robert couldn't hear them. All he could hear was the laughter of the demon in his head.

## 22

Robert sat in the hospital waiting room. It was small and private, reserved for grieving families. There was a couch, chair and end table, which held a large box of tissues.

He didn't need tissues anymore. His tear ducts felt like they were dry and useless. He sat on the couch with his face in his hands. The final seconds of his mother's life played over and over in his brain, like a highlight reel. He pushed the heels of his hands against his closed eyes, stars and galaxies erupted from the darkness, but the images of his mother's mangled corpse remained. He was whispering to himself.

He never heard the door open.

"...phegor. Motherfucker. I'll kill him. Never should've done it...Sarah," he mumbled through his hands. His throat was phlegmy, but Cardinal Carafa heard more than enough.

"Robert," he said, easing the door shut behind him. He stared at the mumbling young man. "Robert," he said again, a little more force in his voice.

Robert looked up, finally realizing someone else was in the room. His eyes were red-rimmed and bloodshot. His hair was a mess, sticking up in different angles.

Cardinal Carafa put a hand on his shoulder.

"May I sit?"

Robert didn't speak, but did slide over. The couch groaned under the weight of the two men.

Carafa's nose twisted; there was a smell of sulfur and shit in the air around Robert. He did his best to control his reaction, knowing it was a smell not of this world. He was silent, his hand still on Robert's shoulder. If he rushed into it, the younger man would clam up and the truth would never come out.

"Robert," Carafa said, squeezing his shoulder.

Robert, who had placed his face into his hands again, looked at the Cardinal.

"I know this is a difficult time for you and for me as well." He paused, looking him in the eyes. "The funeral arrangements have already been made, so there's no need to worry about them."

Burying his mother had been the furthest thing from his mind, but it was something he knew he'd have to address sooner than later. It was hard to believe she was gone. Fresh tears, tears he thought were long gone, welled up in his red eyes. They fell to his pants, making dark marks on them.

Carafa took his hand off Robert's shoulder and grabbed the box of tissues.

Robert removed one and blotted his eyes. He sighed and looked up at the Cardinal.

"It's my fault," he whispered. Robert hadn't said a word since talking with the police, but even that was brief. He didn't realize how raw his throat was. He turned his body as best he could so he was facing the Cardinal.

Carafa didn't speak, but looked at the grieving young man and nodded for him to go on.

"It's my fault she's dead and there's nothing I can do to take it back."

Carafa reached up and touched the crucifix around his neck. It was a relief, the power of God in its metal.

"You can't change the past, but we mustn't let this get out of control." He hoped his gentle prod was enough to get him to open up.

Robert looked at the Cardinal in silence. The flood gates opened and he told him everything.

---

CARAFA SAT AT A RED LIGHT. The crimson eye stared at him and bore into his brain. His eyes drooped, but his mind raced over what Robert had told him.

It was nearing 2 am and he'd just dropped Robert off at home. There was nothing more to be done at the hospital. The young man had signed all the necessary paperwork, releasing the remains of his mother to the funeral home. The funeral director who came to the hospital, a mid-thirties, muscular woman, told him to call them in the morning to set up the date and times for the services.

The light clicked to green and Carafa moved through the intersection. Ahead was the motel. There was no way he was going to be able to drive back to New York City at that time of the night. He'd woken one of the priests at his parish, telling him to cover his masses for the next few days. He didn't specify why, just telling the man he had official business of the church.

Carafa grabbed the small duffle bag, something he kept packed for instances like this and walked into the office.

Minutes later he was standing under the lukewarm water in the shower.

He had a phone call to make, but he didn't know how to proceed. He knew his old friend would be fast asleep, but this was an emergency, and didn't mind waking him up. Explaining to him what he'd been told and what he planned to do was a different story.

Carafa dried off and dressed in an old college t-shirt and a pair of sweatpants. He unlocked his cell phone and scrolled through his contacts. He found the one he was looking for, took a deep, calming breath, and dialed.

CARDINAL HECTOR TIGO was fast asleep. He didn't normally dream, at least ones he could remember, but there was a shrill sound invading his sleep. His weary eyes opened, and reality came back into focus. On his nightstand, his phone was lit up and ringing.

He picked it up, the light from the screen making his eyes water. It was Philip Carafa and it was 3 am. Something was certainly wrong with his old friend. He answered.

"Philip?" he mumbled. He sat up and looked for the desk lamp next to the bed. His eyes were already assaulted by the phone, so the soft white light didn't bother him.

"Hector," Carafa said on the other line. "I'm sorry to wake you, but this is an emergency."

"My friend, are you ok?" He was finally awake, blinking the last of the sleep from his eyes.

"Yes, but I have a problem and need your help."

"Anything."

"I need the blade."

Hector gasped, loud enough for Philip to hear him on the other line.

Philip and Hector had come up through the seminary together. As young priests, they devoted their lives to the Church. Often they would do missionary work, traveling around the world spreading the word of God. Their work was good, but it also exposed them to the evils of the world. Murder, genocide, famine, war; these were just some of the unpleasant things they saw in their travels. Both were devout to the faith and knew if there was good in the world, evil was the counterpart. If there were angels, there were demons. Each of them made it their life's work to study these otherworldly beasts, writing many papers on the subject. The other priests, some not as devout, thought they were two boys chasing shadows of myths and metaphors. They knew differently. In each area of the world where pain was abundant, talks of demons spread. No one had seen anything, but rumors of possessions, animal death, and corpse desecration ran rampant.

When they were in their tenth year of study and priesthood, they were summoned to an archeological dig in Syria. The two of them flew to the country, Hector designated the lead priest on the dig. The ruins of an old church had been found when a construction company broke ground for a building. One of the machine operators, a devout Catholic, saw the markings immediately and halted the dig. His boss wasn't happy, but desecration of any holy site was bad karma. Many old texts and scrolls were discovered. They were quickly secured and sealed, preserving them. Something else was discovered, something untouched by age. A knife. This was no ordinary knife, and both men knew that. Its handle was pure black, but neither could identify the material. It looked smooth and unwieldy, but in their hands, it felt snug and secure. The cross piece was red metal, a substance neither had ever seen before. It looked as if it were plated metal, but that was a modern technique and this was hundreds, if not a thousand years old. The blade was polished to a mirror finish and had just a slight wave to it, giving it a wide belly. Each of them looked at it with awe. They knew right away what they held. A true Seraph blade. Something neither had seen, only read about in their studies.

They made a possible career-ending decision and took the blade from the dig. A weapon of legend didn't belong in the bowels of the Vatican. No, it was meant for the hands of men who would wield it against evil. Both of them risked everything but did it together. The blade was never archived with the rest of the items found on the expedition, and with a couple of small bribes, Hector was able to smuggle it back to the US.

Hector swung his legs off his bed, his bare feet searching for his slippers. He was wide awake now.

"The blade from Syria?" he asked, as if there were any other.

Philip paused and for a second Hector prayed his old friend would tell him this was all a joke and he had a few too many sips of the sacrament.

"Yes."

Hector put the phone on speaker and rested it on his dresser. He opened a middle drawer and pulled his clothes out. The bottom of it was false, only covered by a thin wooden panel. He removed the panel, his eyes taking in a cloth-wrapped object.

"I think I have one," Philip said. He swallowed hard. He wanted to say demon, but the word was bitter on his lips. "Truthfully, I'm terrified, which is why I haven't confronted it yet."

Hector unwrapped the knife. It almost sang to him. The blade seemed to glow from a hidden, ethereal light. Gently, he fingered the blade; not the edge, only the spine. He feared what power it held.

"Hector, are you there?"

Hector snapped out of his trance, covering the blade and replacing the false bottom.

"Yes, I'm here," he piled his clothes back in. He'd refold them in the morning, which was fast approaching. "It's just a lot to take in. An old friend calls you in the middle of the night to tell you he may need an ancient blade, whose only purpose is to kill denizens of Hell." He chuckled a little, taking in the totality of the conversation.

"I'm leaving first thing in the morning," he paused, "which is in a few hours."

"You're really serious, aren't you?" Up until this point, Hector thought this could still be an elaborate joke. He wasn't convinced yet.

"Yes, I'm serious. The drive should take about 12 hours or so. Have a bottle of bourbon in the freezer when I get there and I'll fill you in on everything."

Hector laughed, sitting back on his bed. He kicked his slippers off, but didn't lay down.

"Oh, don't worry, I have that covered, my friend."

"Great, I'll see you tonight."

"Get some sleep, Philip."

"I will," and without another word, Philip hung up.

Hector checked to make sure the line was dead. He dialed a number he knew by heart. A number that wasn't saved in his phone and would be deleted after the call. It would be 9 am where he was calling, so his contact should be awake.

The phone rang twice before being picked up.

"Ciao, Hector," a husky voice said in Italian.

"We need to talk."

## 23

THREE DAYS LATER, Robert buried his mother.

The day of the funeral was beautiful—seventy-five degrees, birds chirping, the smell of fresh-cut grass in the air, and budding trees opening to the world.

Robert smelled none of it. In the funeral home, he only smelled death. Death and the sickly, sweet smell of flowers. It wasn't the pleasant smell of a corsage or even a bouquet. No, it was a cloying odor that permeated every pore in his body. It made him want to vomit.

He stood near the casket, staring straight ahead. Pictures of him and his mother decorated the room and, of course, the flowers. He asked for people to donate money to cancer research instead of flowers; clearly they didn't listen.

One by one, the few friends Helen had filtered through the old house turned into a funeral home. The floor creaked under their weight as they made their way to the closed casket.

"I'm so sorry for your loss," an older woman, who had red lipstick on her teeth, said to him.

He'd never seen her before and would never see her again, but he played the part.

"Thank you," he said, offering his cheek to hers. Her whiskers poked him. He was electric, a live wire. His thirst for the death of Belphegor ran through him like a lava flow, hot and unstoppable. Waiting the three days for Carafa to return was the hardest time he'd ever had. He wanted to go to Josef's and summon the creature, to fight him, rip him to shreds, but knew better. There was nothing he could do, only sacrifice himself to the beast.

"So sorry," an old man, the husband of lipstick-teeth, said. He shook Robert's hand with bone-crunching strength.

"Thank you, sir." Robert winced, but part of him liked the dull ache. It made him feel alive. Since the accident, he'd been numb. L-Mart had given him some time off, but it didn't matter, he had no intentions of going back to work. His days were filled with nothingness, only brooding. He did the minimum for the funeral arrangements; most of it was taken care of by Cardinal Carafa.

Esther knelt before the casket. She bowed her head in prayer, saying her goodbyes to her friend.

"Oh, Bobby, I'm so sorry," she said, wrapping him in a tight hug.

She was the only one he was happy to see made it. He hugged her back.

"Thank you, Esther. She truly did love her time with you," he said, staring at her moist eyes.

Both of them turned as Cardinal Carafa walked out of the backroom. He would give a small eulogy before the services were moved to the cemetery.

The room quieted and people took their seats.

Robert sat in an old, cushioned chair as if he were special. He locked eyes with the large picture of his mother, the one sitting on her casket. Carafa began talking, but Robert didn't hear a word.

---

Robert drove home in silence. He was on autopilot, navigating the car through sparse traffic. The funeral was over and his mother was in the cold, dark ground.

At the burial site he thought he was going to lose his composure, but didn't. He didn't show any emotion at all, just a blank stare at the gaping hole full of wet roots and bugs. Bugs which would eventually find their way into the casket, making a meal of his mother's corpse. When Carafa spoke about the afterlife and all of the angels and saints, Robert thought of fire and pain. He'd seen what waited on the other side: demons, pestilence, torture and pain. He didn't even know if he believed in heaven, but he certainly knew there was Hell. He'd seen the dark black eyes, sharp teeth and putrid phallus of one of the seven princes of Hell. That was a certainty.

Before he even realized what he was doing, Robert pulled into his driveway. He sat in the car with it running, radio off, and staring.

Before the services, Carafa stopped by his house and spoke with him. That conversation still clung fresh in his memory.

"I can kill it," Carafa had told him a few hours ago.

It was the first time Robert had seen him since the hospital. The old Cardinal looked rough, like he hadn't slept in days. Robert knew he didn't look much better.

"Josef said there was no way to kill it, only banish it back into the stone," Robert told him. He was sitting on the couch, surrounded by the scent and memories of his mother.

"Robert," the old man said, looking at him. His eyes were drooping and bloodshot. Even his skin looked unhealthy. "I've dedicated my life to the church and keeping these foul beasts in Hell."

Carafa sighed. Could he kill Belphegor? Did he even have the strength in his senior citizen body to fight one of Hell's princes? With the Seraph blade, he believed he could. He prayed he could.

"I can do it. You must trust me."

Robert was looking at a picture of him and his mother at a petting zoo when he was a kid. They were both laughing as he hand-fed a llama tiny pellets of feed. It was one of the few times they were able to afford a little trip. He remembered making the twenty-five-cent handful of feed last as long as he could. He broke his gaze and looked at Carafa.

"I know you can, but do not underestimate this motherfucker,"

Robert whispered. He had to clear his throat, but didn't. The slight discomfort was his penance.

Carafa didn't wince at the profanity. He'd heard it all and knew if he was truly dealing with an Arch Demon, he would hear much worse.

"We'll get this done tonight," he told Robert. "But first, we need to escort your mother into her eternal rest." Carafa stood, his knees popping. He left without another word, leaving Robert alone with his thoughts.

Robert reached up and turned the car off. The sun was low in the sky, but it was far from night. He and Carafa didn't pick a time, but Robert knew he'd come. Tonight, they'd end this, one way or another.

---

THREE HOURS later headlights cut through the open window of the house.

Robert was sitting on the couch again, an untouched plate of Esther's lasagna in front of him. He was still wearing his suit, which was wrinkled. His tie was somewhere and the collar of his shirt was open.

Carafa didn't knock, just walked in. This task was above formalities.

"Ready?" he asked Robert.

He wasn't, but at this point, there was no turning back. Robert stood, leaving the food on the coffee table.

Carafa wore a long, black jacket, but Robert could see the hem of his robes underneath. He'd swapped out his normal, white vestments for black. On his head, he wore what looked like a red yarmulke, but Robert knew it wasn't. His mother had told him years ago Catholic Cardinals wore a hat similar to that of Jewish men, but it was called a Zucchetto.

"Yes," Robert replied, his voice flat. The two men left the house, closing, but not locking, the front door.

JOSEF'S HOUSE stood silent and foreboding. Robert had been in there a few times, but this was different. The house had changed. He couldn't put his finger on it, but it had. Sure, it had windows and doors, but it also contained something else. It seemed like the house was its own entity, as if it were grinning at them, welcoming them like a spider welcoming a fly to its web.

*Won't you come in?*

The front door was unlocked. Robert opened it with a clammy hand. He expected the demon to attack from the darkness, but nothing happened. The stale air wafted out, mixing with the spring night. Polluting the freshness of it with its cloying scent of death.

Of course, there was no smell of death as there weren't any corpses to decompose.

Robert flicked on the switch and recoiled. A shadow cast by the chair looked like a crouching beast. He stared at it for just a moment as the shadow shifted on its own. What was once a coiled demon lurking in the corner, was again the shadow of a chair.

Somehow, from the depths of his stone prison, Belphegor knew they were there. Not only that, but knew what they were there for.

Carafa looked around. He had a leather bag in his left hand. Casually, as if at a realtor's open house, he walked around. He touched pictures, books and other nick-nacks of Josef's. His eyes lingered on some more than others. Finally, he reached the small kitchen.

He looked around, but didn't see anything that stood out to him. The table, which once was covered with pictures of death from the Holocaust, was bare. An acidic burp rose up from the depths of his stomach. Something chunky and wriggling came with it. Carafa swallowed by instinct, the wriggling moving back down. He knew there was nothing in his throat, but the power of the demon was strong. He'd have to be stronger. With a sickening feeling, he walked away from the table and turned to Robert.

"Robert," he said, trying to get the young man's attention.

Robert's eyes were locked on a framed picture next to Josef's chair in the living room. It was a picture of his family before the war, before the camp and before death swept them all away.

"Robert," Carafa said again, walking the few steps from the open kitchen area into the living room.

He snapped out of his trance and looked at the Cardinal.

"Yeah?" he questioned, his head swimming as if he had a few drinks.

Carafa stood face to face with him. He set his bag on the ground and put his hands on Robert's shoulders.

Robert could feel the clamminess through his clothes.

"In my car is a box with an address on it." He swallowed hard, thinking of what to say. "If this goes," a deep breath, "wrong, please put everything in the box and mail it."

Robert stared at him like he wasn't real. As if the last few weeks, no the last year, hadn't been real.

"Do you understand?" Carafa asked, shaking him slightly.

It wasn't a lot, but enough to jar Robert back to reality. He blinked, the realization of what they were about to do hit him like a truck.

"Yes, I understand." His resolve was creeping back in.

"If he bests me, dispel him and get rid of it all." Carafa still wasn't sure Robert understood. "Say it back," he ordered.

"If he bests you, I will take the box from the car and send it all away."

Carafa patted him on the shoulder, "Good. Let us finish this." He picked up his bag and walked to the basement door.

Robert followed him, knowing what awaited in the darkness below.

Carafa opened the door. The steps were bathed in shadow. He reached for the light switch. In every horror or suspense movie ever written, the light would've never worked. For a second, he didn't think it would. The switch turned on, a urine-colored bulb lighting the way. He couldn't see past the bottom of the stairs, but it looked like the rest of the room was lit up as well.

Carafa's body was slick with the cold sweat of righteousness. He began walking down the stairs.

Corruption, foulness, greed, lust, murder and shit were in the air. He knew it wasn't something Robert could smell. The boy wasn't close to God, but Carafa was...at least he hoped he was. Each step was slow and deliberate. He whispered a prayer, one of protection, under his breath with each labored step.

Robert followed, dreading seeing the demon again. Each step felt like one closer to death, like the condemned walking to the gallows.

Carafa reached the bottom and looked at the display in front of him.

The pentagram was drawn, never touched by Robert. It was surrounded by candles, which still had some life left in them. The writing on the wall looked the same as before, but to the Cardinal it was all new and macabre. A book, a very old book, sat on a stand in front of the circle. These things were all secondary to what was in the center of the star. A piece of black hell sat, hunched as if it were waiting to pounce. Evil poured from it, seething into the air like poison. To the naked eye, it was just a chunk of volcanic stone, but he knew better.

Robert walked in behind Carafa, watching the man take everything in. He didn't panic or seem disturbed, but looked around like he was in a museum. Inside he may have been a maelstrom, but outside he was a still pond.

Carafa took off his overcoat, looking for somewhere to set it.

"Here," Robert said, stepping forward to take the coat.

"Thanks," Carafa said, his voice betraying his calmness with just the slightest of tremors.

Robert hung it over an old chair, careful not to let it hit the ground.

Carafa was dressed for battle. Not in the armor and plate-metal sense, but the sense of holiness. His long vestments were black, a deep black Robert had never known existed. Almost as black as the stone prison of the demon. Around his waist was a purple sash, giving him a pirate look. Blood red buttons tip-toed up the center of his body, all the way to his throat. Hanging from his neck was a crucifix, but it wasn't gold. It didn't even look like metal, but more like bone. His ring, the one given to him by the Pope when he ascended to Cardinal, reflected the gloomy light of the room. Around his neck and shoulders sat a purple stole. The holy relic was embroidered with gold stitching and rested on the chest of the Cardinal.

Carafa rested his bag on the stand, covering the book used to summon Belphegor. He opened it, removing three items.

The first was a crystal vial of holy water. The crystal seemed to glow, but it must've been a trick of the light.

The second was a Bible. It was old, the edges of the paper blood red, looking like it was just dyed. The cover was soft leather, with a deep-etched cross in the center. Nothing else adorned it.

The third item made Robert shiver. It was a knife, but not any knife. It was the most beautiful piece of weaponry he'd ever seen. The curve of the blade was almost sexual and the white metal looked otherworldly in its luster.

Carafa slid the knife, ever so carefully, into the sash on his waist. The tip of the blade stuck out just past the bottom of the fabric. He opened the Bible, resting it in his left hand. Silently, he began an incantation. He closed his eyes and spoke softly. His right hand was held up as if projecting his holiness over the area.

Robert watched, the feeling of dread growing. He knew soon what would happen and there was nothing he could do to stop it. It was like being on death row, watching the days tick by, knowing your date with the executioner was coming.

Carafa slammed the bible closed and opened his eyes. He felt like a live wire, as if his body were buzzing with electricity. The power of God was with him. The knife, tucked firmly against his body, seemed to hum like it was alive. Without saying a word he held the Bible out.

Robert stepped forward and took it, setting it on the chair.

Carafa handed him the holy water. "Only if I fall," he said, not wanting to use the word *die*.

Robert nodded, taking the vial. It was cold, feeling like it should have a layer of frost on it.

Carafa looked at the closed book on the stand. It was a vile tome, a disgrace to his religion and all of humanity. The touch of the cover repulsed him, like a handful of chunky vomit. His throat clicked as he swallowed and opened the book. Revulsion washed over him like nothing before. For a fleeting moment, he didn't think he could go on. He thought of just taking the stone and sending it away for someone stronger to deal with it. No, this was his problem. He was a man of God, a soldier of the righteous, and would fight evil and win.

Carafa flipped the pages and read.

"Te invoco a profundis inferni." The words were filth on his tongue, but he continued.

The stone began to weep. Black ooze poured forth. It rose, shifting from black to red as it took a humanoid shape. With it came a stench of shit and sulfur. Fat, black flies buzzed around the room.

Robert swatted one, watching its bloated corpse smear on the wall. He didn't know if they escaped the circle or were drawn to the smell. Either way, they were floating around the room, impossibly small wings carrying their fat bodies.

Carafa held his nerve as the demon entered their realm.

Belphegor was pestilence. His nude body, slick with sores and pus, crawled with maggots. Parts of his demonic skin seemed to pulse with them. Fissures of his corrupted flesh split, spilling ichor and more vermin. His clawed hands grabbed at the pile of fat bugs and ripped them free. Greedily, he ate, the rows of teeth making quick work of the writhing mass. Some crunched, some squished, but they all became another meal for the demon.

"You have brought me another treat so soon?" Belphegor asked, his black eyes flicking from Carafa to Robert. "What, are you trying to reverse Mommy's accident?" He smiled his wide smile, bits of blackness and chitin, stuck in his teeth. "Oh, even I can't help her now." He put a claw to his chin, as if in thought. "Well, I can't help her in your world, but in my world…" he grinned. One hand reached down and began stroking his large, pus dripping penis. The grotesque phallus wept fluid, not from the opening, but the mass of sores. Eight legs appeared at the ragged piss-slit on his member, poking out. Slowly, the arachnid began spreading the opening, bringing forth putrid slime. Wider and wider the hole became until a tarantula worked its way out of Belphegor's body. The bristly fibers of the spider were coated in gore and filth, but it didn't stop the demon from plucking it from his shaft and devouring it.

Robert tried blocking it out, but couldn't. This he couldn't ignore. Tears of rage welled up in his eyes.

"The truck did me a favor," the demon said. "It gave her a bunch of extra holes. Believe me, I've tried them all." A twitching spider leg poked out from his teeth. He was fully erect now, using the slime from his numerous sores as a lubricant.

"Robert," Belphegor said, but not in his voice. He was using Helen's voice. "Robert, please help me."

He stepped forward, almost shoulder to shoulder with Carafa, who seemed locked in a trance.

"Mom!" he yelled, remembering the barrier. "Leave her alone, you fucker!"

"Robert, please. Get me out of here. They hurt me, oh do they hurt me. The things they make me do." She was crying, but not hard. It was a defeated sobbing. "And the teeth. Oh, Robert, they bite me and bite me, taking chunks that always grow back." The pain in her voice was almost too much to bear. "And then they," her voice shifted, a blend of hers and Belphegor's, "fuck me." The demon laughed, bloody spit spraying from his mouth. "They fuck me and fuck me. They use their claws and teeth to open me, keeping it slick with blood." Her gravelly voice cut Robert to the bone. "And guess what? I fucking love it!" The crying turned to laughing. "I fucking love it because I am a slut, a fucking whore. How do you think you were born? I never knew your father because I fucked everyone. I was so full of cum, you could be anyone's."

Robert shook his head, willing his ears to close. Praying for deafness.

"Fuck you!" he yelled at the demon, who was still stroking himself.

Belphegor laughed as he ejaculated. Instead of semen, a thick rope of viscous blood shot from him, hitting the invisible barrier. It slid down, seemingly floating in mid-air. Tiny, black worms wriggled in it.

Robert clenched his fists and took a step forward.

A strong hand grabbed his shoulder and stopped him from crossing.

"No, I will handle this," Carafa said, breaking his trance.

"Oh, you will?" Belphegor licked his teeth, cutting his tongue. His blood ran down his chin. "I will relish the fight, Red Man." He turned his gaze to Robert. "Next time bring me another girl. They are more fun." He shook his now flaccid penis at them, drops of blood flying from his urethra.

Carafa pulled the knife from his sash. The holy light seemed to be gone from the blade, but he had plenty of faith in his body. He mumbled a prayer and stepped forward.

The barrier burned and hissed as his holy vestments penetrated them.

Belphegor backed up, seeing the knife. He circled the man, head low and claws ready. He was hoping to ram his crooked horns into the holy man's belly. That was one of his favorite ways to kill his food.

Carafa was holding the knife tight, the handle felt slick and loose. He thought back to the first time he'd held the ancient blade. How snug it felt, no matter how sweaty or grimy his grip was. His heart sank.

It was a fake. An expensive replica given to an old man who was seen as paranoid and delirious.

Belphegor knew it. He could see it on Carafa's face. He knew it as soon as the man crossed the barrier. He was carrying nothing more than a toothpick, which he'd use after his meal.

Carafa turned, pushing into the barrier. The invisible wall may have been brick for all the give it had. His nose broke on nothing more than thin air.

Robert's eyes went wide, looking over Carafa's shoulder.

Carafa turned as the demon attacked. He thrust the blade forward, striking corrupted flesh and sinking it to the hilt. It did nothing.

Belphegor's right horn took Carafa full on in the mouth. His teeth shattered and his tongue was ripped free at the root. The wooden-like horn burst from his cheek, taking the tongue with it. Belphegor bit down on Carafa's right shoulder. Bones crunched as he severed the arm, it falling to the floor in a shower of blood. He collapsed on the man, dragging him to the ground. The force and weight of the demon caused Carafa's leg to shatter, white bone poking from his black garb. Belphegor ripped into his throat, eating with greed, the knife still sticking from his belly.

Robert watched bewildered as the beast ate the man who was supposed to be the savior. The coldness of the holy water brought him back to his senses. He uncapped the vial.

Belphegor, sensing he was about to be dispelled, looked up. Gore dripped from his mouth, shreds of flesh hanging from his teeth. The bone crucifix was wedged in there as well, a final insult to the Church.

"See you soon," the demon said, smiling a bloody smile.

Robert threw the vial, the holy water splashing on the demon and corpse of Cardinal Carafa.

Belphegor laughed as he was sent back into his prison. "Soon," he growled, turning into ooze.

---

Robert lay in his mother's bed.

The package with the stone, the book, and Cardinal Carafa's bible, were wrapped with half a roll of tape. It sat on the front steps of his house waiting for the mailman to get it in the morning. The poor mail carrier had no idea what he'd be delivering and Robert didn't care.

The bed was comfortable even though it was old. The room smelled like her. Not the sick version of her, but the healthy, vibrant version. The one he'd always remember. He had pictures spread out all over him; he'd randomly grab one here and there, weeping at the memories. Robert had to force the image of her mangled corpse wrapped in the undercarriage of the truck from his mind. Her formaldehyde-preserved body, just starting to rot, was buried deep in the earth. More importantly, her eternal soul. He knew the demon spoke lies, but it was difficult to unhear. Helen Sinclair was a great woman, a loving mother and devout Catholic. If there was a Heaven, she would be there.

# CHAPTER 23 | 225

As for him, he knew there was no room at the table of God. He thought of Sarah and the final moments of her life. Her innocence and fear. The shame of his betrayal and life snuffed from her. He didn't cry for her. He made his decision and, given the option, he would've made it again. Saving his mother was the most important thing to him and he knew what hell awaited.

Robert found the bottle of Fentanyl when he'd gotten home. It was full of the powerful narcotic, the little pills staring up at him. He sat up and opened his mouth. He upended the entire bottle down his throat. With fervor, he started to chew. He gagged on the bitter taste, but kept eating. He held a bottle of bourbon and chugged from the mouth of it. The fiery spirit burned his throat, washing the poison into his body. When his mouth was empty he threw the liquor bottle across the room. He could hear the remaining alcohol pouring onto the floor.

Robert relaxed, grabbing a handful of pictures. He shuffled through them as the drug and alcohol began slowing his pulse and breathing. His fingers touched a picture of his mother's face. It was taken at his tenth birthday party and was one of the happiest times in his life.

Blackness crept into the sides of his vision and his eyes fought to stay awake. He'd never been as tired as he was right then. Slowly, with the finality of death, his eyes closed, and there was nothing but darkness.

And then, there were flames.

# EPILOGUE

Cardinal Hector Tigo wasn't expecting any packages, so when a priest told him he had one, he was surprised.

The heavily taped box had his name on it alright, but he was still confused...until he saw the return address.

"Oh, Philip, what have you done?" he asked himself, carrying the box to his bedroom. He set it on his dresser, the dresser where the real Seraph blade was secured, and grabbed a letter opener. He sliced and cut the tape away, revealing what his friend had sent him. An envelope was on top of the items.

Hector,

Well, old friend if you're reading this, then I am dead. Do not weep for me, for I will be with our Father in the Kingdom of Heaven. My final task was to leave this to you and I hope I succeeded. These items need to be taken to the Vatican and studied, after which destroyed. Please, do not attempt to study these alone, as I have been bested by the demon. I trust your judgment and *wisdom and know without a doubt you will succeed where I have failed. Say a prayer for me, brother.*

Respectfully,

Cardinal Philip Carafa

Hector set the note down and took the items out of the box.

Evil seeped into his skin as he touched the stone. The book felt like it was alive and warm. When his fingers touched it, he could've sworn it moved. His pulse raced, and for a split second, he thought he was having a heart attack. He put everything, including Carafa's Bible back into the box. This wasn't something he could handle on his own. He grabbed his phone and began dialing.

---

"I'm sorry to ask, sir, but will I get overtime for this?" Fred asked.

Hector put his arm around the janitor's shoulders. "Fred, I would never have you stay past your shift if there was no overtime pay."

The janitor's face lit up. He'd been saving for a new TV and a couple of hours of overtime would help out. Normally he just cleaned around the church and outbuildings, but when the Cardinal asked him to help move some old pews in the basement, he couldn't say no. He needed the money.

The sound of Hector's soft slipper-like shoes was barely audible next to the heavy-soled work boots worn by Fred.

The stained-glass windows that lined the hallway were dark. Sconces, lit by light bulbs as opposed to fire, illuminated the corridor. They reached the door.

"We're getting a few boxes in the next couple of days and I wanted to get this basement straightened up before then."

Fred nodded, not really listening. He was daydreaming of watching football on a crisp, clear TV.

"Sorry it's so late, but my schedule is quite hectic."

"No worries." Fred dismissed him with a wave. "I'm happy to help out. I'd be a bad Catholic if I didn't." He turned on the light leading down the basement steps. "Ah, something stinks." He started down the stairs quicker. Hector was right on his heels. "I hope there's not a septic leak or I'm going to be here all night." He reached the bottom and turned the corner.

At first, Fred's mind couldn't comprehend what he was seeing.

Five figures stood in front of him, all of them wearing hooded black robes. Their faces were bathed in shadow and anonymity. A ring of candles burned on the floor. His eyes, finally starting to comprehend, drifted up, taking in the monster in the circle.

Hector smashed him in the back of the head, causing a starburst in his vision.

Fred stumbled forward, his arms grabbed by the figures in robes. He was barely conscious, but he could see enough. The demon paced in front of him.

Hector approached the ring of candles, his hands in his sleeves. Abruptly, he dropped to a knee.

"For you, Master," he said, lowering his head in subservience, but only for a moment.

The robed figures threw Fred forward through the barrier and dropped to their knees, staring at the ground.

Sounds of screaming, ripping, and chewing filled the air.

Hector was the only one to watch. He did so with a smile.

# ABOUT THE AUTHOR

Daniel J. Volpe is an author of extreme horror and splatterpunk. His love for horror started at a young age when his grandfather unwittingly rented him, A Nightmare on Elm Street. Daniel has published with D&T Publishing, Potters Grove, The Evil Cookie Publishing, and self-published. He can be found on Facebook @ Daniel Volpe, Instagram @ dj_volpe_horror , Twitter @DJVolpeHorror and DanielJVolpeHorror@gmail.com

## ABOUT THE EDITOR / PUBLISHER

Dawn Shea is an author and half of the publishing team over at D&T Publishing. She lives with her family in Mississippi. Always an avid horror lover, she has moved forward with her dreams of writing and publishing those things she loves so much.

*D&T Previously published material:*
  ABC's of Terror
  After the Kool-Aid is Gone

Follow her author page on Amazon for all publications she is featured in.
  Follow D&T Publishing at the following locations:
  Website
  Facebook: Page / Group
  Or email us here: dandtpublishing20@gmail.com

Copyright © 2021 by D&T Publishing LLC All rights reserved. No part of this book may be reproduced in any form or by any electronic or mechanical means, including information storage and retrieval systems, without written permission from the author, except for the use of brief quotations in a book review. This is a work of fiction. Names, characters, places, and incidents are a product of the author's imagination. Locales and public names are sometimes used for atmospheric purposes. Any resemblance to actual people, living or dead, or to businesses, companies, events, institutions, or locales is completely coincidental.

Produced by D&T Publishing LLC

Edited by Patrick C. Harrison III

Formatting by J.Z. Foster

Cover Art by Don Noble

**Corinth, MS**

Left to You

Printed in Great Britain
by Amazon